Caught Dead

Books by Andrew Lanh

The Rick Van Lam Mysteries
Caught Dead

Caught Dead

A Rick Van Lam Mystery

Andrew Lanh

Poisoned Pen Press

Library of Congress Catalog Card Number: 2014938565

ISBN: 9781464203305   Hardcover
       9781464203329   Trade Paperback

Poisoncd Pen Press
6962 E. First Ave., Ste. 103
Scottsdale, AZ 85251
www.poisonedpenpress.com
info@poisonedpenpress.com

Printed in the United States of America

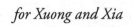

for Xuong and Xia

Prologue

It's always the same dream. Except it's not a dream; it happened. This moment again and again drifts back to me during restless, sleepless nights. I lie in bed, pushing covers onto the floor, and I remember. But I can't really remember, even though I *was* there. My mother told me the story when I was a five-year-old boy, running around the dusty streets. It was her favorite story, and I plagued her with questions. So now it is, in fact, my own story.

You see, I'm probably a year old, living with my mother in Saigon. She's nervous, a little frightened—she holds me too tightly, as though she knows she will not always have me in her lap, in her life.

I've just learned to crawl. The long war is over but the killing and screaming and pain never seem to end.

Her mother—or some older woman in the bombed-out neighborhood—tells her that the little boy will have a tough life now that the Americans have fled. My mother nods, her eyes dark with fear. She looks at the half-Vietnamese, half-white son she holds. She tightens her grip.

Everyone has a bowl of rice in the afternoon. The scarce drinking water is so murky some people spit it out, curse. The sweet aroma of jasmine battles the stench of burnt wood. The stone house where the baby is cradled is missing part of a wall.

"We'll see his future." The old woman takes the whimpering baby boy from his mother's arms. What follows is familiar Vietnamese custom. Let the crawling baby reveal his destiny. People drift over, gathering outside the tiny house with the missing wall, the roof partially caved in. In the dusty, hard-packed courtyard, swept free of papers and chicken bones and dog droppings, the old woman draws a lopsided circle with a stick, positioning the boy in the center. He cries, looks for his mother, falls back onto his side, and then struggles to right himself. Five feet away, the women place small objects, speckled around the edge of the sloppy circle. My mother remembers a pencil, a stale moon cake, a bowl of rice, other bits and pieces. But over the years my dreams have added other items—crumpled paper money, a vial of some elixir, a torn newspaper. I add others with the years.

The mood is festive, buoyant. The neighbors watch. A woman slices an overripe mango; the juices run over her hands. Nearby some men abandon their game of *tam cuc,* leaving the cards still spread on the table. They joke, cigarettes bobbing in the corners of their mouths. My mother waits, but the baby doesn't move. In a small voice she calls out to little Viet Van Lam, "Come, my boy, come." The baby stares at her, a smile on his skinny face. Finally, joyful, he crawls.

They wait. The laughter stops. Now the baby will choose his life. They wait, believing. If the baby crawls to a pencil, he will become a writer, perhaps. If he crawls to a cake, a baker. Money—a banker. Rice—a farmer.

But there are traps, my mother whispers to me later. There are evil omens, symbols of darkness, of loneliness, of disease. Pieces of crumpled black crepe paper. A jagged rock from the nearby fields to suggest a life laid low by nagging want. The tattered shirt of a life of abject poverty, a seeker after alms. The incense stick of early mourning.

They watch. The baby crawls.

Grimy and gurgling, he approaches the bowl of rice. They nod approvingly. He will be a farmer in the fields outside Saigon, now Ho Chi Minh City. Yes, a hard life, but respectable. A life of getting by.

But the toddler shifts direction. Suddenly, in a rush, he lunges toward a tiny wooden dragon painted deep black with a fiery-red shellacked tongue, shiny eyes, razor-sharp tail, and triumphant outstretched wings. With his thin little fingers the boy brushes the miniature emblem.

But then, turning slightly, he grabs a grotesque figurine, a black-stained gargoyle, a fearsome demon. An old farmer had tossed it onto the edge of the circle, this roughhewn clay figure, purposely awful, with its big head, bulging eyes, and terrifying grimace. This, they know, is darkness, evil. This, they know, is the path away from light. At that moment the people gasp, unhappy. The old woman closes her eyes. His mother starts to sob. For the baby has chosen a life of wrongdoing and woe, the sinister clay demon that foretells crime: thievery, brutality, lying, corruption, even murder.

No one breathes.

The boy holds the figurine over his head, waves it, while his mother weeps.

But then little Viet Van Lam grabs it with both hands and, displaying a strength not shown before, he smashes it to the ground, breaking off its head, snapping off the twisted arms. The demon lies broken by his bare feet, covered in dust. The boy looks for his mother.

She remembers that he grins as he grasps the wooden dragon, tightens his fingers around it.

Everyone starts to applaud. Laughs and yells. The men nod at the boy, grinning. The old woman leans into the mother he will lose within a few years. "Your son," she whispers, "will be a policeman." She touches the head of the little boy, now back in his mother's lap, his unusual blue eyes wide and alert. "A seeker after justice," she says. "Buddha's boy."

Chapter One

Everyone had heard of the Le sisters. Even outside the closed Vietnamese community in Hartford, "the beautiful Le sisters" were talked about. They'd been stunners in their twenties, but even now, well into their forties, they caught your eye. So when Hank phoned me one night, waking me from an early sleep, all I heard was "the Le sisters," and I supplied the obligatory adjective: *beautiful.*

"Rick, wake up," Hank yelled. "Mary Le is dead."

I wasn't fully awake. "What?"

I could hear annoyance in his voice. "Mary Le Vu. You know, one of the beautiful Le sisters."

One of the beautiful Le sisters. Twin sisters. I scratched my ear-lobe, sat up on the sofa where I'd drifted off to sleep around nine.

"What?" I yawned.

"You listening to me?" Hank yelled again into the phone.

I tried to picture the sisters. I'd met them a few times, usually at some Vietnamese New Year's wingding, some Tet over-the-top frenzy, once at a wedding where all the men got drunk, and another time at a Buddhist funeral.

"I'm sleeping," I explained.

"It's not late."

"I had a long day." I'd gotten up to jog at six, avoiding the hot, relentless August sun of a heat wave that was in its third day.

"She's dead," he blurted out. "She's been *murdered.*" He waited. "Did you hear me?"

I was awake now. "*Xin loi,*" I mumbled. I'm sorry. I knew the sisters were distant cousins of Hank's mother, a vague connection reminding me that many of the Vietnamese in metropolitan Hartford were somehow biologically or emotionally connected—intricate family bloodlines or spirit lines that somehow radiated back to the dusty alleys of Saigon and forward to the sagging, fragmented diaspora of Connecticut and Massachusetts. Sometimes, it seemed, everyone was an uncle or aunt to everyone else.

"Which one was she?" I stammered.

He didn't answer. "Can you come to my house? It's important."

"What happened?"

Again he didn't answer. "Can you meet me here?"

"Now?"

"Yes."

◇◇◇

After throwing on shorts and a T-shirt, retrieving my wallet and keys, I drove from my Farmington apartment to the poor East Hartford neighborhood off Burnside where Hank lived with his family in a small Cape Cod in the shadow of Pratt & Whitney Aircraft. I knew better than to refuse Hank's request. Not only the insistence—and mild panic—of his voice, but the unspoken message that Hank, the dutiful son, was doing this for his mother. In his early twenties, taking the summer off from the Connecticut State Police Academy where he was training to become a state trooper, Hank was a former student of mine in Criminal Justice at Farmington College. He'd become my good buddy.

He opened the door before I knocked, shook my hand as if we'd just met last week, and nodded me in. A lanky, slender young man with narrow dark brown eyes and prominent cheekbones, he wore sagging khaki shorts and a T-shirt. It was a sticky August night, even though the sun had long gone down, and he was sweating.

His mother, Tran Thi Suong, embraced me, and then burst into tears. "Rick Van Lam." She bowed. "*Cam on.*" Thank you. Hank looked uncomfortable. His grandmother, quiet as a shadow, drifted in, nodded at me, and then disappeared. She was wearing her nightclothes, a small embroidered white cap on her white curls. As she left the room, she touched her daughter on the shoulder, and whispered, "*Y troi.*" God's will.

Hank's mother said something in garbled, swallowed Vietnamese, burst into tears again, and turned away. Hank, bowing to her, motioned for me to follow him through the house. Passing through the old-fashioned kitchen with the peeling wallpaper, I saw the narrow makeshift shrine high on the wall by the door. The plaster-of-Paris Virgin Mary stood next to a tubby Buddha, both surrounded by brilliant but artificial tropical flowers, a couple of half-melted candles, a few joss incense sticks, and some blood-orange tangerines. Scotch-taped to the wall nearby was a glossy print of Jesus on the cross.

Outside, sitting in my car, Hank apologized. "I'm sorry, man. Let's drive. I didn't realize my mother would, well, shatter like that when you walked in."

I was rattled now. "Hank, what the hell is going on?"

He drew in his breath. "I told you. One the two beautiful Le sisters—murdered." I winced at that. "Mary was my mother's favorite, someone she was close to as a small girl in old Saigon, someone she would meet on Sunday morning for *mi ga* and French coffee." Chicken soup for the Asian soul.

"And?"

He sighed. "Mary was murdered earlier tonight at Goodwin Square in Hartford, you know, that drug-and-gang neighborhood. It seems she got caught in some gunfire, some drive-by shooting with local drug dealers who…"

"Wait!" I held up my hand. "I'm not following this."

He looked exasperated. "Mary, who never left her home in East Hartford or her husband's grocery in Little Saigon, for some reason wandered into that godforsaken square and somehow got herself shot."

"In her car?"

"I don't know."

"Why was she there?" I knew that notorious Hartford square—shoot 'em up alley.

"Hey, that's the million-dollar question, Rick. She *knew* better. Everyone in Hartford, especially the Vietnamese, knows better than to go there. That's no-man's-land. You get that. It's not even near Little Saigon."

We hadn't left the driveway, the two of us sitting there, now and then staring back at the house. His mother's shadow slowly moved across the living room. A woman who couldn't sit down.

"Where are we going?" I turned on the ignition.

"To the scene of the shooting."

"Why?"

"Well," he dragged out the word, "when the news came tonight, an hour or so ago, when Uncle Benny called and then it was on the news, Grandma held her hands to her face and said, 'No!'"

"No?"

"She was quiet a long time and then she said 'No!' again. When I asked her what she meant, she told me, 'This is not as easy as it seems. If this seems to make no sense, then there is nothing but sense involved.' I said, 'Grandma, I don't get you.'"

I smiled at Grandma's words. In my head I could hear her soft, melodious rendering of ancient wisdom. Hank was raised a Catholic by his father, but his mother's mother held to the tenets of Buddhism, the two religions coexisting in the often volatile household, with Hank caught in the middle. The Virgin and the Buddha.

So now I said to him, "Well, Hank, she's telling you she thinks something else is going on here."

"I don't see it."

"What I don't see, Hank, is why I'm here."

He smiled, a little sheepishly. "Your name came up."

"Why?"

"Grandma always thinks of you. You know, you and her, the two Buddhists in the house. In fact, she said something about a hole in the universe that only you can fill."

I groaned. "Wait, Hank. She expects me to find the drug dealer with a semiautomatic and a posse behind him? In Hartford? Where the local economy is sustained by drug trafficking and life insurance?"

"You are an investigator."

"I do insurance fraud."

"But you know Grandma. She thinks you can see through plywood."

"And she asked that I get involved?"

He smiled again. "As I say, your name came up."

At Goodwin Square, off Buckingham and Locust, the usual late-night drug dealers on duty had decided to go for coffee or to oil their revolvers in the privacy of their own cribs. A beat cop stood by his lonesome on the southwest corner of the square, outside the obligatory yellow tape. A crew of evidence technicians, scurrying back and forth to a van, was still working the scene, photographing, charting, measuring. But the body had been removed, I noticed. There was some slow-moving, rubbernecking traffic, a few local idlers huddled nearby, but the square was eerily quiet. Storefronts looked beat up and tired. Just a narrow block of broken sidewalks, flickering streetlights, hazy neon signs with burned-out letters, and two stripped, abandoned cars by an alley. And fresh blood stains. Satan's Little Acre, the locals called it.

Hank glanced at the old-model Toyota with all its doors open. Mary's car, I figured.

"Just talk to the detective." He stepped closer to the yellow tape.

"All I see is a cop." I pointed. "And he's looking at us like we're the Yellow Peril."

I approached him, leaning in to catch his name: Lopez.

An unfriendly look. "Help you?"

I told him that the murdered woman was a relative of Hank, and I was a private investigator from Farmington.

"From Farmington?" His clipped voice said the name of the moneyed suburban town with a hint of contempt. "What do you investigate there? Lost stock portfolios?" He looked pleased with himself.

"Who's the detective on this case?"

He pointed over his shoulder, past the yellow tape, past the busy evidence team, through the plate-glass window of a storefront that announced: "Cell Phones! Phone Cards to South America!" I saw a short, wiry man, late fifties, mostly bald with a fringe of hair over his collar. He reminded me of an aging fighter, a tough bantam rooster. He looked bored. He scratched his belly absently, and then, for some reason, licked his index finger. When he walked out, the cop called him over and nodded toward us.

"Family," the cop said, "and a country-club PI."

The detective didn't look happy to see us. "Yeah?" He stepped around the yellow tape, yelled something to one of the members of the evidence crew, and then purposely stood ten feet back, watching us.

"My name is Rick Van Lam." I was bothered by the space between us. "And this is Hank Nguyen, a relative of Mary Vu's. I'm a PI with Gaddy Associates, and the family asked…"

"It's a drive-by." He cut me off. "Some loser drug dealer speeds by, maybe sees competition strolling on his turf, opens fire, bang bang, and the innocent lady who just got out of her car and didn't know where the fuck she was—well, she gets it in the head. The lowlife scum drives off to annoy another one of my days." He reached for a cigarette from a crumpled pack, lit it, and exhaled smoke. His face relaxed for a second. "Satisfied?" He turned away.

"How do you know all that?" I spoke to his back.

He turned. "Witness."

"In this neighborhood?"

He grinned. "I'm very charming. People tell me their life stories." He nodded at Hank. "Sorry for your loss, son." But he looked away as he spoke, glancing over Hank's shoulder, eyes hooded, checking out the street, scanning the walkers and loiterers, a couple teenaged hip-hop kids in baggy jeans sagging around their ankles. Eyes vacant, they looked straight ahead. I followed the detective's eyes. This was an old pro, I realized, someone who grasped a message in the flick of an eyelid, the sly twisting of a mouth corner, the turning of a lip. "I'm Detective Tony Ardolino." He walked closer. We shook hands.

He agreed to talk—"for a minute"—in a bodega-and-café across the street. "Could use a cup of coffee. Christ." He strode across the street with the cockiness of someone who knew no car would dare smash into him. Hank and I followed. Inside the small café, a place with three lopsided tables for coffee drinkers and a light fixture that hummed loudly, we sat by the front window. "The fact of the matter," he summed up, sipping iced coffee and twitching for a cigarette he couldn't have, "is that Mrs. Vu was in the wrong place at the wrong time." He wiped his sweaty brow. "Fucking heat." He looked up at an air conditioner that seemed to be dying.

"But why was she there?" I wondered.

"We guess—that is, *I* guess—she was headed for Little Saigon where her husband got this grocery, and got confused—got lost or something."

Hank protested. "But she's done it many times before."

I added, "And Little Saigon is in the West End, not near here."

He shrugged. "What can I say? People get lost."

"But," I explained, "she would have had to have made a couple of wrong turns."

"It happens."

"It doesn't make sense to me," Hank said.

"Hey, she just got lost. As I say, it happens. The wrong neighborhood. You know, they've closed off some streets near the highway—detours. Construction. Maybe she couldn't read English."

Hank got angry. "She reads English just fine."

Ardolino narrowed his eyes. "Hey, I'm just talking. It's getting a little dark. Like eight o'clock. It's goddamned boiling. She's low on gas. She gets lost. We've had four drive-by murders here in the last year. *Four*—count 'em. All drug-related shit. One just a month or so ago. Remember the little girl that got shot?"

It came back to me: the horrific drive-by in Goodwin Square that got national attention. A father pulls up before a bodega around midnight, his wife runs in for milk, his three-year-old daughter crawls into his lap, half asleep. A gang car passes, the driver thinks he spots an enemy, opens fire, and the girl is shot in the head. Big news on CNN and Fox. Welcome to Hartford.

"You ever get the killer?"

"What do you think?"

"And Mary Vu's the fifth?" I asked.

"A real sad case, this one." He sighed. "For me, at least."

"Why?"

"Hey, she was a simple woman caught in the cross fire among assholes. The punk kids selling drugs go their merry way."

"So the odds of catching her killer are what—minimal?"

"At best." He grinned. "Surprised?"

"So where's this going?" Hank asked.

"Well, we'll do the routine. Round up the usual suspects, but don't hold your breath."

"So that's the conclusion you're making?" I asked. "And the matter is dead?"

Detective Ardolino locked eyes with me. "What are you saying, PI Lam? Like she was murdered on purpose?"

I shook my head. "Yeah, that does seem farfetched."

He chuckled. "Like from out of space."

"Are you gonna talk to the Vietnamese community of Hartford?" I asked.

"Sure. I talk to everyone. My job. I am curious how she ended up here, but we may never get an answer to that."

"They can be a little nervous around cops," Hank said. "Some don't speak English well."

"We'll see." Ardolino was getting ready to leave.

I slipped the detective my card. "If you need me to be, well, a liaison, I'll be glad to help."

The cop slid the card back to me. "I don't share my work with amateurs."

I started to mention that I was once a New York cop, now a licensed PI in Connecticut, but I stopped. The look on Detective Ardolino's face was telling—closed in, tight, the eyes cloudy. He looked at his watch. Hank started to say something, but I touched his wrist. I stood up and Hank, clearly angry, did too.

I pushed the card back across the table. "Don't close off all your options, Detective."

Hank and I left.

"Asshole," Hank said, once outside.

"We'll see."

◇◇◇

It was almost midnight when I dropped Hank off at his home, and he rushed out of the car, already late for his job. He was spending the summer vacation doing kitchen prep overnight and some early evenings at a Chinese take-out in Glastonbury, a job his dad secured for him in repayment of some cloudy family obligation. Hank hated it—he had wanted to be an intern with a local police force. Or, in fact, to do nothing but tag along after me as I did routine insurance fraud investigations that were the bulk of my daily workload. But his severe father was adamant. Hank worked for meager wages paid under the table and put up with the mercurial spurts of anger and irrational demands of the entire Fugian family that ran the restaurant.

"They claim chopping bok choi is an art form," he complained to me. Mornings, he told me, he went swimming or played tennis. "There has to be some summer for me." So now he waved good-bye to me, yelling back that he'd check back with me in the morning. "I'll text you."

"About what?" I yelled back.

"What you've learned."

"I'm not on this case, you know."

"Oh, but you will be. You love Grandma."

"So?'

"Think about it."

Chapter Two

The next morning I called the Farmington Valley Police District and got transferred to Liz's office.

"Liz Sanburn here."

I smiled. I loved the way she answered her phone—a rich whisky voice, throaty, a sensual greeting that always struck me as incongruous in a police station, especially coming from the on-staff criminal psychologist.

"Oh, it's you." She laughed. "What's got you out of bed before noon?" For a second she turned away from the receiver, talking to someone nearby. "Sorry." She came back on the phone. "Madness takes no holiday here."

"Meet me for drinks at the Corner House?" I asked. "Around seven this evening."

"Are you buying me dinner?"

"Will you be hungry?"

"I am if you're paying." She sighed. "What do you want now?"

"Information."

"Have you heard of 411?"

"Yeah, but I have more of a history with you."

"Ancient history." A pause. "You know, we are divorced. I had the papers laminated and tacked to my dart board."

"But you've always had bad aim."

"What I had," she chuckled, "was poor judgment."

"Ah, terms of endearment."

It didn't matter that she was my ex. Liz was a part of my old life in New York City, my student days at Columbia University, and my failed life as a city cop. And now, strangely, my days in Connecticut.

We'd been married right after Columbia College, yet by the time I'd joined the NYPD, our marriage was crumbling. Three years later, when I left the force and headed to Connecticut, it was over. The divorce was my idea, and she agreed because we couldn't live together. But love somehow stayed in place—it was as if we always had to know where the other one was. Because of that, I figured, she followed me to Connecticut. She said she was drowning in Manhattan—alone. The skirmishes and spats, the late-night telephone calls, the silences, the shared confidences, the volcanic angers—all finally resulted in a peaceful coexistence. Sort of. We were, well—friendly. We had dinners together. We spent too many hours together. We joked dangerously with each other. All the wounds stayed open.

I heard someone asking her something. She covered the mouth of the receiver. "Liz, you're busy," I said when she got back on.

She sounded harried. "It's okay. Really."

Quickly I summarized the drive-by at Goodwin Square, Mary's murder, Ardolino's reluctance to look beyond the obvious conclusion. I could hear Liz scratching something on a pad. "I'm curious about Ardolino."

"Poor Hank," she said. "You know how I adore that boy."

"Seven o'clock."

"I already said yes."

◇◇◇

For most of the afternoon I played computer Scrabble, paid some bills, organized an investigation I was working on for the Hartford Insurance Group, and then got restless. I switched on the air conditioner, but my rooms on the second floor of the creaky old Victorian were still stifling. I lounged in running shorts, considered going down the street to Farmington College for a swim, changed my mind, and tried to straighten up the place. Invariably I kept circling back to Mary Vu's murder, my thoughts centering on my role in this hapless event—that is, Grandma's utter faith in me. But…to do what? Rick Van Lam, the miracle worker? A murder that was impossible to imagine.

Hank texted me, then phoned, pushing me, and I told him I'd make calls on people, but I didn't want to pester family members yet. "I'll wait a day. Let them grieve."

He wasn't happy with that. When I hung up, I washed the kitchen counter. Bored, restless. Then it hit me—I didn't want to get involved. My connection to the Vietnamese community was tenuous at the best of times.

So I vacuumed my carpets.

My apartment is on the second floor of a wonderful painted Victorian lady on Cedar Lane, a quiet street, maple-shaded and elegant, that runs off Main, steps away from Miss Porter's School. With its gingerbread moldings and rococo turns and surprising angles and widow's peaks, with its floor-to-ceiling bay windows and rippled glass panes, the house is a throwback to days when families were gigantic, stayed at home, and huddled by blazing fireplaces in winter. Gracie, the landlady, had painted the house a shrill canary yellow, which compelled some unhappy souls to malign it as the cheap blonde on the corner. I liked that.

My apartment is a complicated two-bedroom, with deep, walk-in closets, but what I really like are the window seats in the two bedrooms, both with faded burgundy crushed velvet from decades back, both overlooking a backyard of overgrown oaks and sunshine-hungry maples. There's also a lush garden with wild honeysuckle vines covering a white picket fence. I love my apartment because of its sudden surprises: cobweb-like nooks and unnecessary crannies, quick turns into meaningless alcoves where octagonal stained glass catches the morning sun or the late afternoon twilight. High vaulted ceilings, the one in the kitchen covered with tin plating, many times painted but still making the room echoey. Ornate carved oak molding wherever you look. Floor-to-ceiling living room bookcases with milky leaded-glass doors. Early on, I filled the shelves with old leather-bound law books I bought for a few bucks at a garage sale, alongside rows of gilt-edged family-parlor volumes of Tennyson and Thackeray I picked up at a church rummage sale.

Yet the place has my own Rick Van Lam touches, such as they are, because the apartment certainly needs no help from anyone to make it charming. I added old couches and deep, worn leather chairs, spreading a frayed oriental on the dark oak floor. I wanted it roomy but homey, a place I could fall into at the end of a day. Hank, when he first visited, squinted and called it the backroom of the Salvation Army. That was the perfect comment.

I spent the rest of the afternoon moving the furniture around, then shuffling it back to where it was originally. I worked up a sweat.

Later I strolled down the street past Miss Porter's, where girls in summer dresses were headed to some dressy function, their high laughter sailing across the sidewalk. Usually I saw them in shorts, talking into cell phones. I stopped at Farmington College, checked my mailbox, and retrieved essays from my summer session Wednesday night Criminal Justice class.

I dressed for dinner with Liz, donning iron-pressed khaki slacks, a pinstriped tan shirt with an art-deco design tie, and a tan summer sports coat, finished off with tasseled oxblood loafers. In the hall mirror I saw a long dark face, thick and sleek black hair inherited from my mother, and the sharp jawline—chiseled as a fashion model's—I got from my American father. And his blue eyes. I'm decent looking, I know. That isn't just vanity. Women like me. I tell myself it's the slanted lazy eyes that widen to reveal deep baby blue irises. People don't expect such eyes from an Asian.

We met in the parking lot of the restaurant. She was waiting when I pulled my ten-year-old BMW into the lot, positioning it next to her creamy beige Lexus, parking it just a little too close. Psychologists love worrying about territory. She was smiling. Liz is a snob about cars. My treasured black BMW, still a looker, keeps breaking down, and she chides me about it.

I kissed her on the cheek. She was wearing lilac, I noticed, a scent she knew I didn't care for. It reminded me of family funerals and old grief. Inside, I watched as she walked ahead of me—a white cotton summer dress, stark against her tanned skin, a string of pearls, and very high heels that I'd seen before. They reminded me of lethal weapons. They probably were. Liz once told me heels on women were male-mandated torture. She wore them only on special occasions, she'd said.

"Like what?" I'd asked.

"First dates, last dates, funerals. Sometimes"—a wink of the eye—"the last two are one and the same."

So now I had to say something. "Heels?"

"It's the place, not the company." She loved the eighteenth-century ambiance of the Corner House, which is why I chose it: hand-hewn stained beams, warped wide-board floors, fieldstone fireplace, pewter wall sconces, and candlelight illuminating the stylized oil paintings of severe-looking New England patriarchs on the walls. A place for Yankee pot roast and dumplings, for apple butter and molasses-baked beans. Spiffy customers in suits that held fat wallets. A corporate expense account haven for the Farmington tax attorneys and their Arts League wives. All the women wore pearls. All the men talked of golf and handicaps.

Sipping her dry martini while I worked a scotch-and-tonic, Liz got serious, rifling through her handbag for papers. Though she protested my occasional use of her local police connections—and her easy access to inaccessible records, something I lacked—she once told me, in an unexpected burst of familiarity, that she enjoyed "helping" me. Her job, though stimulating at times, had become routine. "Levels of aberrant behavior are surprisingly limited."

Now, tapping the sheets she placed on the table, she shrugged. "Nothing much, Rick. The *Hartford Courant* largely had it right this morning. Supposedly Mary Le Vu was in the wrong place, et cetera, et cetera. The reporter simply mimicked the police report, which I got a copy of. My limited connections at the Hartford PD—my counterpart and her captain lover—say the same thing. The death of an innocent Asian lady did give them some pause, I hear. But they're swamped. Too many murders happening in that happy city. Too much gangbanger violence. Too many drugs. Especially in Goodwin Square. They just want to close this one out—make it go away."

"Sounds like they're blaming the victim, Mary Vu."

"Sort of," Liz agreed. "She *shouldn't* have been there."

"And if the story goes on too long, they don't look too good, do they?"

"Based on track records for that neighborhood, they're not gonna find the shooter, that's for sure, unless they lean on a rival gangbanger. But nobody snitches to the police. And so we can't have a middle-class, middle-aged respectable housewife on the first page of the *Courant* for a week. People stay out of Hartford as it is. Make it go away. Chalk it up to: *oops!* End of story."

"And Ardolino?"

She smiled. "I knew you'd get to that work of art. He actually mentioned you to someone—showed them your card. Doesn't like interference but can't leave a question unanswered. Following up on you. Very thorough. Nice touch, Rick."

"He wants me out of the picture."

"Think about it—he doesn't want the Asian angle to get any bigger. To begin with, Hartford doesn't understand Asians, especially the cops. You know how inscrutable you people are. Someone joked that the mayor just learned about Little Saigon, like it's a brand new geography. But the Vietnamese don't vote. So who cares? And Ardolino, I hear, is a loner who doesn't even have a buddy on the force. He's two years from retirement to Miami, he's got acid reflux big time, and there's a rumor that he has a silver-dollar-sized mole on his left buttock."

"All valuable info, Liz, but…"

"But the talk is that he's a real good cop most of the time, pretty thorough, but of late he's getting a little lazy. He can surprise with excellent, on-top-of-it work some days. Some days they're surprised he even shows up."

"Maybe he'll surprise us."

"Don't count on it."

"Drinker?"

"What detective isn't?" Liz leaned in. "You want my advice?"

"Of course."

"Stay clear of him. If you've got to, work around him. Quietly. I gather that's your intention. You're in this, thanks to Hank and Grandma."

I held up my hand. "No, I'm not. I'm just asking a few questions…"

"Of course you are. You feel some obligation to Hank and the Vietnamese world you claim to be a part of. Guilt, shame, whatever you lost souls are going through."

"I love snap judgments from a trained psychologist."

"Nothing snappy about it. Don't forget I lived with you for years."

"I still have the wedding photo over the fireplace mantel."

"The one I drew a moustache on?"

"Yeah, but it's not a look you wear well."

She laughed.

Over dessert we caught up on each other's lives. Liz had grown quiet during the meal, her eyes half closed some of the time, chuckling at some funny story, but dreamily, a little far away. Whenever I told her a story—I embellished the boring routines of my investigations—she leaned into me, a weak smile on her face. It always made me feel like a little boy, a happy, wanted child. In the scant light of the candles her olive-toned skin looked silky. If I hadn't already been married to her once, I might have been intrigued.

"So how are you?" I asked. "I haven't seen you in a while."

She turned her head away. "I'm okay. Been busy."

"Busy at work or busy social?"

Her eyes darkened. "Busy at work. I was seeing this guy for a while—a homicide detective, would you believe? Talk about neurosis heaven."

"Didn't work out?"

"What do you think?" She paused. "What about you?"

"Nothing. Some investigations. I'm teaching one summer class on Wednesday nights. Almost over."

We were quiet for too long, Liz distant, while I fiddled with a napkin. Then suddenly she said, "I turned thirty-eight. Two weeks ago."

I shook my head. "I'm sorry. I forgot." I leaned forward to kiss her, but she backed away.

She gave me a broken smile. "Don't be. I know you. Even when we were married, you never paid attention to birthdays. That's what comes from being an orphan. You…" She stopped. "I'm sorry. That was cruel."

I swallowed my words. "Sometimes we don't do well when we get together, do we?"

She reached across the table and touched my fingers. I had been drumming them idly on the table and I didn't know whether her touching me was affectionate or simply a gesture for me to stop being nervous with her. I stopped.

Back at home, I switched on the local news, and Mary Vu was still the lead story. They ran a snapshot of her with husband Benny, taken when they were in their twenties. I had to admit that she was a stunner. Even the newscaster termed her "a local beauty," quoting someone in the Vietnamese community. Near bedtime, I sat there, the room still warm, and I stared at the air conditioner. Three days into a heat wave. Grimly, I thought—people kill people when the thermometer stays over ninety degrees.

The phone rang.

"Rick, it's Hank. I'm at work, and not happy. People who don't speak English are waving meat cleavers at me."

"They must have a reason."

"Jealousy."

"What's up?"

"I smell like stale soy sauce and look like leftover mu shu pork."

"Is that why you called?" I yawned.

"What did you find out from Liz?"

I shook my head, grinning. "How did you know I called Liz?"

"You always do when you're on a tough case. Like this one. She's your, well, lifeline."

"Hank, I'm not on a case."

"Of course you are."

"Hank…"

"After the funeral Thursday, you will be."

"I'm not going to the funeral."

"I'll pick you up at nine. We can get coffee first. You can buy me a doughnut."

Chapter Three

The next morning I woke up bloated and tired, last night's wine leaving me headachy. Yawning, I pulled myself out of bed and showered. My muscles ached. I really needed my morning jog. I'm not out of shape but in need of muscle on my long, lanky body. It's a jogger's body. I have great calves, but I have the upper body of a teenage drug addict. Drying myself off, it suddenly dawned on me: birthday. Liz's birthday, her thirty-eighth. In a month I would be thirty-eight, too. We were the same age, though I'd always ragged her that I was the baby.

I was turning thirty-eight on September 15. It's a phony date, I know, given me when I arrived in America, a thirteen-year-old boy who, until then, had no birthday at all, or, at least any that I remembered from the orphanage. September 15. It was birthday by fiat. Catholic Charities and Immigration Services giving me puberty, America, and a birthday all at the same time. Talk about your hat tricks.

I decided to hit the gym before the heat settled in, do some prep for my Wednesday night class. The college has a rich man's health facility, with state-of-the-art wall-to-wall workout equipment and free weights, even a jogging track, but I like to use it early in the morning, before the droopy-eyed undergraduates drag in for fun, games, and rendezvous. A few inveterate muscle boys who ignore everyone always arrive early, but the rest don't arrive until eight. I got there at six-thirty.

While swimming laps in the pool after the workout, I felt distracted, unable to focus. Images flooded me: one minute poor Mary Vu shot to death in a forbidden drug zone and, in the next moment—me. I couldn't escape my birthday. My American birthday. The mingling of these two events—one a sad death, one a legislated birth—overwhelmed me, stunned. I stopped swimming, resting on the side of the pool, my hair in my eyes, heart pounding, veins in my hands jutting out as I gripped the side of the pool. Liz's comments about my being an orphan bothered me more than I thought.

My name is Rick Van Lam. My real first name is Viet. Most Americans can't pronounce the distinct monosyllabic Vietnamese inflections. No matter. In Vietnam I was Lam Van Viet. In America, resting in a foster home in the Bronx for a month, I was Viet Van Lam, and then I allowed myself to become Rick Van Lam at the insistence of Father He from Catholic Charities, my English-speaking conduit to my new American culture. I didn't mind—I was thirteen and I wanted to become American.

I'm that curious breed produced by the Vietnamese Conflict—I'm Amerasian, one of the so-called children of the dust, the dirty secret, the *bui doi*. I have no idea who my mother was, except that she was a Vietnamese woman who, in the final days of the war, carried a child by a white American soldier, also nameless and now forgotten. Left at an orphanage when I was around five, I have trouble remembering my mother, but sometimes I recall her holding me tight. I remember her story of the baby boy attacking the clay demon. That's an important story I hold in my heart. So I grew up hated by most Vietnamese—"Your mother was a whore, your father a pig"—as I struggled through childhood in a Catholic orphanage. I was hated by white people, too. Dust boys, that's what they call us. But it also explains why I have those violet-blue eyes encased in sleepy slanted sockets, my tall lanky body, and the bone structure of an all-American soldier, probably some milk-fed boy from Des Moines or—I don't know, maybe Pensicola. God knows. I never will.

One document I own suggests that my real last name is indeed Lam, which, like Nguyen, is as commonplace as Smith or Jones or Garcia in America. And supposedly the Van and the Viet are real. But there's no mother to guide me, as they say. And for a long time, in America, I would look at older white men and think, Hey, is that you, Daddy? What did you do in the war?

Sometimes I find myself still doing that.

I was a bright child, alert, the darling of the severe, unyielding nuns, a cute little bugger who played every manipulative game because I wanted to survive. I knew the odds were stacked against me. I'd sneak out of the home at night, maneuvering my way through cluttered, hostile Saigon streets, hiding in the shadows of walls plastered with posters of benevolent Uncle Ho, the leader who saved us from America. Those days I was always hungry. Soon I wormed my way into America. Being half-white was a liability in the best of worlds, but it also afforded me guilt-laced entry into the country of my father. So at thirteen I was sponsored to America by the good Catholics, who found me a permanent home in Port Elizabeth, New Jersey, where I excelled in school—of course—making my adopted parents, Jesse and Connie Greeley, inordinately proud, but not currying much favor with the less-bright natural siblings, Judith and Harry, who still don't speak to me to this day. Jesse Greeley was a lawyer, and that was to be my career. Full National Merit Scholar at Columbia College, Phi Beta Kappa, American success story, until my senior year when bouts of depression kept me in bed.

In the words of my adopted father: "What the hell's your problem all of a sudden?" I'd been a model teenager.

I never knew how to answer him. I still don't, to this day. I see my parents whenever I can, though they still look at me with the same pitying expression they wore when I stepped out of Brother He's limping station wagon onto their suburban lawn. They never lost that expression. There I was, poor boy, frightened, trembling, in a Salvation Army sweater, in baggy jeans with frayed cuffs, carrying a battered GI Joe toy I got at a Goodwill toy bin. Half-eaten Oreos in a Catholic Charities tote bag. Thirteen years old, with a war toy. Years later, with BA from Columbia College in hand, they hugged me like the orphan I was—a barefoot boy with cheek.

How was I to tell these wonderful people, my deliverers into a safe America, that I would wake in the night in a cold sweat, hungry for something besides law and money, hungry instead for quiet and order. I wanted something to stop the shaking, the nighttime sweats. Sometimes I still get them. I wake up feeling lost and homeless. I'm drifting in space, no rock to cling to. Helpless, screaming.

In my senior year, riding the IRT subway from 116th Street down to Times Square, I saw an ad for a master's program in Criminal Justice at John Jay College. At that moment a transit cop was shoving a homeless black man into a sitting position across from me, shaking him out of a sleep, kicking him, and it seemed the only route to go for me. I wanted the front lines, not the three-piece-suit world of the corporate courtroom. I wanted my blood to boil. Fire in the belly, fury in the marrow.

"What?" I can still hear Liz's precise intonation—clipped, a tinge of hysteria. I'd been dating Liz Sanburn throughout my senior year. A psychology major from a Riverdale family of psychiatrists and tax attorneys, she acted as though I'd slapped her in the face. Our romance had been magical. Madcap, stupid, filled with laughter, a little bit taboo, but it had become serious in the last spring semester. Suddenly we were talking about marriage because we were both drunk with each other. I couldn't believe there could be anyone else for me. We'd see each other in the stacks at Butler Library and burst out laughing, out of control. But when she fought me on my going into police work—I wanted the master's and then the police academy—something started to die in me. Stupidly, we married anyway, hoping the marriage certificate and the settled life in Manhattan would jump-start our love again. It didn't. And the more I withdrew, the more Liz—so aware of my distance, my moods, my running away—tightened her hold.

We stayed together for three years, she getting a psych master's at Hunter while I became a foot patrolman in Chelsea. She cried every night. I never wanted to go home. My brief stint on the force was a blur, a kind of manic, headlong assault on crime and injustice. One day, collaring some piece of trash who'd just beat up an old woman for her purse and a few bucks, I found myself up against a .22 pressed into my neck. I flipped out, overreacting, fighting the scumbag. He fired, grazing my left shoulder—I still have a jagged, lighting-bolt scar—as I tried to wrestle the gun from him. He was stronger than he looked, a wiry drugged-out maniac who fought for his life. As did I. I won, getting out my revolver and blowing him away.

But something happened to me as I stood over him, my body virtually connected with his, pumping lead into him. My head became light and airy, echoey, and I found myself staring into the man's face, and I kept yelling, *Take that, take that take that, you fucking bastard*, until I was pulled off him by my partner. Years later, when I dreamed about it, things got mixed up. In those feverish awakenings, I found myself yelling, *Take that, father, take that, father, take that, father*. Over and over. The day the little Vietnamese boy struck back at his white daddy. Today on Dr. Phil.

Months of police-mandated therapy and my own mournful introspection compelled me to leave the force. Frankly, I was happy to go. But when I did, I realized I had to clear up a number of nagging lies, and one was my sputtering marriage. I needed a fresh start, so I asked for a divorce. Liz knew it was coming.

An old police friend had connections in Farmington where the College was initiating a new degree in Criminal Justice. He got me the job, I made the move out of the city, I connected with a private investigator named Jimmy Gadowicz because I still wanted to be active in the profession—out there in the field—and that's how I ended up where I am. Jimmy took care of me, maneuvering me through the medieval criminal justice red tape of Connecticut. Proudly he gave me tours of places like the Connecticut State Police Forensic Crime Lab in Meriden.

The Connecticut Police Academy. He has buddies everywhere. Everyone likes him. He took care of me.

Now, years later, Connecticut—this town, Farmington, so far from Manhattan and the frantic life I led there—is the only home I want. Quiet, quiet. I teach undemanding kids—a little too pampered, a little too dumb—at the small liberal arts college that struggles to stay afloat. I do knee-jerk fraud investigations and slimy divorce investigations with Jimmy. Quiet. Life hums along, the heartbeat of the dead.

I wanted nothing to do with murder.

Chapter Four

Hank and I were late arriving at St. Lawrence O'Toole Roman Catholic Church in the South End of Hartford. We'd started out in my BMW, which chose to sputter to a halt in the middle of Main Street, directly in front of Miss Porter's school.

"How ignominious," Hank whispered. "And not even a newer model."

So we walked back, got into his rusty Chevy, skipped coffee, and ended up in the last pew of the church. At ten in the morning the temperature was ninety-one. Mourners wilted in pews with paper fans and soggy handkerchiefs. A packed house, the entire Vietnamese community gathered, it seemed, largely because of Mary Vu's spectacular and senseless death, but also because she was a well-loved woman. Local TV crews were set up on the sidewalks on New Britain Avenue, interrupting the mourners for local color vignettes. A photographer from the *Courant* leaned on a car and watched us walk by. Hank and I rushed past another latecomer, an old Vietnamese man, who was stopped by a news stringer with bleached blond hair and oversized sunglasses. When he started babbling in Vietnamese, she simply turned away. The old man stood there, perplexed, then followed us in, sitting next to us.

At one point Hank's mother looked back anxiously, checked out the mourners, spotted Hank, and was satisfied that he'd made it there.

The Vietnamese priest was conducting a High Mass in the native language of virtually all the mourners, who were mostly Catholic but with a generous number of Buddhists. The singsong rhythms, coupled with the incense and the intoxicating aroma of flowers, lulled me, made me drift off.

Sitting there, I remembered that I was born a Buddhist. I believe that because one of the few items I carried to America from the Catholic orphanage was a tattered, brown-cover paperback, slim as a calendar, that my mother had supposedly left with me when she dropped me off at the orphanage. *The Sayings of Buddha*. I still cherish it. In college, hanging with friends, I'd glibly quote bits I translated from my little book. Like: *All things small are as all things large when boundaries disappear.* Everyone would smile. Sometimes I'd deliver them a little mockingly. But one night someone called me Charlie Chan. It meant nothing to me then. But when I suddenly became addicted to late-night black-and-white movies and heard the drippy maxims, I shuddered. I stopped my joking—and hated the way I'd acted.

Well, Charlie Chan and number one son. Rick and Hank. Someday, Hank insists, he wants us to be partners in a detective agency. Tan and Viet. Our Vietnamese names. TV Associates. Chopsticks—with surveillance cameras. *All things small are as all things large.*

Those pithy, wonderful sayings come to me every so often. They warn me of danger. They humble me, level me.

So now, dwelling on Mary, I found myself thinking:

The act cannot separate from the actor;

The actor cannot separate from the act.

But I didn't think Buddha could help me find Mary's killer.

I shook myself out of my reverie. What was it about churches that always brought me back to my childhood? The music? The solitude? The incense? The resonance of bells? The coldness of shadowy stained glass? Suddenly I heard raspy, choked noises erupting from the front pew, jolting me to attention. One minute absolute silence, then the garbled rasp of overweening grief, covering our heads like rain. Everyone leaned forward, expectant.

Hank whispered, "It's Benny Vu."

Mary's Vu's husband, a small squirrelly man with almost no chin, was making guttural, desperate sounds, a man suddenly lost to shock and explosive grief. For a moment he stood, looked around him with wild, passionate eyes, his head lolling to the side like a rag doll, and then he was tucked back down into his seat by his children, Tommy and Cindy. They looked embarrassed.

When I looked at Hank, there were tears in his eyes.

A reception was held in the church hall, with platters of home-made dishes arranged on long rows of folding tables. There was *goi cuon*, the aromatic spring roll of mint, shrimp, pork, vermicelli noodles. Small bowls of *nuoc mam*, the savory fish sauce. *Tom ram man*, salted shrimp. *Ga xao gung*, chicken with ginger. Dish after dish, mouth-watering. Parched from the heat, Hank and I reached for *cha fe sua*, the iced coffee with condensed milk, so cold and sweet it made my teeth ache. Nearby were pitchers of *nuoc mia*, the sugar cane drink, and *tra da chanh*, lemonade. But I also spotted the influence of such American gatherings: bowls of baked ziti and meatballs, chicken wings, potato chips, and Sara Lee cake. One table held a huge aluminum bucket packed with ice. Inside was Budweiser. And more Budweiser. Already, the men huddled in the doorway were smoking Marlboros and drinking.

Benny Vu sat quietly at a table, relatives hovering protectively around him. His two children were sitting across the room with friends. I thought that odd. In his rumpled suit and cowlicky hair, their father was lost in a sea of cold comfort. Someone had placed a dish of food in front of him, which he ignored.

I didn't know much about him, and on the drive over Hank had filled me in on a few details. Part of the first wave of much-televised Boat People of 1975, Benny had bummed around for years, lost in America, a handyman at an apartment complex, a janitor at a school, even a hot dog vendor at the UConn football games out at Storrs—a drifting sort known for his easygoing demeanor that disappeared only when he drank beer with his cronies. Then his face would turn beet red, the spittle would fly, and the fiery condemnation of the Viet Cong—as well as his enforced exile in an America he could never understand—would first startle, then scare, his drunk listeners at Bo Kien, the bar-restaurant where he hung out. Then, after making a few bucks off a vending cart parked in front of the Aetna Insurance building on Farmington Avenue, where he sold lunchtime Chinese food, he opened a small Asian grocery on Park, right in the heart of the burgeoning Little Saigon, a cluster of similar grocers, lunch places, nail salons, gift shops, and beauty shops. Tucked between My Xuyen Clothing and Song Ngoc Dental Office, his Vu Pham Market was one of the few struggling stores on the bustling strip. For years I used to stop in the neighborhood at Nha Trang Noodle Shop for the best *pho,* beef noodle soup with basil, or go for the best *bun* at Viet Huong. His piddling market barely made a decent living for the family, Hank said, because Benny wasn't much of a businessman. Sometimes he'd close shop on a busy Saturday afternoon, when most Vietnamese did their shopping for the week, and head to Foxwoods Indian Casino to gamble.

In the car I'd asked Hank, "He has a gambling problem?"

Hank shook his head. "Dunno. No more than most Asians. You know, it's a part of the culture. Look at Foxwoods or Mohegan Sun on Christmas Day or New Year's. More Asians there than in all of Thailand. Don't you get those glossy mailings in the mail from the Indian casinos? All in impeccable Vietnamese."

"But some have problems. Maybe he's in debt."

Hank nodded. "Could be. My dad bitches that Benny closes the store at odd hours. He drives there to find that handwritten sign on the door: *Dong cua.* Closed. Tommy works there some days, but not always. He's not loyal to the store."

I told Hank about my only venture into Benny's store, back before I knew Hank and his family, days when my encounters with the Vietnamese community were minimal. I'd gone into the market looking for some Vietnamese bean pudding, a weakness of mine, but there was not a soul in the store. "I didn't like the place," I told him. "It had a musty, leaden smell of uncleared shelves and unswept floors."

"Sort of like your apartment."

I ignored him. "Then I heard noises. Some loud voices, laughter, and in the back of the store I saw a stairwell. Stupidly, I walked down into what was a storage room and found four men playing poker at a table, piles of American dollars on the table. Benny was there, though I didn't know him at the time, but the whole bunch jumped up, nervous. Apologizing, Benny followed me upstairs, introduced himself, shook my hand, and took my money for the food I bought. But he wasn't happy at being discovered down there. I could have been Hartford undercover. There's gambling like that going on all over Little Saigon."

"Probably his son was supposed to be working and cut out. Tommy does that," Hank said. "My cousin is a slacker."

I joined Hank's family at a table at the back of the hall as the room filled up. His grandma motioned me to sit by her side, smiled, and held my hand. I leaned in to kiss her cheek. "This is a great sadness," she whispered in Vietnamese, and I agreed. Hank's grandfather wasn't there, and I didn't ask why. Hank's father, Nguyen Van Tuan, barely nodded at me. Hank's younger brother and sister, Tinh and Phuong, fifteen- and thirteen-year-old kids, were giggling over something one of them said to the other. Grandma frowned.

Hank's older sister Linh, who called herself Anna, sat stone-faced, pensive, looking at no one. Anna was taking a leave of absence from her job at Travelers Insurance—she'd been a scholarship student at Miss Porter's and an economics major at Trinity in Hartford—to spend three months in Vietnam. Sometimes, after a little wine at New Year's, she only spoke Vietnamese, refusing English as a language, a woman caught between cultures. Sometimes she smiled at me, but sometimes her cold stare dismissed me as a diminutive insect.

Hank said to his mother, "Why aren't the kids sitting with Benny?"

His mother glanced at Grandma, then shook her head. "I guess they're embarrassed by their father."

Grandma clicked her tongue. "American children."

Hank smiled. "Unlike me, right, Grandma?"

Anna looked at him and grunted. "Self love…"

"…is all I have sometimes," Hank finished. "Anna, you've been telling me that since I was five."

"Because you think you're God's gift to the earth."

"Only women."

Grandma interrupted, not happy with their conversation. "Quiet, you two. We are in a Catholic church."

Hank insisted, "Not really. It's the hall connected to the church."

Grandma pointed at him, unhappy.

"How did the Le sisters get to be Catholic?" I asked Grandma. "Your side of the family is Buddhist."

She waved her hand in the air. "Their ancestors lived in a different province. I guess the power of a Catholic God was stronger there."

I watched Benny's two children, sitting across the room. Tommy was the older, perhaps twenty-five now, a few years older than Hank. I'd met him a few times. Tommy had started his rebellion against his traditional and poor Vietnamese-American family early on by shoplifting plastic action figures at Walmart at age ten. One stupid, infantile arrest after another, loitering, sassing a teacher, petty theft, a smart-alecky boy who hated his parents—or so family lore went. Now he sat with friends and his sister, all of them picking at the food. Tall, skinny, with a bony, pushed-in face, his dark skin the color of nut bread, he usually cultivated a slacker appearance, wearing a weathered leather jacket with too many buckles and twists, a string of glittery earrings up and down both lobes, a tattoo of a green dragon with red fiery tongue on his upper left bicep, and a shaved haircut with a Mohawk sliver of hair left intact. Stomping boots, even in the dreadful heat of August. Today, for the purposes of grief, he did not have on his leather jacket. Instead, he wore a simple military camouflage jacket over a T-shirt, as tasteful as public urination.

At the other end of the table Cindy sprawled out, eyes half-closed, glossy red lips parted, listening to a chatty new-wave Asian boy with bright red hair puffed so high he could be taken for a streetlight. Whatever he said must have amused her, because I noticed the trace of a smile. Idly, she checked her cell phone—tapped out a text message. She looked like a candy cane confection with her white-powdered face, kohl-rimmed eyes, purple ribbons in her hair, too much costume jewelry, and mismatched pieces of clothing, colorful if not downright eccentric. Her miniskirt rode high over long legs encased in boots that were best worn in seasons other than summer.

Hank saw me sizing up her outfit. He leaned in. "No one dresses like Madonna anymore. Sad."

As I got up to get some jasmine tea for Grandma, I sensed a shift in the currents in the cavernous room. People, sitting back after finishing eating, suddenly became alert. Every head suddenly shot to the entrance. Hank's mother and grandmother were talking about the new super-sized Asian market, A Dong, that had high-quality lemongrass for ginger chicken, but stopped the conversation midsentence.

The Torcellis had arrived. Of course. Always the late entrance. Mary Le Vu's twin sister, Molly, swept into the room, striding forward, trailed by her husband, Larry, who looked the way he always did at Vietnamese functions—*why the hell am I here?* Behind them, walking as though they'd been promised Porsches if they behaved, were the two children: Jon, the aloof young man of twenty-five and heir to the vast car dealership franchise, and his younger sister Kristen, the fashion-plate daughter with the brain of an aquarium pebble, gorgeous and wide-eyed and personally happy that she was so stunning. Okay, I admit to a certain bias in these belittling descriptions, despite my scant acquaintance. I'd sat at a New Year's table with them one time. It was very easy to dislike them. All four of them, Benny and Mary's two kids, and Larry and Molly's two, were kids who struck me as appropriate metaphors of a twilight of the American dream. Only the presence of Hank in this world—purposeful, smart, compassionate—saved me from utter disaffection with that Vietnamese-American generation.

But Molly always intrigued me. I loved the way she floated into any room. She'd always been, of course, one of the "beautiful Le sisters," so she was used to flattery and attention. But unlike her dead sister Mary, she'd married a very rich man, Larry Torcelli, the ambitious son of a local hotshot Hartford politico and businessman, once questioned by the FBI for illegal contributions to a gubernatorial election fund. Larry was a striking, charming man who'd inherited one of the most lucrative automotive enterprises on the Eastern Seaboard. He'd also fallen in love with the stunning Molly Thi Le, a romance that surprised him, but especially alarmed his unhappy father. He took her off to a sprawling estate in the Farmington hills, where she produced Jon Dinh and Kristen Thi, cookie-cutter pretty children, the envy of absolutely no one. And so, over time, Molly became the "rich one" of the beautiful sisters whom people saw only at holidays and funerals.

Last winter, at a Vietnamese New Year's party at a VFW hall in East Hartford, in the shadow of poor neighborhoods whose souls struggled to make ends meet, Molly swept into the dreary room, late as usual, very Ethel Merman with her booming voice and over-the-top Broadway gestures, and the room stopped. I remember that she wore an expensive fur. A mink, I was told. "She has three," someone whispered. But she also had on a traditional *ao dai*, the high-neck silk dress, slit to the waist, worn over black satin slacks. Very eye-catching on a woman so beautiful. Now, striding into the late August sweltering hall, she struck me as still in silk and furs—the effect was always there, despite the simple blue dress she now wore.

At New Year's I remember hearing Mary Le Vu, sitting with Benny at a nearby table, announce, "That's why I'll always be the one that people talk of as 'the poor one.'" There was neither rancor nor envy in her voice, only a world-weary resignation to the unpredictable and heartless fate that had hooked her up with poor—and always to be poor—Benny Vu, nice guy with no bank statement.

Everyone at the table had laughed uncomfortably.

So the beautiful Le sisters had found disparate destinies: One had a subsistence life, lived off a struggling Asian market, life in the slow lane. The other had a Learjet housed at JFK in New York and a beachfront cottage in the Bahamas.

Now, in a room that became electric with the dramatic entrance of wealth and privilege, I watched the stylized routines as Molly embraced Benny, burst into tears, clung to him, then sought out Cindy and Tommy and embraced them. No one in the crowded room said a word, everyone eyeing the drama. Benny started sobbing again, but his kids didn't.

Molly's Larry stood behind her, not so much awkward—this guy never had an awkward moment in his life—but wholly deferential, waiting for his turn to shake Benny's hand, say the appropriate remarks, nod at the kids, and then find a folding chair against the back wall and sit and wait for his wife to be finished. The Vietnamese community, a little intimidated and a whole lot nervous, didn't know how to deal with him. He wasn't friendly. Hank had told me once that people suspected he didn't like the Vietnamese. He'd married Molly Le for one reason only—he couldn't take his eyes off her ravishing face and her drop-dead body. No other reason. And he'd admit to that. He was inordinately proud of her beauty. He had no interest in Vietnamese culture—and he only followed certain obligations, like all-important New Year's celebrations, funerals, and occasional weddings, because Molly looked good at those occasions. People didn't like him. No, that's not true—they didn't want to know him. They felt that knowing him would be too much baggage to carry around.

"The rich are not as we are," Hank whispered.

I'd had one conversation with Larry, the two of us standing outside during a New Year's party, getting fresh air. Staring straight ahead, he asked me what I did for a living, and then told me he was rich.

"I know you are," I'd commented.

"You do?" he'd responded.

"That's what people know about you," I'd said.

He walked away.

No one spoke to him now.

Larry hadn't been at the church service, only Molly and her two children, arriving late, ushered to a front pew, and then leaving quickly. They didn't linger to talk on the sidewalk with the priest or the mourners. They avoided the TV cameras. Nor did they show up at the gravesite at Cedar Hill.

Jon and Kristen sat down at Tommy and Cindy's table as Hank darted over to join them, though I noticed he sat quietly, listening. No one paid attention to him, but Tommy did nod at him. Tommy talked on his cell phone for a minute. Kristen never let go of hers. Meanwhile Molly wandered throughout the room, hugging, weeping, and whispering. When Hank wandered back a while later, he was shaking his head.

"What's up?" I asked.

"You know what the kids are talking about?" he grumbled. "Jon just got a new car from his daddy. He showed us a picture he uploaded on Instagram."

I shrugged my shoulders. "Well, what else is there to talk about?"

Hank squinted, gauging just how serious I was. He tapped me on the shoulder. "Let's go. I wanna get out of here."

In the car he wasn't happy. "They're talking like nothing happened." He paused. "You know, these families are somehow related to me through my mother."

"I know."

"That doesn't make me happy."

"It has nothing to do with you."

"I overheard someone ask Molly about Mary, and she just turned away, almost angry."

"Asked her what?"

"About the sudden loss."

"Well, maybe she was too hurt."

Hank grinned now. "God, you are so…so forgiving at these funerals. Where's the old cynicism?"

"Well, Hank, this is a blow to the family…"

"I *know* that. You know something else?"

"What?"

He turned in the seat. "Everyone avoided talking about the murder. I heard people talking about how good Mary was, how her death was so sudden and such a shock, how Benny looked horrible, what is he going to do because he loved her so much, how the kids looked like rejects from some MTV video—on and on, over and over. But no one used the word *murder*. No one."

I sighed, thinking back to my days as a New York cop. "It's a hard word to wrap your lips around."

"Spoken like an ex-cop living in the suburbs." The words came out too sharply.

"What's the matter, Hank?"

"For God's sake, Rick. Mary was murdered. *Murdered*. It's not like *she's* the *murderer*."

"Here's another cliché for you, Hank. Murder makes people uncomfortable."

He sucked in his breath, then gazed out the window as he drove along. "I don't give a damn. To ignore the way she died is to, well, dismiss her life."

I quoted Buddha: "'The killer and the one killed are the same. Parts of the whole.'" I glanced at him. "Forevermore she and the killer are one."

"You sound like Grandma."

"That's the nicest thing you've said today. When you were away from the table, she said to me, 'We need your eye on this tragedy, Rick.'" I laughed. "Then she added, 'There is an incompleteness that the universe hates. When there is a void, there must be an end to a void.'"

"Avoid what?"

"Never mind. She thinks I have some power that the police lack. She *insists* I talk to people."

"Are you going to?"

"Do I have a choice?"

He grinned. "No, you don't."

"But you're wrong about one thing, Hank. Some people did talk about the murder. In my earshot. A couple of times the talk was about what Mary was doing in that neighborhood. Why in God's name would she venture into drug war territory? Goodwin Square. Christ, it was a *Courant* banner headline just a month ago. I even heard Molly telling one of the old ladies, 'Mary wouldn't be caught dead there.'"

"But that's exactly what happened."

Chapter Five

Later that afternoon, I stopped at my office to check the mail. Though I do most of my investigations out of my Farmington apartment, I am officially part of Gaddy Associates, Private Investigation, Inc., housed in the historic Colt Building in the South End of Hartford. When I pulled into the half-empty parking lot, I noticed the air conditioner whirring in the sixth floor office. Gaddy was there.

Gaddy is Jimmy Gadowicz, a rough-and-tumble PI, a man in his sixties, overweight, at times overbearing. He likes truck-stop diners and all-you-can-eat home-style buffets. Fat-free is a four-letter word.

Jimmy made me his only partner years back—"Don't need no partner, so I don't know why I'm doing this"—gave me office space, helped me get a Connecticut license, mentored me, and maneuvered me through the cumbersome ropes. He lent me the money to post the bond for my license—my right to investigate and gather info on criminal and noncriminal matters. His firm—our firm—does mostly insurance fraud. Hartford is the insurance capital of the world, of course, with Aetna, Travelers, Cigna, the Hartford, you name it—and where there's insurance, there are people trying to rip somebody off. A lot of my work is fielding cases Jimmy can't get to. That's how I make my money. We don't get into murder, Jimmy and I. We play it safe among the white-collar insurance execs.

I took the elevator to the sixth floor. The Colt Building is a nineteenth-century derelict factory building, once owned by Colt Firearms. You know, the gun that tamed and maimed the Wild West. With its dilapidated façade, dreary and bleak, it houses public TV access shows, fundamentalist religious crusades, starving artists, karate or tai kwon do classes, left-wing political action groups, and fly-by-night business ventures. A world of spirited people living off nothing. A catacomb of cheap, partitioned rents.

Gaddy Associates—everyone calls Jimmy by the nickname Gaddy except his friends—is a straight-arrow firm, no doubt about it. Yes, Jimmy's a man of incredible bluster, but always principled. I swear I've never met a man so honest…and so infuriating at times. He'd fought in Vietnam and that's why he had me around in the first place, why he discovered he could actually tolerate someone else around the office. So many Vietnam vets hold a lingering affection for the land of their early manhood. A shattering experience, one you couldn't get away from, lodged in the bone marrow, deep as death. Jimmy saw me as part of that past—his past. His dangerous rite-of-passage days.

"What the hell you doing here?" Jimmy greeted me. The room smelled of thick cigar smoke and old tuna sandwiches and stale breath.

"What are you doing here?" I asked back.

He clenched his fists. "Got a goddamn deadline on this Aetna fraud case. Fact is, I was making no progress until a few minutes ago. Think I got the answer." And again, "Why are you here?"

I told him about Mary's murder, the funeral, Grandma's request that I investigate—he scrunched up his face—and I even told him about my dinner the night before with Liz. His frown deepened.

He's old fashioned. When you get divorced, you don't go out to dinner with the ex-wife, just the two of you. You just don't, even though he adores Liz. Now Jimmy never married because—well, "Nam ruined me for a good woman," something that made no sense to me. But he has a lot to say about marriage. And everything else.

He's a big pile of a man, unshaven half the time, always sweating even in winter, mopping a grainy forehead with a gray handkerchief, a man poured into extra-large sweat shirts that ride up a tremendous belly. When he gets drunk on his celebratory rye-and-ginger highballs, his thinning blond hair stands on end, and he announces that he is the Polish Prince. Last year he didn't talk to me for three days when I told him I thought Bobby Vinton had that title. Didn't he watch late-night TV music offers? The Best of Bobby Vinton, the Polish Prince. Like the Best of Jerry Vale. The Best of Vaughn Monroe. On some sleepless nights, I sometimes wondered: Who *are* these people?

Jimmy doesn't give a damn about most things that don't matter, and a lot about things that do. We get along great—my good friend. I'd trust him with my life. I don't know if it would ever come to that, but I would. I don't say such things lightly.

"Murder?" he barked. "And you took the case?"

"It's not a case. I'm just gonna talk to…"

"I think you lost your mind. The money is in fraud, not murder. Murder is too messy." He was getting ready to leave. "Turn off the air conditioner on the way out."

I invited him to dinner that night at Zeke's Olde Tavern.

"Maybe. You paying?"

I nodded. I knew he'd be there.

"I'll close up in a bit," I yelled after him. "Check the mail. Play with my computer." That was his expression. When I became his associate, I computerized and streamlined his chaotic office, which he grudgingly accepted. He knew it was time, but he fought the idea. Nobody from Aetna or Travelers hires an investigator who keeps notes on slips of paper in his breast pocket. The man tucked important information in outdated Manhattan phone directories and then, forgetting, recycled them. He recorded crucial facts on the backs of gas station credit card slips.

So now I could bring up files via Wi-Fi in a split second, information that used to cost him weeks of foot traffic, as well as favors traded with people in high and low places. "Holy shit" is what he usually says when I give him instantaneous access to personnel and personal files of people he's investigating. Most of it is matter-of-fact online data available at the public library in Hartford.

"Go play with your computer" is his way of letting me know whose office it really is.

That night, after a dinner of steak and potatoes at Zeke's, Jimmy and I lingered over coffee—me—and tepid beer—him. He didn't want to return to the one-room efficiency he rented in the West End of Hartford, and he brightened when my landlady Gracie wandered in "for an early nightcap," joining us at the table. I shredded a placemat while the two flirted with each other, danced around their mutual attraction. They'd been playing this game for a long time. Gracie's in her late seventies, maybe early eighties, a tall woman, a string bean, her hair tied back into a chaotic bun, her face pale. She refuses to wear makeup but creates the illusion that she does. I can never quite figure it out: a flick of an eye, her tongue rolling over her lips, even an upward thrust of her head into a shaft of window light. She has high, pronounced cheekbones and an aging dancer's spent body, all angle and wrinkle. She looks like she got lost, years back, on the way to the opera, what with her scarlet-lined Dracula cloaks and oriental scarves and whalebone hairpins. Sometimes she has the mouth of a street thug.

Gracie often stops in at my apartment, lingering, gabbing, annoying, trying to convince me to get remarried as quickly as possible, to eat more, to go to church. Some of the time Gracie is flamboyant and wacky, but other times she's rock-bottom rigid. She'd been a Rockette at Radio City Music Hall a thousand years back, had entertained the troops with Bob Hope in Korea, done some minor acting in failed Broadway reviews, and then followed a wealthy businessman husband to Connecticut. When he died, she inherited the elegant, sparkling Victorian home. She lives on the first floor, rents out an apartment on the second to me and one on the third to an old guy. Gracie considers us her boys, smothers us, loves us, admonishes us, abuses us, tries to run our lives. Her mission is to steer us into lives she would never want for herself. And we often let her.

Her smile reveals a showgirl's faded teeth: chipped caps, murky as puddles.

I ordered her another beer and she nodded her thanks. She always drinks from the bottle. Like a man, she says. After all, she entertained troops, in her words, "north of Seoul." Sometimes she recalled it as "north of Panmunjam." One time Jimmy, a little too drunk, said it was north of Jersey. She gave him a look that would have withered a lesser man.

Finishing her beer, she stood to leave, convinced she'd left some burner on or some gas jet flickering in the basement or some water running somewhere. It was always the same. Jimmy watched her leave.

"Christ, you two love playing this game," I told him.

"And what game is that?" Snippy. He sipped his beer.

"Never mind."

"You're damned right—never mind."

My cell phone rang. Liz was in the neighborhood. "But let me guess, Zeke's?"

"Right."

"The land that time forgot. The place where the bodies are buried."

"Only the dreams of mankind."

"Then you must be real comfortable there."

"Are you joining us?"

"Who is 'us'?"

"Jimmy and me."

"I love that man." She waited a second. "I'm a couple streets away."

Jimmy was happy to see her, the two of them hugging like father and daughter. She gave me a quick peck on the cheek. She asked about Mary's funeral, but was shaking her head.

"So what I still don't get, Rick—and this is a big what-I-don't-get—is this: What does Hank's family want you to do about this drive-by shooting? If the Hartford cops can't locate any past shooters in those little urban bang-bang episodes, then what can you do? I mean, you're not a homicide investigator. Especially, too, if Mary Vu's killing was just wrong place, wrong time."

"I don't know," I agreed. "Grandma thinks I'm Superman."

Jimmy was nodding furiously. "Yeah, I can see if there was a *motive* for Mary's killing, like someone knew she had hidden money in her home, broke in, surprised her. Or something to do with business, maybe. Like she was actually *targeted*. Then I'd say, it needs a look-at, especially since the Hartford cops have written it off."

"Do you know Detective Ardolino?"

"By rep," Jimmy answered. "Never met him. Heard he could be a hard-ass."

"He's written off Mary's murder already." I tapped my fingers on the table. "Or so I'm guessing."

Liz was opening her purse, pulling out a sheaf of folded sheets. "Does anybody here wonder why I was circling the neighborhood?"

"I thought you were stalking Rick," Jimmy smirked.

"Well, there is that. But no, sorry to report, I called to say look at this." She handed over the sheets, more printouts. "I'll cut to the chase. Mary was killed by a bullet from a Glock 19, right in the head. One shot. Dead on. The gun of choice of street gangs. But I think you may be curious to learn that a kid was also shot. A known dealer, picked up a couple of times near that square and for some reason released over and over by a myopic judge, checked himself into the Hartford ER around six the next morning. Until then nobody knew there was a *second* victim. Gunshot—a slug extracted from a baggy-clad shin. Kid scared he was gonna lose a leg. Turns out it's the same gun. Big surprise. Kid said he was 'walking by' on his way to see his baby's mama when a car he didn't see drove by and shot him. Oh yes, he saw the 'old lady' hit, but he was too busy ducking into an alley."

"Shit," Jimmy roared. "Sounds like maybe *he* was the target."

"Police were slow to release news on him to the press, questioning him, but to no avail. You'll read about it in tomorrow's *Courant*."

"Lots of priors?" From me.

"Like a hundred. He claims he's clean. No longer selling—has no beef with anybody."

"And the cops say?" I asked.

"What do you think? Detective Ardolino is crowing like a rooster in a hen house. Proves his case. More gang-bang rivalry."

"But," I insisted, "it doesn't explain why Mary was there. And out of her car. If you find yourself in the wrong neighborhood, you gun it, find your way back home."

Liz spoke, "Maybe she got disoriented?"

"Over what?"

"You're the detective."

Jimmy sighed, rubbed his belly, made gestures of leaving.

"I'm curious," I began. "Do we have specifics on the earlier shootings there? Besides the notorious one where the little girl died in her father's lap."

Liz took back the sheaf of papers from me, found one in the middle. "Well, four deadly shootings in the past year alone, but there may have been more attempted murders, unreported. One kid was Julio Sanchez, another Marcus Lopez, a third Mario Lucia. All gang members. The Latin Kings. It's their turf. And the sad little girl, member of no known gang. In the second one cops spotted a kid in a stolen Jeep, gave chase, lost him, but a cop knew him, a gangbanger from rival Los Solidos. Tracked him down an hour later at his sister's, but he was clean. That is, the stolen gun in his pants was not the shooter, no residue on his hands."

"So?"

"So police are convinced he's the killer, and they suspect he did a quick gun exchange with a brother—everyone has more than one stolen gun these days—and then washed his hands in tomato juice. These kids are one step ahead. He knew they'd expect him to have a gun."

"Are they looking at him for *this* shooting?"

"No reason to. Someone shot him six months back. In the head. Dead at eighteen. Right in front of the State Legislative Building."

Jimmy snickered. "A loss for civilization."

"That's cruel," I said.

Jimmy got up to leave, mumbled good-bye, but Liz lingered, curling the edges of the printout absently. She looked up at me, smiled, and asked if I wanted some wine.

We ordered a carafe, and I was glad she suggested it. A glass of chilled wine on a hot, hot night. "Good idea." We touched glasses.

"You know," Liz leaned in, "there's one thing that bothers me about the killing."

I tapped the sheet of paper in front of me. "I think I know what you're gonna say." She waited. "Mary was shot around eight o'clock, still early, lingering daylight, on a busy intersection, with all the mom-and-pop bodegas bustling with people buying their lottery tickets, malt liquor, and smokes. It's a street that's alive that time of night."

"Exactly," Liz nodded. "Every other shooting happened late at night, early in the a.m. in fact, the streets were closed up. Only the dealers manning the corners while the suburbanites cruised in over Avon Mountain in their Land Rovers to buy some coke."

I agreed. "Even the little girl's murder was at midnight, her parents coming home from somewhere, running in for milk. After eleven or so all the decent citizens are sheltered in their apartments. No one wanders out—at least not there. You'd think no one lived there. But not at eight o'clock. People flood the streets."

Liz sipped her wine, rolled her tongue over her lips. "Don't you find that odd, a killing in a busy city square on a brutally hot night when people sit on stoops or hang out windows?"

"We can't be the only two that noticed that."

"Right. Ardolino is no fool, Rick." Liz stared into my face. "But maybe it means that the drug-traffic turf wars are escalating…that this, this"—she checked the sheets for the wounded kid's name—"this Jose Santiago was targeted, and it took him off guard."

"Whatever happened to after-midnight, deep-in-the-night sales?"

Liz grinned. "Lord, I've driven down Washington Street, headed for a doctor's appointment near Hartford Hospital at ten in the morning, and there are hookers in fake red-leather mini skirts and not much else, sashaying their rumps in the parking lot across from McDonald's."

"I should make note of that."

We laughed. I drank more wine. She looked at her watch but made no effort to leave, yawning, but trying to hide it by smiling. Finally, hesitant, she said, "It's getting late." She stood up.

"I'll walk you to your car."

Before she got in, jiggling her keys, she paused. "This was fun, seeing you and Jimmy." She hugged me and kissed me on the lips, lingering a little too long. I smelled perfume and wine on her, and I stood there as she drove away. I loved Liz—always would—but sometimes when Liz got lonely in that apartment of hers, years away from the life she remembered in New York, times when she had no romance in sight, she looked back at me. I was always there in that rearview mirror, the tarnished knight of all those New York nights.

I walked home, feeling the wine now and sticky from the unrelenting wash of still, hot air that hugged the dog days of August. But I was also afraid of the delicious scent of perfume that stayed with me, like soft humming in my ear.

Chapter Six

The next morning Hank plagued me to do a walk-through at the crime scene, ignoring my halfhearted protest and reminding me that his grandmother loved me, trusted me, expected some Buddhist comingling of spirits, even promised me home-cooked chicken soup on Sunday. And, well, I agreed. I picked him up in East Hartford in my repaired BMW. The third-floor tenant of Gracie's house, a retired mechanic she'd dated a hundred years before, checked it out for twenty bucks, replacing a switch. I knew nothing of cars. I always assumed they'd keep running.

We drove to Pho 501 on Burnside, had beef noodle soup for breakfast, the savory *pho,* the comfort soup of the Vietnamese, North and South, and everyone in between. Sitting in the crowded restaurant, I leafed through the *Hartford Courant.* The reporters who'd covered Mary's funeral described it as a sad day, with a photo of the coffin carried into the church on page one, "Story on page 3" under it. It was already becoming back-burner news, but there was a reiterated statement from the police that the shooting was an accidental drive-by. The reporter mentioned the grazing of Jose Santiago in the leg, with the glib speculation that the drive-by shooter had been trying to kill that hapless young man, who was quoted as saying, "Hey, it gotta be a mistake. Me and that dead lady was in the wrong place, like everybody says."

"Like everybody says," Hank echoed, spooning vermicelli noodles into a wide plastic dipping spoon, biting into a basil leaf.

"I guess it's official," I summed up. "So why are we going to the scene of the crime, Mr. Nguyen?" I stressed my words so they were capitalized—The Scene of the Crime. I waited. Hank slurped his soup, made a disgusting digestive sound that suggested his utter satisfaction with the meal, and then smiled. "Grandma *feels* it in her ancient bones. The spirit of the legendary Truong sisters rising up against the Chinese."

I interrupted. "Makes sense to me." I nudged him. "Hurry up. I got things to do today. There's a file clerk in the bowels of the Aetna building who's siphoning off billions of misdirected health benefits intended for the old lady from Dubuque."

"What the hell are you talking about?"

In Hartford we pulled the car onto Zion Street, headed down Maynard, and crept through the desolate streets near Goodwin Square. The yellow tape was down, of course, though a few fragments remained wrapped around a parking meter, entangled with an empty Coke bottle. As the two of us stood on the sidewalk, a Hartford cruiser slipped by, the two officers inside eyeing us warily—and the square. The car slid through a red light and nearly hit a hip-hop kid who assumed he had the walk light, a kid who shot the officers the middle finger. The cops disappeared onto a side street. Two out-of-place souls, Hank and I stared at the sidewalk, with me dressed in Eddie Bauer unpressed khakis and a faded J. Crew polo shirt, in loafers with no socks. Very Farmington Country Club. Hank, at least, was dressed in knee-length cutoffs and a baggy tank top, looking like something out of an MTV self-indulgent reality show, a hip young man who knew when the cameras were on him. I suddenly felt old and I thought—My God, we've produced a generation of young kids who spend their lives dressing and acting and speaking as though cameras are always rolling.

The square was largely Hispanic with a smattering of blacks, a few old white shopkeepers who looked glazed and unhappy as they stood in doorways of shops that sold used furniture and bric-a-brac. One ran a check-cashing operation, with bulletproof barriers between him and the world.

We walked along. "I look out of place here."

Hank grinned. "I don't."

Midday, the street sang, families on the sidewalks, vendors setting up to sell knockoff Rolex watches and phony Boston Red Sox baseball caps. Kids sucking on raspberry sno-cones. The sidewalks were so hot a wavy film hovered in the air like a hot-air ghost. Folks moved slowly. At the end of the block someone had opened a hydrant and half-naked kids hurled themselves joyously into jets of cold, cold water. We talked to a lot of people. We found out nothing. As Detective Ardolino had suggested, the square was infamous for silence, that numbing blankness that answered any question.

"Could I ask you a few questions about the shooting here the other day?"

"Are you guys cops?"

"No, I'm a PI working for the dead woman's family, just looking for some answers." I repeated the line over and over. I displayed my license, handed out my card with my office and cell numbers. Most didn't take it. But some examined my Connecticut State PI license with the care of a scholar examining the Dead Sea Scrolls right out of an unearthed pottery jar. But it didn't matter because nobody saw anything. Shaking heads, shrugged shoulders, quick turning away, tight lips, furrowed brows, palms out like a traffic cop. "No, nothing. Sorry." Most times we didn't even get the "sorry."

"Everyone is afraid," Hank said.

"I know, but a lot of these people work and live here. The stores are open till nine. People sitting on stoops. Somebody saw something."

Hank pointed out a young kid, maybe sixteen or seventeen, in a T-shirt that bore the name Bob Marley and displayed a bold marijuana leaf, a boy in baggy pants and work boots, who was lounging against a brick wall near an alley, dealing openly. But when we walked toward him, he bolted, disappearing so quickly into a half-boarded-up building that it was easy to believe he was never there in the first place.

"He thinks we're cops," Hank muttered. "He's seen us going in and out of stores."

So we talked to a clerk and the street customers in Baby Doll Video, a XXX adult video parlor that featured blinking lights in a painted-over window. The clerk was talky and funny, but wasn't working the five-to-midnight shift that night. In some of the groceries the owners only spoke Spanish—or claimed to. The guy in the check-cashing establishment turned his back on us. The Jamaican woman who was singing at the top of her lungs as we strolled into her discount women's dress shop decided to take a vow of silence. When we walked out, the singing began again. The owner of South American imported gifts was a sweet old woman who talked only to Hank, grinning into his face, but she said, "*Lo siento. Nada nada nada.*" A dashiki-clad young man in an apartment rental storefront—No Fees! No Hidden Charges!—wore drop earrings that made noise when he shook his head. "I no seen nothing. I go to the back parking lot when I leave anyway." We had thick, potent coffee and lunch at a small Peruvian café, but the owner and patrons claimed there'd been nothing to see. Two of the customers said they'd been at the café that night, as was the waiter, who recalled, "Suddenly there's a bang bang, and then there is silence. I look out and the cops are speeding through. A body on the ground. It's over. Like that. We say, hey, another killing."

And so it went, until we approached the old shopkeeper of a dreary pawnshop on the southeast corner: Meyer and Meyer, est. 1937. The faded contents of the grimy front window—a folk guitar, a set of mismatched barbells, some LP records, one of which was Harry Belafonte, and a console model 1960s hi-fi—appeared frozen in a past lifetime. Stuff no junkie would "smash and grab." The burglary gates were half-down now, as if stuck in place.

The shopkeeper was a gruff, blustery soul who first warned us off. "What you expect in this neighborhood? Look around you. Not like the old days, let me tell you the God's honest truth. Now the punks bring in garden hoses they steal from people's garages and want top dollar. They walk in with DVD players with no backs, fresh from being pulled out of the wall. If I didn't own the building, I couldn't stay here. I still can't stay here. Look around. I'll be dead in…"

I cut him off. "The woman who was shot raised this young man here." I lowered my voice. Hank tried to look mournful, but succeeded merely in looking like a melodramatic circus clown frowning for the kiddies. But the old man stared into Hank's contorted face, said something in a language I assumed was Yiddish, and made a guttural sound.

"This is what the world has come to," he stammered. "You"—he pointed to Hank—"come to America and find not gold in the streets but gold in people's teeth and across their knuckles and chunks so big around their necks they got back problems if they live to my age." He chuckled, pleased with his observation. "Look," he added, "it's a sad story like all stories around here." His lips trembled. "But I got nothing to tell you. I read the papers. I saw no shooting car, and if I did would I ever tell you about it? Not in this lifetime. But I did see your mother." He looked at Hank, who was startled that the old man assumed Mary was his mother. "I'm closing up. It's eight or so, I go to lock the door, but, you know, having trouble with the old key, so I turn and see the woman walking out of a car and standing on the sidewalk. She's standing there under the streetlight, and I think, what's with the Oriental lady being here? But I think maybe she's working in the Chinese takeout one block over so I don't look back. I went back into the store to turn off a light I left on in back because I forget every day, and I close the front door behind me. Next thing I know—bang bang."

"Two shots?'

"Two shots. I stay inside until the police come. Then I go home to watch it on the eleven o'clock news."

"Thank you," Hank told him.

"But I'll tell you, young man, a strange thing. In the split second I spot her standing there, she's there like she's looking for someone. That was the look on her face. Like she's supposed to meet someone there. Like a person would look at a watch, you know."

"Did she look disoriented?"

"What does that mean? I don't know. I'm telling you, she might have been on the wrong corner by accident, but she'd come from somewhere looking for something."

"Or someone." I looked at Hank. "Maybe she was looking for someone."

Chapter Seven

On Sunday I drove to Hank's home for *mi ga*, chicken soup, the Sunday morning ritual of Vietnamese the world over. Invited many times to his home, I still felt a twinge of nervousness whenever I turned the car in that direction. There was a time when I wouldn't have agreed so quickly to such an invitation. Hank's father and grandfather, defenders of the idea of Pure Blood, stared at me too long—me, the mixed-blood violator of the Vietnamese household. But Hank had made it his mission—once he got beyond his own bias inherited from the men in his family—to integrate me into the family. It worked. Sort of.

Inside the front door I removed my shoes, pushing them into the pile outside the kitchen door. I checked whether I had a hole in my sock. I didn't.

Hank saw me looking. "How Americanized you are."

I grinned. "Look at you."

Hank's big toe jutted from a white athletic sock. He wiggled it. "I'm at home."

Hank's mother greeted me, hugged me, and her fingers touched my hot cheek. "Sit in front of the fan. Please."

We sat at the huge Formica table. The life of the family was centered in the kitchen where all friends and family gathered. American guests sat in the little-used living room.

His mother handed me a glass of Vietnamese coffee, a potent brew sweetened by condensed milk. The glass was ice-cold to the touch. It tasted like a creamy dessert.

"I know you like it extra sweet."

"*Cam on*," I told her. Thank you. *Cam on nhieu.*

No one spoke English now, so I stumbled a bit with my fractured Vietnamese. We discussed the heat of the day. His mother choked out a word: *Nong*. We all nodded. Hank, wide-eyed at some of my stuttered words, jumped in to save me from total embarrassment once or twice, my incomplete sentences hanging in the air. Yet I managed somehow, perhaps feebly.

I heard soft muttering in the hallway, and Grandma walked in, followed closely by Grandpa. Old, old, Hank's grandfather creaked along. I had been talking to Hank, facing him, and his eyes got cloudy, a wide, uneasy stare. The old man, small and withered like a gnarled twig, took a seat at the table, away from me, and looked at me as though I were a horrible nightmare, perhaps your worst enemy come to poison your table.

Hank cleared his throat, but said nothing. Maybe the old war had a few more battles left to fight. He'd been through this before, of course—warring with Grandpa's dislike of me, the visiting pariah, a dust boy from under a rock.

So I turned to Grandma, greeted her in halting but very respectful Vietnamese, and she smiled, leaned over the table for the obligatory kiss. I liked her, this woman so small she barely came up to my hip, her ancient face lined and blotchy. A woman given to generosity and love, she motioned her daughter-in-law to ladle delicious *mi ga* into my bowl. I nodded. Yes, please. Soon the whole family settled into chairs around the table, chopsticks clicking.

But today a film of grief covered that warm kitchen, quieting the tensions and angers that sometimes surfaced there between Hank and his father, Hank and his grandfather, and Hank and his older sister. This was a family that never understood their bright, clever, good-looking son, especially when he decided to become a cop. It made no sense to them. Good Vietnamese boys went to UConn, majored in finance or computers, and bought houses for their parents in Avon or Simsbury. Why else the arduous trek to America way back when?

Hank once told me, "Mom said I was too good-looking and too smart-mouthed for my own good. They would have been happier with a squat, chunky son with thick glasses and an obvious overbite, who could do math in his head. *That* is the son of choice in Little Saigon."

We sat at the table, close together, even the younger kids. And the talk today was about the murder. Everyone had something to say, and the family talked over one another excitedly. Only Grandma, tucked into a kitchen chair by the open window, her head turned toward whatever breeze seeped into the room, kept still, though it was clear to me she was listening to every word. Hank's father talked of hatred of the Vietnamese. "We are the Jews of Asia," he declared. "Mary's murder…"

Hank raised his eyebrows. "Why does everything have to be a conspiracy?"

"What does that mean? What conspiracy?" His father's tone was cutting.

"Maybe Aunt Mary made a mistake, that's all," Hank's younger brother said, a little shyly.

"I'm tired of hearing that," his mother groaned. "Everyone talks as if the woman was an imbecile."

"Death by confusion." Hank cleared his throat. His father cast him a withering look. "I mean…"

"The soup is delicious," I cut in, looking first at his mother and then at Grandma. I knew both women created the aromatic *mi ga* together, a careful concoction of savory broth, diced scallions and herbs, tender bean sprouts, and pieces of chicken. I also knew that a concession was made for half-white and wholly American me. While the family ate the chicken soup with all the dubious parts of a slaughtered chicken tossed in—bones, cartilage, flabby skin, neck—my bowl held a floating layer of pristine, elegantly sliced pure-white breast meat.

Grandma once told me, "Foolish boy. White meat is inferior. The flavor is at the bone."

Hank's grandfather, that moody, irascible man, given these days to spurts of gagged coughing from his three-packs-a-day Marlboros, monitored the conversation with the restlessness of a man sitting among inferiors. He shook his head when Hank's mom concluded, "We may never know what happened to sweet Mary. This is one of the mysteries that will linger in the Vietnamese community forever."

"No." Hank's father frowned. "It should be easy to nab a madman, some deranged American." Hank's father believed the world had gone crazy after 1975. When he drank, he blamed the white man, who ruled the earth and ruined his life.

"Well, it's not like we don't kill each other," Hank said, probably reading his father's mind. And he started to catalogue the domestic disputes of recent years in the Vietnamese community. Husbands strangling wives, wives bludgeoning husbands, homes ransacked, infidelities that led to street brawls, women slapped in West Farms Mall and their incredulous husbands, since a man can do whatever he wants to his wife, led off by overweight security rent-a-cops.

Mr. Nguyen boomed. "Enough. This is what you do in front of an American guest? You put down your people?"

Everyone looked at me, then at Hank, red in the face, sheepish. Until that moment I'd been feeling very much a part of the community, despite the curse of being mixed blood. Now, conspicuous, I blinked too much. I slopped *mi ga* on my white man's shirt.

Hank stammered. "Dad, Rick is Vietnamese."

"If you say so," the man sneered.

I looked at his mother. She wore a bewildered look, and when she noticed me eyeing her, she turned away, a hint of color rising in her cheeks and neck.

Grandma was following this unpleasant exchange with a glint in her eye. "Rick is like my son." She stared down her son-in-law. "This is a good man. He's looking into this case…"

"Mmm." I smiled. "I'm not really on any case here. I'm just asking a few questions."

Hank's mother whispered, "Mary had no enemies. None. You have to *talk* to people, Rick. Find *out* things. She had no enemies." Anger in her voice.

Grandma spoke quietly. "Of course she did. We all do. Even you." She pointed at her flustered daughter. One of the kids actually giggled. She paused. "I know she had an enemy because I dreamed it."

Immediately the whole family groaned. Grandma's dreams were notorious: cautionary tales of woe and doom, though they sometimes had silver linings in otherwise dismal landscapes. Hank once told me she could end a meal with a few dark images she carried from her dream life. Hank's father would walk out of the room.

"I'm not on the case," I repeated slowly.

Grandma patted my hand, resting on the table. "I have faith in you, Rick. You understand that we all suffer but there are roads that shift, change direction, lead away from pain…You are a man with questions, and questions lead to answers."

"Not always," Hank insisted. "Sometimes questions don't have answers."

I found myself staring at the Buddhist shrine in the corner—a bowl of blood-red oranges, sticks of incense, gaudy icons pasted to a board. That shrine always took me back to Vietnam and comforted me. In this typical American kitchen—with the Mr. Coffee and toaster and microwave oven and juicer, surrounded on every wall with calendars from Chinese or Vietnamese restaurants, perhaps five in all—I could always detect the peculiar smell of incense and Asian cooking, the curious mixture of sweet and bitter, a hint of jasmine.

Grandma reached over and tapped Hank on the shoulder. "You have a lot to learn, love." But she was smiling at him.

When we were finished, Hank and I left the kitchen. Outside, Hank apologized for his father's insult to me, but I held up my hand.

"Sometimes I hate him," he fumed.

"No, you don't."

He actually trembled. I put my hand on his shoulder, but he shook it off. "Don't feel sorry for me, Rick."

I waited.

Finally he stammered, "He *is* a good man, Rick."

"I know that."

"But I will never be like that. Never."

We drove to Benny Vu's home to make our condolence call. "I'm not on a case," I repeated. "I don't recall receiving a retainer from anyone involved, nor did Benny and his family hire me."

Hank grinned. "Of course you're on the case. I've already told you that."

"I forgot."

"Besides, you wouldn't take money from family. That's not how you're built."

I groaned.

Benny Vu lived on the other side of East Hartford, on Maple Street, a small dead-end street off Main Street, a row of squat houses whose backyards faced a moribund textile plant and a city incinerator. From the street I could see darkened smokestacks, a cell tower, and elaborate electrical grids. Overhead wires, strung on poles with red blinking lights, stretched and towered behind the small weathered Cape Cod house, company houses originally, that looked like hiccoughs of one another. The neighbors to the right still had their Christmas decorations hung, those redundant white-light icicles hanging off every eave and over their garage.

"One hundred shopping days left to Christmas," I joked to Hank.

We parked on the street, and I stared at the house with its peeling paint and sagging front porch. Hank had mentioned that the grocery was closed now—and no one knew when it would reopen because, family gossip suggested, Benny had lost his spirit. Since the murder, he sat at home in front of a large-screen TV that stayed on the same channel, smoking cigarette after cigarette, the long trace of ash of each one finally falling onto his lap.

"That's what my mother told me," Hank confided. "She's worried he'll burn down the house." Family dropped off food. Neighbors stopped in but quickly left.

The doorbell was broken, the cement landing was cracked, and the laminate on the cheap front door had buckled and split. The chain-link fence surrounding the front yard was rusted and, in one place, bent, as though a runaway car had plowed into it. The gate no longer latched. This was a house its owners forgot.

A woman Hank didn't know let us in—"I'm Melissa from next door"—and we slipped off our shoes in the hallway. We sat in the tiny front room, the TV on, though the sound was turned off, and Benny mumbled something about tea. No, we both said. Then we all got quiet. The neighbor waved good-bye, looked relieved, and disappeared out the front door. Benny lit a cigarette. I noticed ashes on his shirt. He was staring at the images on the TV, as if he forgot we were there.

"*Xin loi.*" Hank leaned in. I'm sorry.

"*Xin loi ong,*" I echoed, apologizing for the intrusion.

He nodded, smiling thinly.

In contrast to the outside of the house, the living room was spotless, a hard-polished look to it, and I imagined Mary's deft and passionate hand on every surface. But everything was old, threadbare. A boxy floor fan whirled hot air around us, but the windows were shut. The room was stifling. This would be a short visit. I found myself staring at a thumbtacked calendar from an Asian marketplace, not Benny's, with the wrong month— July—still showing. Why hadn't Mary changed it? Hadn't she noticed? The house showed her attention to detail, so that fact bothered me. That, and the oversized flat-screen TV that seemed too large, too emphatic, for the tiny room.

A cousin Hank recognized walked in from the kitchen, carrying a pitcher of iced ginger tea. A woman in her forties, she nodded at Hank and smiled at me. "I'm Hyunh Le." She bowed and handed Benny a tall glass with a sprig of mint floating near the top. She sat down next to him, looked at us, and sighed. "Well."

No one said anything.

Finally, struggling, sitting there with Benny and Hyunh Le looking into their laps, we began forced, idle talk about the unrelenting dog-day heat, the solemnity of Mary's funeral, the recent flooding in the southern provinces of China. Benny, I realized, was still in shock because his voice was calm and deliberate, the words spaced out as though he were drugged. In fact, I wondered whether he'd been put on some medication. That might explain the narrowed eyes and the drumbeat monotone.

All of a sudden, at Hank's mention of our visit to the crime scene—I'm not sure why he did it—Benny started to gurgle, a deep, bubbly sound erupting from the back of his throat, rising like vomit, until he stammered, "Somebody has got to pay for this. Mary needs justice." The words hung in the air.

"Benny," I began, "the cops have decided it was an accident. They say she got lost or…"

He stared directly into my face, and I involuntarily jerked my head back because his look was so raw and haunted.

"No, there's more of an answer," he cried out. "Mary did everything with purpose. You hear me. She was *not* a woman who made mistakes."

It was an effort for him to say so many words, and he mumbled at the end, as though losing his train of thought. But then he summed up, his voice loud again. "Somebody didn't *love* her."

That sentence stunned me. "What?"

"There's someone out there that killed her."

True, I thought, but that didn't mean the shooter knew her, wanted her dead, even cared whether she died—but I kept my mouth shut. Again, that full, stark look into my face.

"He has a name that somebody knows. Murderers have names."

I swiveled toward Hank. He shot me a look. We sat there, our eyes riveted to the glass pitcher of iced ginger tea, beads of sweat running down the side.

The awful silence was broken by the sound of a slammed car door. Tommy and Cindy arrived, traipsing in from somewhere, rapid footsteps in the hallway and into the living room. Cindy was yelling at Tommy for something he'd said, which I didn't catch. Suddenly the house had noise as Benny's two children settled into armchairs, adjusting their bodies as if they were late for a good movie. Benny didn't even look up at them. The cousin, unhappy now, with steely eyes and angry mouth, chided them for going out.

Tommy spoke into her face. "We can't sit around here like zombies, Aunt Hyunh."

"Your mother is dead."

I thought that a little cruel, and even Benny looked at her.

Tommy closed himself in like a turtle, tucking in his neck and folding his arms. The pale sunlight filtering through the blinds caught the irregular shape of his metal earrings and his eyebrow ring, and he sparkled there in the shadows like a glittering store mannequin. I stared at him, this twenty-five-year-old who was a little old to be so punked out, so deliberately and calculatingly tough. Beneath the tattoos and ripped T-shirt, the stomp-you boots, the thick chains hanging off his studded belt, the last-of-the-Mohegans haircut—beneath it all was a gangly, feckless Vietnamese boy with a long narrow face and intelligent eyes, but eyes filmed with a spacey blankness I couldn't penetrate. Something was going on there, for sure, but what? A drifter from one dead-end job to another—used-music store clerk, pizza delivery boy, various stock boy jobs, now and then a clerk in his father's grocery. Tommy wanted nothing to do with his Old Country family. The son of one of the most beautiful women of Hartford, he had once told Hank that he had little use for his parents, born as they were into the woeful poverty and endless war of Saigon.

"They're strictly FOB," he told Hank. Fresh Off the Boat— that dismissive and insulting phrase. He, however, was ABV— American-born Vietnamese. That made all the difference.

I said, "Tommy, I'm sorry about your mom."

For a second he looked ready to hurl a flip comment my way, because I saw his lips purse. But then his body sagged, folding into the armchair, and his arms fell like broken tree limbs against his side. It was like watching a puppet loosed from its strings. For a second his face crumbled, but then immediately tightened. He nodded. "Thanks, man. She was—okay." That was a strange remark, but maybe not. It came out like a perfect epitaph for the mother he couldn't help caring about.

And somehow those words, so casual but so apt, elicited an unexpected dry sob from Cindy, sitting opposite him. Her cell phone chimed, but she ignored it.

"I hate this." We all looked at her. She was looking at Hyunh Le.

Cindy, I realized, must have had a brutal adolescence, living in the shadow of the legendary beauty of her mother. No one ever said the "beautiful" Cindy Vu. Not by a long shot. And they never would. She'd never approached even a suggestion of the sensuality, the allure, the dead-in-your-tracks beauty of her mother and Aunt Molly. It wasn't that she was unattractive, I realized. It was that she was abysmally plain, as though fate had willed her the dull out-of-proportion features of her father, the flat round face, the loopy ears, the disappearing chin, the undersized head. She'd done everything possible to correct this. I'd never seen her without an overabundance of makeup. As she was now, in fact, sitting there with her Asian new wave wardrobe, the laced-up boots and tight halter top, that tattoo of a heart where her almost nonexistent cleavage began. And the spiked, magenta-tinged hair. But the face: the shrill whore's lipstick, white Kabuki powder too generously applied, thinned out and repainted eyebrows, arching too high on the flat face. She'd done everything possible to hide the face she could not love. At twenty-four she was a young woman trying to disappear.

"What?" From Tommy, looking at her.

She was shaking. "I just hate this. This is not the way…" She fumbled. She looked at Hank. "We had a fight that morning. Like we always did, her and me. The same stupid, stupid fight over nothing. I told her that I *hated* her. I ran off and left her alone for the whole day. I was supposed to *be* with her that day. I didn't go home." A long silence. "Then someone calls the house that night and tells me somebody murdered her. How can your mother get murdered? How? She stocks shelves at a fucking loser grocery store. She washes the kitchen floor. She…"

"*Dung ngay*," her father demanded. Stop it!

Cindy, trembling, stood up suddenly, ready to fall. Hank rushed over, wrapped his arms around her, and held her. Tears rolled down that powered face. I thought of mountain rivulets, water coursing through spring snow. She whispered, "Mommy."

Tommy jumped up, chains rattling against his side. "For shit's sake, Cindy, what the fuck's wrong with you? We talked this out in the car, no?"

"Talked what out?" I asked.

Tommy looked at me, disgusted. "It doesn't do any good to fall apart now."

"What does that mean?" From Hank.

"It means, we gotta pull the pieces together and keep going." The words sounded harsh and unfeeling, but there was a barely-controlled edge to them. Unhinged. Wound too tight.

"Dien," Benny said, using his son's Vietnamese name. "It is okay to grieve for your mother."

Tommy looked from his sister, still held by Hank, to his father. He spat out angrily, "You never had a clue, did you, Pop?"

"Tommy!" From Hank.

"None of this is your business, Hank. Why are you even here? And why'd you bring *him*?" Pointing at me. "The white guy."

They all looked at me. "Actually I'm half-Vietnamese." I immediately regretted the words.

"Which is the half that made you stumble into our house?"

With that, he left, but not before hurling another angry look at his sister. Cindy moved away from Hank now, sitting in a chair with her arms folded around her chest.

Benny turned to me, his face sad. "My children don't know how to grieve for their mother. They forgot that they loved her." He lit another cigarette.

When Hank and I left, Benny was in his chair, slumped over, staring at the floor. He glanced up when we said good-bye, then went back to staring at the carpet.

"Well, that went well," I said to Hank in the car. "Any other ideas?"

"And we didn't really learn a thing."

I shook my head. "Actually, Hank, I think we learned quite a lot in that house."

"But none of it useful."

"That remains to be seen."

Chapter Eight

Molly Torcelli opened the door before we rang the doorbell. "You're early."

On the phone I'd said five o'clock, and it was ten of the hour. "Sorry."

She turned, walked back into the vast foyer under the chandelier, and Hank and I followed. She hadn't said come in, but she was used to people following her. To her back I mumbled my traditional Vietnamese condolences.

I'd never been to her home in Farmington, but I was surprised when Hank said he'd never been there either. Molly didn't entertain stragglers from the Vietnamese community. Lost in the leafy, mountainous hills, the estate was set far back in a cove of towering maples, far inside the gated acreage, unseen from the narrow road we drove in on. A white sprawling Colonial, with Greek columns staggered across the front, it looked like the forest had grown up around it, sheltering it. A circular driveway followed a rise of land, with beds of flowers speckling the overwatered blue-green lawn. A bank of garages masquerading as a carriage house was off to the left. The neighboring estates were barely seen—a hint of chimney, a suggestion of attic windows—tucked away in their own private forests.

"I've been waiting for you," Molly said as we sat in a sunroom, all wicker and polished green ivy. "People have been coming all day, and they look at me for answers." She sighed. "What answers can I give people? What? Tell me that. My twin sister is gone. Stupidly gone."

Suddenly she was quiet, staring from me to Hank, but I could see her body tighten. She sat still, her hands folded into her lap, a study in fragile self-control. She was dressed in a light yellow cotton summer dress, with yellow sandals. A gold bracelet. In her hands she held a crumpled yellow handkerchief, wadded and damp. Only her hair held slight reddish highlights. And her nails—fingers and toes—were a shade of pink. Of course, as I looked at her, I pictured the dead sister, her dark flashing eyes in the oval, delicate face. Here was a woman who'd known nothing but being beautiful since she was a child. And the redundant yellow of her appearance simply reinforced her exquisite look. I was impressed.

A maid entered the room, almost apologetically, and set a large silver tray on the table. I saw a pitcher of iced tea and an array of Italian cookies. Four tall glasses, chilled. "Anything else, Miss Molly?"

Molly looked into her face and suddenly burst into tears. The maid nodded, made a sympathetic sound, looked ready to cry herself, and backed out of the room. Molly sobbed into her crumpled handkerchief. In between the giant, sloppy gasps, she tried to apologize, tried to control herself.

"No need to apologize," I told her. "Maybe we should leave you alone."

"No, no," she protested, half rising. "I can't get used to—can't believe—Mary is gone. Unbelievable. Un*bear*able. Someone *shot* her. Mary. Quiet, simple Mary."

Those quaint, sentimental words—"quiet, simple"—jarred me, maybe because I sensed a little patronizing tone, and I found myself adding the obligatory final word—quaint, simple, *poor* Mary. Probably this was unfair of me, I told myself, as I watched Molly pull herself together, pour herself a glass of tea. She forgot to offer us some. Her hand trembled.

I repeated, "Maybe now's not a good time."

She breathed in. "Will there ever be a good time for something like this? I don't think so. Oh no."

"Are your children here?"

She waved her hand in the air. "Somewhere." The flighty hand suggested they were lost, out of satellite range, in some distant wing of the large palatial estate, doubtless playing violent video games on a Sony PlayStation in the lower forty.

Then, her sobbing under control, Molly looked at Hank, her voice all business. "Your mother called this morning. She told me about your grandmother wanting Rick to ask around." She glanced at me.

Ask around—what did that mean? I tried to distance myself. "Mrs. Torcelli, the truth of the matter is that I don't even know if there's any reason *to* ask around. The police are pretty sure about this."

"Please—my name is Molly." Then, blunt, to the point. "But isn't that why you're here?"

"I suppose so. I told her I'd *talk* to people. But also, of course, bring my condolences."

She almost smiled. "Like a good Vietnamese."

She started to nibble on an almond cookie, collecting the crumbs in the palm of her hand.

"I'm not the kind of investigator who takes on murder…"

The word *murder* startled her, and she choked on the cookie. "I'm sorry," she stammered. "Just the way you said that hit me to the quick. It's not a word I'm comfortable with."

I apologized.

"No, no." She leaned toward me. "It's me. I had a sleepless night last night. I expect I'll have a few more such nights ahead of me."

"How's your family doing?"

She ignored me. "I expect I'll have to see someone." She looked away, as though running through a list of therapists on call.

It dawned on me that Hank had said nothing since we'd arrived. After offering his own condolences, he'd closed himself up. Glancing in his direction, I saw him leaning forward in his chair, elbows on knees, hands on the sides of his face, staring wide-eyed at nothing. Not at Molly, to be sure. His lips were drawn into a thin, disapproving line, bloodless and tight. In the car on the way over he'd confessed that he never really cared for Molly, what little he saw of her.

"Money has made her different."

"It has that effect," I'd told him. "How different?"

"She likes it too much."

"That's not a sin."

"She learned it from her husband Larry. He's the dean of that school, let me tell you." He sounded angry.

"Well, think about it, Hank. She came from nothing, born in Saigon during the war, airlifted out, dirt poor, you know, and now she's on the Board of Directors for the Athenaeum in Hartford. That's a leap."

Hank made a face. "I don't trust people who don't have any self-doubt."

"But we can cut her a little slack in light of her twin sister's death, no?"

"We'll see."

So now he sat still, Rodin's *The Thinker* meets the young kid in *Home Alone*—that pose. Frozen, the prisoner in the tower.

When Molly confided, "You know, I've had to cancel four appointments this week alone," Hank stood up, coughed, and gazed out the bank of windows at the rolling acres that swept down the back into a thicket of hemlock. The muscles on the back of his neck looked like rough thick rope.

Molly paid him no mind. "How do you go about questioning drug dealers?" she asked.

Good question. I had absolutely no response to that.

"Well?" Impatient.

"This really is not a case, Molly. Right now, I'm just exploring. I'm just talking a bit…"

She interrupted. "Rick Van Lam, it's either a duck or it's not a duck. You either do something or you don't." She half-closed her eyes. "I'm sorry. That's not me talking. That's my husband Larry. That's his philosophy of life."

"Drug dealers—or gangbang shooters—are not known to talk about themselves. Even the police hit a brick wall there. I'm more concerned with Mary's behavior that night. *Her* decision to go there."

Hank returned, sat down, and stared at her.

"Iced tea?" she interrupted, as though just remembering to be a perfect hostess. She leaned forward, indicating the pitcher. The gold bracelet, I noted, was inlaid with tiny diamonds. She handed two glasses to us.

"Molly," I began as she sat back, "why do you think Mary was in that neighborhood, even stepping out of her car?" I waited.

The question took her off guard. She hadn't expected it. Then she composed herself. "You know, I don't have a clue. Mary wouldn't be caught dead in such a place." She looked away.

But in the split second that she caught my eye, repeated the line she'd said before, and then turned away, something happened. I caught a momentary flicker of an eye, a quick bleak flash of fear and terror. When she looked back, the eyes were dull, veiled.

I didn't know what to make of it. I swear I saw something there.

The front door opened, and Larry walked in, undoing a tie and the top button of his blue dress shirt. He didn't look happy to see us there. "I wondered who was driving the ancient BMW." He looked at me.

He sat down, reached for the iced tea. That explained the fourth glass the maid had placed on the tray. I noticed thick graying beard stubble on his afternoon face. Larry had the rumpled, slightly gone-to-seed look of a very wealthy man who once was tremendously handsome, athletic, popular, and aggressive. Now, it seemed to me, the aggressiveness dominated, but it was tempered with a hazy sort of good looks. People would always refer to him as handsome, but they might also comment on the steeliness of his eyes, the harsh wrinkles around the sensual mouth. The Mediterranean good looks—he and Molly must have been Scott and Zelda country club luminaries way back when—had hardened, and the shock of black hair was thinning now, gray at the temples. What he exuded, I felt, was a kind of blunt, no-nonsense force, the authority of stock portfolio and embarrassingly wonderful cash flow.

He was trying to be friendly, joking idly with the totally unresponsive Hank. "Haven't seen you in a dog's age." He punched him in the shoulder. Hank nodded.

Molly introduced me. "This is Rick Van Lam, a friend of Hank's."

Larry looked like he could care less, but he extended his hand, and we shook. His palms were wet.

"Horrible, horrible," he spoke to no one in particular. "Makes no sense to anyone." He undid another button on his shirt. The home was beautifully air-conditioned, but he looked flushed from the heat of the afternoon. He dabbed his face with a handkerchief.

Molly smiled thinly. "You know how we said the police were doing absolutely nothing, Larry?"

"What do you expect? It's Hartford. Most of the cops are on the take, if they're not boinking some crack hooker on Asylum Hill."

"For God's sake, Larry." She looked at me, then back at her husband. "Larry is a man of definite opinions." Her face crumbled a bit.

He smirked. "Molly hates it when I'm candid."

"Rick here is an investigator and he's looking into the case…"

I raised my hand in protest. "Wait. It's not a case…"

"What case?" From Larry.

"Hank's mother and grandmother have asked if he'd ask around about Mary. To see if anyone knows *why* she went there. You know, help the police a bit. You know. Talk to people."

Larry looked at me as though he were in the presence of a lunatic. "You're doing what?" Incredulous.

"Just talking to people."

"Like us?"

"People."

"Well, knock your socks off." He shrugged, dismissing the subject. "But it seems to me you'd be better off nailing that lowlife that gunned her down."

"For God's sake, Larry," Molly pleaded.

"Let the Ricans shoot each other. What's sad is that Mary was..."

Hank spoke for the first time, ". . . in the wrong place at the wrong time." I stared at him. His face was red now.

"Exactly," Larry summed up. "Well, I got business I gotta take care of." He stood up. "Molly," he turned back, "where are Jon and Kristen?"

In the lower forty, I thought.

"I told Susie a half hour ago to get them to say hello to Hank and—and to Rick when they arrived." She made a you-know-how-they-are gesture, and smiled.

"I'll tell Susie again." He nodded at us. "See you, guys." He rushed off.

A horrible man. Or maybe not—a man used to having the world fall into line, a world that obeyed his commands.

Eventually, after an awkward silence during which we sipped tea, I heard footsteps on the stairwell, and Jon and Kristen strolled into the room, both looking like they'd been summoned to a gathering they preferred to skip. "What?" asked Jon.

His mother pointed to the two of us. We stood and shook hands. Jon said, "I saw you both at the funeral." He sat down, yawning, but covering his mouth after the fact. I found myself looking at him, thinking of him in ways I often thought of myself. Here was this half-Vietnamese, half-white man, twenty-five years old, I'd been told, comfortable with himself, a BA from Yale, a perpetual student, now living at home during the summer break. According to Hank's capsule summary in the car, Jon was getting a graduate degree in Public Policy, intending to become a lawyer "down the road, maybe."

That was Hank's quote.

Jon looked more Asian than white, though he had a square jaw and a shock of Italian hair. Those narrow eyes. Sepia skin like his mother's, supple and silky, and he'd inherited his mother's looks. Tall, a little too thin, he sat down with his long legs stretched out. He wasn't wearing shoes. Hank had told me Jon had forgotten most of the Vietnamese his mother taught him as a boy. Mary once told Hank's mother that Jon thought speaking Vietnamese made him sound like a Disney cartoon character. The few times I'd spotted him at gatherings he looked sullen and miserable. We'd never been introduced.

"Hi, Hank," Kristen nodded at him. "I saw you in church."

"Hi, Kristen." Hank smiled. "Sorry again."

"Oh, it's just awful. Awful." Then she stopped, as though confused.

"It's all right, dear," Molly said protectively.

We all knew that Kristen was, as one old Vietnamese man announced, "as dumb as two chopsticks trying to find each other in the dark," a cruel barb that had some currency a while back, one that got back to Molly and Larry. Kristen was, well, slow. As Hank told me in the car, "She's *ngu nhu cho*." As thick as two short planks. She'd become a recurring joke in a Vietnamese community that celebrated brainpower. And because she was rich—and half-white—the joking was often vicious and heartless. She said dumb things, not knowing they were dumb. Her father had a long history of enrolling her in progressively more and more expensive girls' schools. One of the last and most unsatisfying had been Miss Porter's down the street from my apartment, a school that talked of Jackie Kennedy as though she were still enrolled there, sitting in the cafeteria adjusting her bobby socks. But Kristen forgot to go to class and was expelled. She didn't care. I'd talked to her once at a New Year's party and I found her a sad young woman who'd come to believe her drop-dead gorgeous looks were all she needed to survive. That, her cell phone, and a checkbook.

Molly turned to Jon. "Hank and Rick have come to talk about your Aunt Mary."

"Why?" From Jon.

I spoke up. "Everyone feels that there has to be *some* investigation, some answer to why Mary drove her car…"

Jon interrupted, brusque. "You mean, *everyone* in the Vietnamese world." He ran his tongue over his lips.

"That's right," I insisted. "Closure, I guess." I despised the handy word. "We may never know."

On the defensive Hank added, "The Vietnamese need to tie all the strings, you know. Right, Jon? To leave little unanswered. What did Buddha say? 'When the line of a circle begins to be drawn, it must go until it finds itself again.'" He looked at me. "Rick taught me that."

I smiled. "Good for you, Hank."

Jon just stared.

"We're Catholic," Kristen said suddenly.

Jon frowned. "I never knew Aunt Mary that well, so I don't know what you want *me* to say. I couldn't even guess why she went *there*. I know Tommy and Cindy, but I knew them better a few years back, when we went to the same school for a while." He stared over my shoulder. "Our lives have gone in different directions. I don't know what they're up to these days. I mean, we're all friends on Facebook, but that's a way of *not* caring about people, right?"

"When we'd hang out with them, Aunt Mary wasn't around much," Kristen added. "She didn't like to talk to us."

"You know, she seemed uncomfortable around us," Jon said. "Sometimes she looked at us like we were dollar signs, two little privileged kids."

Molly spoke up. "You *are* privileged kids."

Jon looked at her. "Thank God for that."

Kristen smiled. "She was always nice to me."

Jon smirked. "Everyone's nice to you, Kristen. They want something."

"What?"

"Nothing. Nothing at all."

Kristen suddenly said good-bye. "Gotta run, gang." Nodding at her mother, she left the room.

Hank and Jon had started discussing Hank's desire to be a state trooper. "Sort of cool," Jon admitted. "Not for me. But sort of cool."

Molly didn't look too happy with the conversation, eyeing her son. I glared at Hank.

"When was the last time you spoke to Mary?" I asked her.

For a second, she got flustered, uncertain. "A day or so before she died, I think. We talked all the time on the phone. I'd got her on a local Asian Relief charity that I chair. She had better connections to the old Vietnamese community, and—and—I, well, I was supposed to pick her up for a meeting. It would have been the day of her funeral." She paused. "I missed her phone calls the day she died. She called me a few times—nothing unusual there. I called her. We played phone tag. Back and forth. We never spoke that day." She began sobbing and reached for a handkerchief.

Jon got up to leave. "Ma." Impatience in his voice.

I nodded at Hank. We said our good-byes. As we stood up, Kristen suddenly bounded down the stairs. Surprisingly, she'd gone to her room and changed her outfit, replacing the silky red blouse and baggy shorts for some tight jeans and a skimpy top.

"Going out?" her mother asked.

"No. Why?"

She disappeared back up the staircase.

Hank hugged Molly, who held on a long time. I could see Hank squirm. The maid stepped into the room. "Susie." Molly introduced her to us. "Do you know Susie? Her name is Suong but somehow, years back, we started calling her Susie." The short woman grinned, uncomfortable. We introduced ourselves. Susie led us into the foyer, but she hesitated on the threshold.

"Yes?" I encouraged her.

In broken English: "I know Miss Mary when she came here now and then. I always like her. A lot. She bring me cookies from her store, and she always asked about me and my boy. So sad to learn what happened to her. So cruel for a woman so good like her." She looked into my face, and I saw her eyes were wet. She held my hand.

We stood there, awkward, the three of us.

Somewhere in the house Larry was barking at his daughter, the words biting and angry. "What the fuck do you think you're doing? You don't have a brain in that goofy head of yours."

Susie saw me glance at Hank. "No listen to Mr. Larry. Please. He's, well, a rough man, but only on the outside. Inside he's a good, good man, let me tell you. I would not work in this house for more than twenty years if a man is evil." She opened the front door for us and watched us leave. I looked back. She was looking over her shoulder in the direction of the father-daughter altercation. The door closed.

In the car I said to Hank, "Why is it I'm not liking these people?"

"I feel the same, and they're my family. But I gotta tell you, Rick, they're distant, distant cousins. Maybe not even real cousins. You know how Vietnamese call lifelong friends family, like brothers and sisters and uncles. We probably don't even share blood...."

"Keep talking." I was smiling. "It's not helping you distance yourself from your, excuse me, cousins."

Hank waited a second. "When you asked Molly why Mary might be at that drug-dealer corner, I noticed her body tighten so fast it caught my attention."

"Not only that." I told him I saw some confusing flicker in her eyes, a flash of fear.

"Does it mean anything?"

"Maybe nothing at all. Grief sometimes is hard to translate."

Chapter Nine

Liz called with news.

"Just a tidbit that may mean nothing. Benny's store was once cited after a municipal-FBI raid. They confiscated bootleg Asian videos, but nothing came of it. No fine, just a warning. But you know how the mom-and-pop Asian markets thrive on bootlegging Hong Kong and Vietnamese tapes. Benny's was one of four shops raided in Little Saigon, a few splashy lines in the *Courant*, an indignant editorial from the paper about the death of legitimate free trade or something like that, what would the Founding Fathers say, and then the shelves were restocked with grainy copies of Jet Li kung fu flicks."

Lying on the sofa, I absently scratched my stomach. "Hartford thrives on an illegal underworld of drugs, hookers, and knockoffs of Sean John sweat suits—and Jackie Chan and Bruce Lee DVDs."

"I lift my torch…"

"Anything else?"

"How'd you know?" I could hear her smile. "The only other arrest was for little Tommy Vu, back when he was a senior at the hoity-toity Chesterton School. He had a couple of minor-league run-ins as a juvenile, shoplifting stuff. Nothing much. But he had one serious count of possession of a controlled substance—an ounce or so of pot. Intent to sell. Some lawyer got the charge reduced, a fine, probation, no lockup. Nothing since."

"How was he caught?" I asked.

"With the goods."

"I mean where?"

"In a club downtown near Union Station, one of those dance clubs for high school and college kids. No alcohol, just Ecstasy and sex in the bathrooms. By the time it wound its way through the courts, it seemed small potatoes in comparison to the high-level street traffic elsewhere in the naked city, what with slaphappy gunfire and all those gold teeth that shine in the dark."

"Doesn't sound like much of anything."

"I agree. But in the original police report a cop noted that Tommy struggled with the undercover agent, tried to flee, had to be cuffed. He said he'd get even with the snitch, even if it killed him."

"What snitch?"

"Report didn't say. You're the venerable PI. You find out."

◇◇◇

The next morning, close to noon, I drove to the Elmwood section of West Hartford, to the three-family house where Tommy lived on the third floor with two roommates. I figured he'd be home, probably still in bed. The first-floor apartment was boarded up, the result of a fire. "No Trespassing" signs were plastered on the plywood sheets covering the windows. But there were fans whirring in the second- and third-floor apartment windows, and the door to the front entrance was wide open. I climbed the stairs, the acrid scent of burnt wood lingering in the stairwell.

He answered on the third knock, dressed only in baggy denim shorts and all those earrings. His chest displayed a sunburst tattoo around his navel, and a painful-looking ring dangled from his left nipple. He looked a little glazed so I figured he was stoned. But it could have been the haze of sleep. He stared at me, eyes half-shut. He stuck his hand under the elastic band of his shorts and scratched a nether region best left unexplored.

"Oh, it's you. The PI. You're…"

"Rick Van Lam."

Confused: "You want something?"

"Can I come in?"

He was uncertain. "Sure, why not? Anything happen?"

"No. I wanted to talk to you about your mother."

But he stood there, vacant eyed, blocking my path.

"Is this a bad time?" I hoped he'd move.

"What?" Did he speak English, I wondered? Finally he turned. "Sure, come in." But he didn't move.

"You have a fire downstairs?"

He grinned. "Small one, in the living room. Crackheads knocked over a candle."

"I can smell the smoke."

"Cool, ain't it?"

I didn't think so.

But he stepped aside and waved me into the room, where I noticed another young man sitting on a stained, patched sofa. At first I thought it had to be one of his roommates, but he looked too much like a visitor—that, or he was going on a job interview, dressed as he was in a suit and tie.

"Tommy, take care of yourself, okay?"

The man leaned in and with his fist gently bumped Tommy's shoulder, some atavistic male bonding that seemed to energize the lethargic Tommy. He grinned, almost shyly. "Mom wouldn't like my manners," he said to me, and I found the statement oddly endearing. "This is my old friend Danny," he pointed. "We went to school together a million years ago."

I shook Danny's hand. He introduced himself. "I'm Danny Trinh."

"If there's anything I can do, buddy..." The young man's voice trailed off. "As I said, I'm sorry I missed the funeral. Bank business in White Plains. You know I couldn't help it." Tommy looked surprised. Danny was saying this for my benefit. Another young guy with proper manners. God, what was happening to the uncivil generation?

"I know," Tommy seemed confused. "You told me."

"It's just that everyone was there but me. The old gang. I wanted to be there."

"Hey." Tommy was dismissive. "What can you do?"

"Well, I gotta get back to the bank." Danny buttoned his sports jacket. A beep from his cell phone. He tapped his pocket.

Danny was a stark contrast to the slovenly Tommy. You could see how muscular he was under the beige summer jacket, the way the shirt hugged his body, the way he walked to the door in lithe, graceful strides. Scrawny, stringy Tommy, his ragged Mohawk haircut looking a little like a bristle brush, seemed a fitness center's "before" ad while Danny was the "after." This Danny was a man comfortable with himself. With his close-cropped hair, with that smooth sepia complexion, and with those expensive designer sunglasses tipped into the breast pocket of an expensive suit, he looked nightclub debonair. Poised and sure—the words that came to mind. If he were a shade lighter and didn't have those slanted eyes, he could be the newest suburban member of the Kiwanis Club, and a Young Republican to boot.

"Nice to meet you." Danny nodded at me in a polished, careful voice. To Tommy: "I'll stop in to talk to your father later this week."

They shook hands again.

"Sit down," Tommy told me after Danny left. I didn't know where to sit, so I sat in the spot Danny had vacated. The place was a shambles, like a freshman dorm room. Empty crumpled Coke and beer cans, a soup-dish ashtray of ground-out cigarette stubs, gamey-looking Chinese takeout containers, open with chopsticks jutting out. A pizza box, open, crusts scattered inside like petrified wood. CDs littered the floor near a boom box. A copy of the *Hartford Advocate*, an alternative newspaper. "Well?"

"Some of your relatives," I began, "want a clearer picture of your mother's last hours. Why she did what she did."

He watched me warily. "I dunno." He paused. "Look, I don't know. You don't think I haven't thought about it? Like…well— Mom driving there to that place. I know the place. Everybody I know does. You drive *around* it. It's always in the news."

"And you came up with nothing?"

"Nada. I swear."

"When did you last see your mother?"

He thought a minute "The day before she died. She stopped at the store and I was working."

"You talk to her the day she died?"

"No. No reason to."

"No idea why she went to Goodwin Square?"

"No."

"People who don't live there go there for drugs."

His eyes got wide. "You can't think Mom was on drugs?"

"God, no." Then, abrupt: "Do you ever go to Goodwin Square for drugs?" I waited.

The question made him angry. "Goddamn it. I was wondering if my arrest was gonna come up somehow. I mean, I hadn't thought about it, but everything online…or on TV…is drugs this and drugs that…in *that* place…and Mom…"

"After all, that was prep school—what happened to you. Right? Years back."

"You got that right, man. Prep school. Another world. Dumb kid shit. Stupid on my part, man. A real dumb-ass move by me. Sure, I toked a little weed, still do, but recreational, like everybody today, including probably you. It ain't like…heroin. But someone says 'drugs,' and everyone in the family looks at *me*. One time—and no other trouble with the law. You hear me? Nothing. Christ, I learned my lesson."

"But your mother…"

He broke in. "Man, it almost *killed* my mom. She was so *crazy* about it. You know, she had this thing about drugs. Scourge of the land, you know. You know the drill. But with her religion crap and her own son involved, well, she thought I was headed to heroin addiction and a psycho ward at Middletown. But if you're thinking that had *anything* to do with Mom…"

"At the time, when you were arrested at the club, you ran."

"So?"

"I'm just curious. You did threaten to get the 'snitch,' as you called it. Did you believe someone set you up?"

He laughed. "My, my, you do your fuckin' homework, don't you? No, that was just trash talk. I got the bag off this dude bartender—we all did—and I'm thinking he's undercover. But no, he's still there, a fuckin' cokehead himself now."

"So that was that."

"Right." He stared into my face. "Whoa, man. Ricky boy, is that why you're here now? Over *that*? What the fuck are you up to, man? That was like eight years ago, got nothing to do with this shooting of Mom. I admit she still hounded me about it, glanced at my arms for needle tracks or something. Years later. Good old Mom. But no, sorry to disappoint you. Are you saying I go to Goodwin Square to cop drugs? Like my mom was hunting me down there?" He made a fake laugh.

"No, just…"

He laughed that false laugh again. "Headline in the old *Courant*: Slacker Druggie Rubs out Mommy Because She Saved His Ass from Jail Back in Prep School. How's that for a big story? Guess not, Mr. Rick Van Lam, PI. Too long for a headline, maybe. You got enough Viet Cong in you, Lam boy, to understand what I have to say to you." He sneered, "*Du ma may.*" Fuck you.

He stood up and stormed into the bathroom, slamming the door behind him. When I realized he wouldn't be coming out, I left.

◇◇◇

I called Hank that afternoon, told him I wanted to talk about the Torcelli-Vu kids, and he suggested we meet for a pizza. "What about work?" I asked him.

"I'm on strike. Besides, I need a break. In a few weeks I'll be back at the Academy."

So, abetting his diminishing work ethic, I picked him up, and we headed down to Pepe's old-fashioned coal-fired pizza on Wooster Square in New Haven. It was a forty-five-minute drive and we had to stand in line with Yalies and the old Italians from the neighborhood, baking in the late-afternoon sun, just to get frosty Foxon Birch Beer and dusty crusted, mouth-watering pizza.

Seated after a long wait, relaxed, I asked him, "Now tell me the story of those four kids. The cousins."

"They're not kids. Kristen is the youngest at twenty-three."

"She's two years older than you."

"What do you want to know?"

"Just talk about them. You know them."

"Only a little bit. We never hung out or anything, like at each other's houses. Just at New Year's or weddings. That kind of thing."

"They like you. I sensed that Kristen does, at least."

"She likes everyone. Well, sometimes I like them." He sighed. "Sort of. Maybe. One or two of them. Most times they irritate me. Especially Jon."

"Well, I'm glad you've thought this through."

He laughed. "You know, for a while, when they were young kids, even through the first years of prep school, the four were good friends. Or so my mother tells me. It didn't matter that Jon and Kristen were rich, and Tommy and Cindy were poor. I guess blood meant something, even though Jon and Kristen— half-white—always had, you know, the best electronic gadgets, the most expensive clothing, ski trips to Vermont, the best of everything. But Mary and Molly wanted them to be friends because Molly and Mary loved each other." He looked me in the eye. "They were the beautiful Le sisters."

"Seriously?"

"Yeah, they took that label seriously. It was like Molly, after she got married, was afraid she'd lose her connection to her family, her sister. Their parents were dead. They only had each other. But you know how it is—time started pulling Molly away. All that money and prestige, Larry's business connections, those business parties, those husband-and-wife cruises to the tropics, the rich friends flying to their place in the Bahamas. But Molly still kept that allegiance to her sister, her twin sister, her only sister, and her sister's poverty rankled."

"She blamed Mary for being poor?"

"She blamed Benny for keeping Mary poor. So she pushed Larry to make things smooth and easy."

"Larry was agreeable?"

"Yeah, Larry's a gruff, loud guy. That's the way he's always been. But he's not a bad guy. Pretty generous, in fact. He likes to keep Molly happy. Lord, he worships her, frankly. It's just that, as he got older, like Molly, the money became more and more important, especially when he had more than he knew what to do with. There were more and more things separating Molly and Larry from her sister. He's never been poor, but he was okay with Benny and his family."

"Sounds like he was more accepting than Molly."

Hank nodded. "Way back when, he used to go fishing with Benny down in New London."

"From the wharf?"

"From his yacht," Hank roared. "For God's sake, Rick, think *rich*."

"Must have made Benny feel good."

"Benny's a humble man. He felt out of place, my mother says. Benny prefers Vietnamese to English. He *likes* Larry because Larry mostly treats people decently, despite his explosive temper tantrums and hard-edge personality. I like him. He *wanted* Mary and Benny around. After all, he landed one of the beautiful Le sisters. That was something."

"Well," I said, "one big happy family."

"You know he paid for *all* the kids to go to the Chesterton School. All of them. Paid the hefty tuition not only for Jon and Kristen, his own kids, but for Mary's kids."

"I didn't know that." The pizza arrived—white clam—and Hank and I stopped talking for a moment of dutiful worship. Hank snapped a photo and immediately uploaded it to Instagram, though he saw me frowning. We each took a slice and ate quickly. "That's quite a chunk of change," I said finally.

"He didn't have to do that, but Molly thought that would sort of level out their futures, give each kid a future."

"But it didn't work."

"Never does, right?" He nibbled at a slice of pizza. "Part of the problem is that his only daughter Kristen, as you've been told, has only one functioning brain cell, and it's covered with a designer label. She flunked out after a year, dramatically so, and continued her odyssey through Loomis Chafee, Kingswood Oxford, Rosemary Hall, and Miss Porter's. Money money money. Larry wrote her applications on dollar bills. Jon graduated, a bright kid, went on to Yale—he's still there, eternal student, talks about being a lawyer. Most likely not—life is a game to him. Likes to spend daddy's money, but he's hostile, nasty to people. But what really got to Mary and Molly was that Cindy, plain Jane, became antisocial, got in trouble all the time, did manage to graduate, but barely. She dragged herself through. Since then she's drifted, this half-assed job, that one. And her brother Tommy, slacker central, never went to class, violated probation, ignored pleas, held on by the skin of his teeth somehow, and then dropped out near the end of his senior year. That rankled—here are poor kids given the chance and fucking it up. You're not surprised when rich kids rebel at prep school. It's like a rite of passage. But charity demands obedience. Larry never said a word about wasted money. He gave them a shot. Molly couldn't complain."

"But she did, I bet."

Hank ate half a slice of pizza before talking, licking his chops. "Molly wanted a perfect world—the four chosen children of the Republic. Ivy League and Junior League. As far away as she could get from the poverty of Saigon."

"She got part of it—with Jon. Sort of."

"Did she? Who knows? He seems to make a career out of looking for that same perfection."

I filled him in on my brief visit to Tommy's apartment. He grinned. "Did the cockroaches get you? I've seen water bugs the size of Detroit carrying pizza crusts to the curb."

I thought of something. "He had a school friend there, offering condolences."

"Who? From Chesterton?"

"A rico suave named Danny, a banker who…"

He broke in. "I forgot about Danny. Trinh Xuan Duong."

"You know him?"

"Oh yeah. Of course. Not well, but he's been around. I'm surprised you don't know him."

I took a sip of soda. "If he doesn't come to Vietnamese New Year's at some VFW Hall in East Hartford, then I don't know him."

"True, I guess. He's actually the real success story of the group. Larry paid for *his* tuition at Chesterton, and the dirt-poor Vietnamese kid who was born in the worst housing project on the East Coast, Dutch Point, flowered, a hungry, bright boy, ready to take advantage of his scholarship. He's never looked back, that kid. Christ, he graduated from Harvard as a finance major."

I thought of the sleek, expensive-looking young banker. "Hank, who the hell is he?"

"I just told you…"

"But why would Larry pay his way through school?"

Hank's eyes got wide. "God, there is so much you don't know. Larry and Molly have known Danny since he was a little boy, since he was born, in fact. A playmate for Jon and Kristen. They watched him grow up."

I groaned. I must have looked stupefied because Hank grinned. "It's not a big mystery, Rick. Just one more episode of Molly's I'm-proud-to-be-an-American democracy. Danny is the son of their housekeeper. You met her today. Susie. Tran Thi Suong. Affectionately renamed Susie way back when."

"The cheerleader of Larry's fan club."

"Now you know why."

Chapter Ten

I woke up thinking of Molly's eyes—that momentary flicker I'd spotted.

I drove to her estate without calling first. She wasn't home. No one answered the door, but I spotted a gardener mowing the back acres. So I frittered the day away, billing clients, stopping in at the Gaddy Associates office, debating whether to call Liz or Hank but realizing I had nothing to say. When I drove back to the Torcelli estate late in the afternoon, I spotted a new gray Volvo in the driveway with the vanity plate: MOLLY2. The hood was warm to the touch, telling me she'd just arrived home.

Susie answered the door, called Molly, who became agitated. "What's happened?"

"Nothing. I hope you don't mind me stopping in?"

She looked flustered. "I feel like you're gonna tell me something bad."

"No, Molly, no," I said quietly. "I just wanted to follow up on a few things."

"Come in." She turned to Susie. "I'll go over that list with you later." She smiled at me. "Susie and I just got back from Springfield. The traffic was horrible." She looked distracted. "We're doing a luncheon." Then she paused. "I'm sorry. You're not here to hear about my day."

She motioned for me to sit down.

"I won't take a lot of your time, Molly, but I was wondering about something. When I was here with Hank, I asked you if you knew why Mary went into that neighborhood. I thought I saw a moment's hesitation—I don't know, a bit of fright in your eyes."

She parted her lips, and then closed them. "You have to be kidding."

"That's why I drove back out here."

"Then, frankly, you wasted your time. Your question took me off guard, I have to tell you, but I guess that's what you're supposed to do. Maybe you did see fright, as you put it. The day after Mary died I made Larry drive me to Goodwin Square, where I'd never been, stop for a minute at the yellow tape. I was trying to see for myself what was there. Trying to *imagine* Mary there, standing outside her car. The *why* of it. I hated it—that sordid neighborhood, boarded-up buildings, street thugs. When I cried, Larry took me home. It was a mistake going there, he told me. Foolish. I shouldn't have gone."

"It's natural. I went there, too. With Hank."

"But it's etched on my mind now." Her eyes watered. "When you shot the question at me, it was like a bullet to the head, Rick. I was suddenly there, right there, with my dead sister. If you saw fright or fear, whatever, you got a good eye because I was looking at the photograph in my head."

"I'm sorry."

A thin smile. "You shouldn't shock people like that."

I got up.

"I know you're trying to make Hank's mother happy. I'm glad. But don't do that to me again." Leaning forward, she touched my elbow, a quiet reprimand.

I felt like a little schoolboy back in the bleak Saigon orphanage, caught by the scary nuns in some foolish boyish prank. Molly had turned the tables on me. Buddha: *A man has within him the child he must always be.* Before I apologized again and reverted to knee-jerk childhood sputtering, I took my leave. I held out my hand, and she took it. "I know you're grieving."

She sighed. "I'm learning how to be an orphan."

The line struck me as strange and obviously wrong, and I almost said, "I know firsthand." But I'd already overstayed my welcome.

Susie was outside, a plastic bag by her feet, a light sweater over her shoulders despite the heat of the early evening. She was going home. Standing in the shadows, out of the sunlight, she smiled at me.

"I met your son Danny at Tommy's."

She lit up, eyes bright. The haggard face, wrinkled and pale, metamorphosed into a doting mother. "Ah. My handsome boy."

"I was very impressed by him."

"Everyone is."

"A banker."

"At Bank of America. Someday he'll be president."

I grinned. "Of the United States?"

She giggled and punched me gently in the side. Then, on reflection, "Nothing is impossible for him."

I waved good-bye and headed to my car. In the rearview mirror I saw her checking her watch, looking down the long curving driveway.

Stopping for gas at a Mobil station a mile away on Main Street, I spotted a sleek Mercedes stopped at a light, and noticed, by chance, Danny in the driver's seat, the young man still in his summer suit, the sunglasses now over his eyes. The dutiful son, picking up his mother? Fascinated, I followed, circled the small road that led up the winding hill to the Farmington estate, and waited, idling in a cove of boxwood hedges and Hawthorne trees, concealed from the street. I didn't have to wait long. The ice-blue Mercedes floated by, quiet as snow on a lawn, and I trailed at a careful distance.

Danny drove with a kind of sensual nonchalance, his body slumped into the exquisite leather, his head slightly cocked at an angle. Even from the distance I could see that he and his mother were having a lively conversation, and the body language suggested laughter and ease. At one point, at a light, Susie threw back her head, and I imagined her laughter.

Danny was in no hurry to get home, and cars passed him, making it more and more difficult for me to trail him.

He turned onto a side street off New Britain Avenue in Elmwood, not too far from Tommy's ramshackle apartment. South of the avenue, small Cape Cods and 1950s ranches, neat as pins, with postage-stamp yards filled with flowers, plastic statuary, and the occasional Virgin Mary in half a claw-foot bathtub. Sloping garages and dated carports. The old post-World War II neighborhood for returning veterans who found available housing—electricians, plumbers, carpenters, firemen, police. A decent neighborhood. Now it was heavily Hispanic with a smattering of blacks, and a few scattered homes occupied by Vietnamese or Chinese families. Some old-time whites who still mowed their lawns with manual push mowers while wearing their VFW caps.

I got close enough to write down the license plate number, and when the Mercedes slid into the one-car garage behind a modest home, I jotted down the house number. I drove past but circled back to see Danny walking into the side entrance with his mother. He was carrying some bags of groceries as well as a briefcase. They were still laughing at some personal joke. Bizarrely, I thought of my mother and the slim book of life's wisdom in my little breast pocket: *A mother bears a child and the child becomes her shadow.* Buddha still talks to me—as does my mother. I had a mother who still lingers at my side. She watches me from the shadows. It's just that I can't remember what she looked like, no matter how hard I try.

I called Hank on his cell phone.

"What?" Impatient. In the background a rumble of loud voices, pans banging.

"You went in to work?" I was surprised.

"What do you want?"

"Did you know that Danny drives a Mercedes?"

"You called to tell me that?"

"But did you know?"

"No, but I'm not surprised. He's a goddamned banker, for Christ's sake."

"And he lives in Elmwood with his mother in a small nondescript Cape Cod, a little run-down."

Hank grunted. "What a detective you are. Living with his mother while working at a bank is how he can afford the Mercedes."

"I never thought of that."

"Some detective."

"What are you doing?'

"I'm busy dicing bok choi for the uninformed masses. If I'm lucky, I get to chop off my finger. I'm happy that you're spinning around town trailing folks as they wend their way home from work."

"I stopped at Molly's to ask about that look in her eye."

He roared, "You're kidding. Did she boot you out?"

"No, but I almost brought her to tears again."

"You have that effect on people, you know. There are times you drive me to slobber like a farmer who's lost his last cow."

"What?" Static on the line. The shrill cacophony of a frantic Chinese restaurant kitchen, the swish of a fired-up wok, the slamming of cleaver against helpless chicken parts, the babble of fast-paced Chinese dialect. "What does that mean?"

"I was trying to be clever."

"You didn't tell me that Danny lived in Elmwood."

Hank yelled, "I didn't know. I hate to tell you this but I don't really know Danny. I've met him over the years, but that's it. Other than by glorious reputation." I could hear more yelling behind him. "They're telling me I'm being paid to work. I gotta hang up. Why don't you go follow someone else?"

"Why?"

Static, sputtering, and the cell phone went dead.

Chapter Eleven

Liz reported back the next morning with information. Yes, Danny Trinh owned the Mercedes he was tooling around town in, but she added smugly, "The alleged vehicle is not new but actually four years old."

"I've never been good with cars."

"And yes, he bought that home in Elmwood for his mother just last year. No big deal here, Rick. Homes in that neighborhood are below current market value. Sounds to me like the dutiful son giving his mother a bit of the old pie."

"Anything else?"

"Susie's worked for the Torcellis for over two decades."

"Interesting."

"It really isn't, right? I mean, where are you going with this?"

I laughed. "My use of the word 'interesting' was purely transitional."

"Well," she dragged out the word, "that's it from police central, Rick."

"What? I hear something in your voice, Liz."

She took a deep breath. "I don't know—this whole investigation you're doing…"

"What about it?"

"You're doing this for Hank's family, I know, I know, but I don't sense any strong belief on *your* part."

I took a long time answering, bothered, I suppose, by Liz's skill at reading me. I finally said, "You're right. I want to find one answer—why Mary drove to Goodwin Square. That little piece of information. But I'm not on a case. As I talk to people, I feel like it's just one long, protracted condolence call."

"Maybe that's all you can do."

I was having lunch with Jimmy and Gracie at Zeke's Olde Tavern when Hank strolled in. "I took a chance you'd be here."

"I have a cell phone, you know."

"Who doesn't?"

"Well, you found me, Hank."

"I'm thinking of quitting my job at the Chinese slave mines. Last night the owner—keep in mind he's a friend of Dad's— called me a fool and a simpleton."

"Ain't they one and the same thing?" Jimmy asked.

Hank grinned. "There are subtle distinctions, I suppose. But I must embrace them both."

"Your father won't be happy." From Gracie.

"My father's never happy with me."

I spoke up. "That's not true."

"I don't want to talk about it." He thumbed through the menu all of us knew by heart, and ordered his usual cheeseburger. He always ordered a cheeseburger. Medium rare with provolone. He knew, as well as we all did, the sandwich would arrive well done, crispy in fact, almost burnt, though pretty good, and the cheese would always be American.

"Danny's car is four years old," I told him.

"And this is a problem in what way, Mr. PI?"

"Just a factoid I'm providing my helper in this case."

Hank mocked me. "It's not really a *case*. It's a…"

I groaned. "Exercise in Asian futility. I've already had that lecture from Liz."

Gracie piped up. "I've never understood Orientals."

"Oh, Jesus," Jimmy moaned, throwing back his head.

"I mean, what's wrong with potatoes? Why does everyone have to eat rice?"

"It's hard to grow potatoes under water." Hank was grinning.

She looked perplexed. "They don't have dirt in your country?"

"Enough," I begged, laughing. "Maybe we should all go back to school. Right, Gracie?"

"I had to skip school. It was Korea. I was barely sixteen. I had to entertain the troops."

Jimmy shook his head. "In Korea, no less, where they grow potatoes."

I drank some coffee, nibbled at the edge of a grilled cheese-and-bacon sandwich. "You don't like Danny," I said to Hank.

He was surprised. "I told you on the phone I don't know him. He's someone I've seen around now and then. He's never said a word to me."

"How'd his mother come to work for Molly?"

"Well, she came out of one of the poor Vietnamese families in Hartford, living in a project after her husband took off. Real poor. Molly hired her through a temp agency, felt sorry for her, liked her—Susie was born in Saigon too—and made her an all-around housekeeper. Still there years later."

"But you don't like Danny. I can tell."

A heartbeat. "You're baiting me. He's a loan officer, junior grade at Bank of America."

"And that's why you don't like him?"

"Once—just once—he nixed a loan application for a young couple I know from our street. Good, hard-working Vietnamese people."

Jimmy perked up. "What's this about Bank of America?" I filled him in. "Which branch?"

"Main Street, downtown Hartford."

"I can make a call." He looked for a wall phone.

"You wanna use my cell?" Hank asked.

"No, I can't talk into anything that small and pathetic."

Jimmy despised the new technology. Cell phones sent him into a rage whenever they'd ring as he rode a city bus or walked downtown—especially if a yahoo near him yammered loudly about what his therapist said about his childhood bed-wetting.

If Jimmy is ever arrested for murder, it will be because he's slaughtered a slob on a cell phone.

"Who are you calling?" asked Gracie, as she watched him struggle to get out of the tight booth.

"I know people."

But he was back in seconds. "My friend gotta call back from the street. On her cell phone." We all laughed at that. We waited, Hank noisily chomping on his burger, the ketchup oozing onto his palms. Within a couple of minutes the phone on the wall jangled, and Jimmy answered it, a little out of breath. The three of us sat quietly, watching the disheveled pantomime that was Jimmy taking a phone call: his huge weight shifting from hip to hip, belly scratching, his smoker's hacking cough making him double over. Only his face remained impassive. Talk about your inscrutable. He returned to the table, a triumphant look on his face as he slid into the booth and drummed the table with his knuckles in a kind of *ta-dah* punctuation. He was not looking at Hank or me but at Gracie, as though he expected congratulations.

"My friend, *she* said…" he began, stressing the *she* and still looking at Gracie. "My friend tells me he's bright, all over the place, an up-and-comer, the pet of one of the vice-presidents, who's like his mentor. The two get drinks sometimes. The vice-president treats everyone else like shit, but he likes Danny. She said nobody else likes him, but that could be jealousy. He's that good at his job, and I quote, 'efficient, unemotional, and occasionally heartless, like all good bankers.' Unquote."

"Ah, that Harvard education." From Hank.

"That's not to say he's all peaches and cream at the soda fountain," Jimmy went on. "Last year he wrote two real bad loans that lost the bank a ton of money. He wasn't the only one. The economy didn't follow predictions, and a couple of banks got themselves burned. But this was very public—some Vietnamese investment group out of Park Street. He took a chance—loyal to his people, maybe. Or so they thought. So all was forgiven. He was warned not to screw up like that. Since then, he's playing it real close to the bone, conservative as hell. Trying to make the bank happy and avoiding the risk-taking mortgage seekers."

"Portrait of a banker as a young man." Again from Hank.

"Money," Jimmy stressed, "is at the bottom of everything. But maybe it's different money you should be looking at. Rick, Danny the Banker doesn't seem to want anybody to have any of his."

"Why are you interested in Danny?" Gracie wondered.

I shrugged. "I don't have a reason." I grinned foolishly. "There's no one else to follow, really. I saw him at Molly's picking up his mother. He's just someone who knows all the players."

Hank frowned. "Pretty lame, Rick."

"Keep in mind that this is not a case…I'm exploring."

"Like I said," Hank prodded me. "Pretty lame."

Back at the apartment I scribbled on note cards, jotting down bits and pieces of information on all the family members, my usual method of organizing an investigation. I was a little tardy in doing this, largely because I didn't see this as *my* case. But I tacked the cards to a pegboard behind my computer, searching for patterns as I shuffled information before me. I didn't know why I was doing this, but my familiar method usually cleared my head, got me to see things a little differently, and started the juices flowing. My scribbling today was perfunctory, idle. My heart wasn't in this. All the family members seemed—well, far removed from that sad Hartford neighborhood.

Mary, Mary, quite contrary, why did you go to Goodwin Square?

Later that afternoon Hank's call was a welcome disturbance. "I'm not going to work today. Sick out."

"That'll make your dad happy."

"Mom wants you to come for *bun*. You can't say no."

I didn't feel like driving to East Hartford and begged off. I stared at my pegboard. "No, thanks."

"You can't say no to Mom, Rick. She's deep-frying spring roll and marinating pork right now. Smell it?"

An hour later, four of us sat at the supper table: Hank, his mother, Grandma, and me. Everyone else was off somewhere, so I could relax and not have to fight the Vietnamese—or as they term it—the American War all over again. I could savor my marinated pork and vermicelli noodles and diced mint and basil, all topped with *nuoc mam*, that special fish sauce, giving the food the attention it deserved.

"*Toi doi*," I said to Grandma. I'm hungry.

"You better be." She'd made her special lemonade. *Tra da chanh*. Pale as water, as sweet as ripe melon, icy to the tongue.

But the two women watched me out of the corners of their eyes, warily, expectant. I avoided looking at them, digging into my food with the feral attention I remember from my days as a scavenger in the Saigon streets.

After an all-American mile-high chocolate and coconut cake, the likes of which they'd never seen in Saigon, we relaxed in the living room, windows open and a creaky floor fan whirling the hot, sticky air from one corner to another. We talked about the heat wave that refused to break, and Grandma admitted she loved the humid nights that reminded her of home. But she was alone in that sentiment. Dripping with sweat, Hank wore a tank top and running shorts. I had no sweat left in any pore of my body. My T-shirt was plastered to my bony chest, and my shorts didn't move when I did. It was going to be a long, hot night.

Despite all the pleasantries, I could sense the two doting women waiting for me to say something. "Great cake." I thanked Hank's mother. Without saying a word, she headed to the kitchen to slice another piece for me, despite my raised hand and the fact that Hank flippantly pointed to the beginning of a paunch on my thirty-eight-year-old body.

Finally his mother spoke softly, "I am starting to feel that the police are right." She glanced at Hank, the future cop. "I think and think about it, and now the feeling comes over me that Mary…"

"No," said Grandma with vehemence I'd never heard before. She tapped me on the wrist. "You have no choice but to continue,

Rick Van Lam." She used my whole name, which I like. "What you are doing for us is the talk of the Vietnamese community, you know. I've spread the word. There are people who will *not* talk to the police. There are people who remember the cruelty of Vietnam, the hated authorities, but they'll talk to one of their own."

"I'm an outsider."

"You got the blood of Saigon in you." She tapped my hand again. "You're one of us."

"Well, the police have their own questions. Mine have to do with only one thing—*why* was Mary *there*?" I looked into her eyes. "That's why I keep talking to the family. *That* angle."

Grandma went on. "If there is anything to be heard, the stories will find you. *I've put the word out on the street.*" The last phrase was spoken in English, heavily accented, but it had its effect. We all chuckled.

"Grandma's favorite show," Hank confided, "are reruns of *Law and Order.*"

"God help us," his mother said. "But no one has said anything."

Grandma stared into my eyes. "But maybe it's the Americans and not the Vietnamese who hold the answer." She kept drumming my wrist. "Sooner or later, if there's something, it will come to you. You have a face people talk to…they trust you."

I caught Hank's eye. He nodded. "The four cousins. Maybe one of them…" He shrugged.

His mother smiled. "Four kids—so different."

"Tell me a little of Danny Trinh." I looked at his mother.

She looked confused but spoke softly. "Well, he's close to all the kids, Mary's and Molly's." She sat there thinking at bit. "Well, maybe not. Not for years, really. Not since prep school."

"He's no longer friends with them?"

"He's friendly and all. Drops in now and then to say hello to everybody. After prep school Tommy used to bad-mouth Danny all the time. They had a fight."

"Danny was at Tommy's apartment the other day."

That intrigued her, but she waved her hand in the air. "Well, he had to go, for old time's sake. He missed the funeral. Susie must have pushed him. I know he stops in at Benny's store now and then. Mary told me that. He's not a bad boy, that Danny. He just tries a little too hard to please everyone. I haven't seen him in—well, years. Before he went to Harvard."

Hank was shaking his head, "You can't make too much of that visit to Tommy's, Rick."

I talked to his mother. "Talk about the falling out with Tommy."

His mother drew her lips into a thin line. "Of course, everyone remembers the drug thing with Tommy. In his senior year. My God, people in this community don't forget anything."

"But Tommy was caught with pot. How was Danny involved with that?"

Hank looked puzzled. "Yeah, Mom. I knew Tommy'd been picked up, but when I walked into the room those days, everybody shut up."

She looked from Hank to me, suddenly hesitant to talk. "Hank doesn't know the whole story. It was embarrassing to the family. Hank, you were what—thirteen or fourteen?"

"I knew about Tommy. I had ears. But people clammed up when I was around."

His mother looked at him protectively. "It's the world we live in. You had to be sheltered. Drugs everywhere. Still are, and guns, too."

"Mom, I'm training to be a cop."

"Don't remind me." She rolled her eyes.

I got the conversation back on track. "Mary, Tommy, prep school, drugs. Okay?"

His mother sighed, as though her words would take away any of Hank's remaining innocence. "When Tommy was picked up in downtown Hartford with those drugs on him, the pot, Danny was there as his buddy, and was also picked up. The two were arrested."

I looked at Hank. "That wasn't in the police report."

"Because of Larry Torcelli, doing a favor for Susie. He used his clout and money to end it all. Danny's name never came up. A few quick phone calls."

"Then what happened to Tommy? You mean Larry wouldn't help the kid? My God, he was sending him to an expensive private school."

"He *wanted* to. That was Benny's doing. He didn't want any favors. A matter of pride, of losing *face*. He didn't want Tommy to go to jail, yeah, but they wanted to teach him a lesson. You know, tough love. Him, and Mary too. Larry got them a pricy attorney, true, and we all know that Larry made some phone calls, and Tommy got probation and nothing else. Thanks to a detective who took a liking to Benny and Mary."

"And so Danny got off."

"Bingo." Hank drummed the table.

"Did Tommy think Danny turned on him?"

"Why?"

"He made some threats when he was busted—about a snitch."

Hank was shaking his head. "That couldn't be Danny. They were arrested together."

"But," his mother added, "it did end their friendship. Tommy didn't talk to Danny for years, we heard. He thinks Danny should have stayed with him, the two together. But Larry wanted nothing to be on his golden boy's record. He invested a lot of money in the poor boy, and when he invests money it's, like, well, an investment. There has to be a payoff."

Hank leaned into me. "They call it Harvard."

"But Danny got a little independent after college. Larry planned for Danny to work at the dealerships, but Danny pulled away. I heard he even got sarcastic with Larry once or twice. I know it hurt Larry."

"But Danny's the success story of the bunch."

"Yeah, Danny's the golden boy. Especially since Jon, Larry's own son, is the boy who never leaves school and maybe says five words a year to his father."

"But shouldn't Tommy resent his own father and mother?" Hank asked. "They're the ones that made him go to court. Not Danny."

She sighed. "He never blamed his mother, I know that. He blamed Benny. A father runs a Vietnamese household. You know that. To this day he claims he hates the man. He says his father ruined his life."

"So he was okay with Mary?"

"Benny did the yelling. Mary just cried. She was afraid Tommy would sink into drug addiction like so many other Vietnamese kids in the neighborhood."

"You know that, Rick." Hank stressed the words. "Right?"

I nodded. I did know. In Hartford some teenaged Vietnamese boys joined loosely organized gangs and peddled drugs on street corners. Or became addicts themselves. These were dangerous boys who carried guns, dressed like rap-video thugs, spoke the hip-hop language their parents despaired of. In the Vietnamese community there were dozens of stories of such nouveau riche boys, barely twenty, cruising in BMWs and souped-up Jeeps, boys who bought three-family houses for their parents in the West End of Hartford, and sometimes did jail time for a year or so. The Vietnamese viewed them warily, and the first generation—the Boat People—feared the loss of a whole generation. Like so many others, Mary, principled, confused, was frightened of that world. She'd rather be poor than live off the ill-gotten profits from street drug sales. Profane and uncivil Vietnamese boys strutted by, tattoos on their arms and necks, crack vials in their pockets, gel-stick in their hair. It made sense to me now—Mary's terror for her son. She wanted to save Tommy from that. And I suppose she did. But I bet she often reminded him of his folly.

"Has it gotten any better with Benny?" I asked her.

"Well, Tommy works in the store now."

"So?" Hank wondered.

"So sometimes they even talk to each other. They share cigarettes and lottery tickets. They drink beer together. They go gambling at Foxwoods."

Hank grinned. "Father's Day rituals. It warms the heart."

Grandma slapped him on the hand. "A fresh mouth will get you nowhere."

Hank winked at Grandma who pretended she didn't see.

Hank got serious. "You know, I still don't understand why everything was kept from me. I was old enough to know about drugs then."

Hank's mother threw a sidelong glance at Grandma. "You were still young then, a boy. It was better that you not know some things."

Grandma added, "There are still things it's better you don't know."

"Like what?"

"It's better that you don't know." Now Grandma winked at me.

◇◇◇

On the drive home, the air conditioner blasting cold air on me, I thought about Hank. A year ago he sat in the front row of my Criminal Investigations course the first day of class. I'd noticed him when I walked in, the Vietnamese name and face, of course, but, more important, the casual posture in the chair, his long legs stretched out in front, his arms folded over his chest. A hard face, hostile—and I was bothered. For weeks he never spoke in class, ignored my questions to him, yet his exams and papers were generally good, well organized, and sometimes the best in the class. He would eventually earn a B from me. But he always glowered, arms crossed, his eyes narrow, hooded.

Once, leaving class, he dropped something, and by the time he retrieved it, he was alone in the room with me. "Hank, see you for a minute?"

He was uncomfortable. "Why?" He approached my desk.

"Have I offended you in some way?"

He looked surprised. "No."

"You seem angry."

He started to walk away.

"Hank."

"Is there anything else?"

I sighed. "No."

By midsemester I understood the problem. I was friendly with some other students, and one afternoon, having coffee with them in the cafeteria, I spotted Hank walking in, spotting us. He turned around and left. One of the guys grinned.

I nodded toward the departing Hank. "What's up?"

They looked at one another, shrugged collective shoulders. "Come on."

"Well, Prof," said one of the group, a beefy ex-marine with a blond crew cut and a tattoo of a dagger on his neck, "he hates your guts."

I was surprised. "But why?"

The guys looked at one another. No one said a word. "Well, what? For God's sake."

Finally one kid, a nineteen-year-old freshman, in a workout shirt and weightlifter pants, all cockiness in class, grinned. "He called you a mongrel." He paused. "Sorry, Prof."

"What?"

Suddenly it was clear to me. All over again. *Bui doi*. The mixed-bloods so hated by the Vietnamese.

Dust boy.

So Hank harbored that age-old Vietnamese dread of impurity. It made sense now.

Deliberately I ignored him, though that wasn't possible. There was a faculty-student tennis competition, one of those embarrassing spectacles someone invariably dreams up, and I was signed up. The day before, realizing I was woefully out of practice, I drove to the college courts off Main Street, only to discover Hank Nguyen practicing. Alone. The two of us. I suggested we play, which we did. Silently.

He was aggressive and wild on the courts. There was no stopping him. I played—or tried to play—a cool, calculated game, all rhythm and theory. It drove Hank crazy. Twice he lost his temper but turned away, biting his lip. An hour later, exhausted, we played a final game that was rough, long, and bitter. I hated the smug look on his face, that haughty superiority I'd seen in one Vietnamese guy too many. I played fiercely, but he countered me point for point. Thirty all. Back and forth. Until, at last, with more luck than talent, I smashed a deliberate, rhapsodic ball into his hesitant backhand and it landed a foot inside the line. I won.

He was furious. I waited by the net, expecting him to say something. When he walked by me, he actually sneered.

"Hank." I reached out and touched his shoulder, trying to stop him.

The effect was electric. He turned, his eyes wide with anger as he shoved me, his hand pushing against my shoulder. Surprised, I dropped back, but when I straightened myself, he pushed again. "Fuck off, half-breed," he muttered. "*Du ma may bui doi.*" Fuck you. Damn you. "*Do chet tiet.*"

A stupid scene, and it immediately got worse. I yelled back at him, also falling into Vietnamese. "*Di cho khac choi.*" Get lost. The hell with you. Suddenly we were pushing at each other, like clumsy wrestlers. I hated the little shit, and within seconds we were rolling on the ground, jabbing at each other, our bodies tight.

But it ended almost as quickly as it began, the two of us falling apart, each toppling onto our backs, away from each other. I was breathing hard.

Finally I sat up. "Why do you hate me?"

He didn't answer.

I got up. "You're a waste of time," I shouted.

The next day he came to my office, a little sheepishly, and we finally had the talk we should have had long before. He said he realized that he didn't hate me—he just *wanted* to. Throughout the semester he liked my class, sort of liked me, liked my humor, my way of dealing with students. And the night before, nursing his wounds, he'd come to realize that his venom—and his father's and grandfather's long-standing and knee-jerk attitudes toward the *bui doi*—had made him despise me from the outset.

"I've never doubted their words. Until now." Suddenly, overnight, it all seemed so irrational to him. "I heard it ever since I was a little boy."

I smiled. "I'm a dust boy."

He looked down. "I'm sorry."

So began the friendship, awkward at first, as Hank transcended his family's parochial views, and, ultimately, integrated me into his household. Early on he insisted Grandma would adore me. That was true. Now Grandma and even his mother—but never the intractable grandfather nor father—looked forward to my visits, and, oddest of all, I was family. Sort of—at least sometimes. Hank's family. Set adrift in America, the dust boy had found his Vietnamese family, with all the idiosyncrasies I would have had in my biological family, had I ever had one. It didn't matter. Hank, now a young man, was my brother.

Being with him always made me happy.

And that night, pulling my car into the lot behind my apartment, I found myself smiling. Out loud I said into the leaden, humid air, "Hank, you're one of the winners."

Chapter Twelve

The next night everyone ended up at my apartment. Jimmy stopped over unexpectedly at seven, claiming he had to drop off some official papers in nearby Unionville, and it was his idea to order a pizza. He carried in two six-packs of Budweiser, because, as he said, "People like you can be counted on to have vodka and scotch, but usually don't stock up on the essentials." As the aroma of tomato and cheese and garlic wafted up the staircase, Gracie drifted into my kitchen where, acting surprised to see Jimmy, she said she'd come just for one slice. She had to watch her figure and twirled a bit, a little awkwardly, as if she were auditioning for some geriatric Rockette reunion. Jimmy grinned through it all like Bart Simpson at a peep show.

Then Hank and Liz showed up, the two bumping into each other on the sidewalk. We first heard their syrupy giggling in the hallway, and Jimmy rolled his eyes. Liz and Hank were fond of each other, and sometimes Liz could made Hank stammer in ways that amused all of us. If Jimmy became Bart Simpson, Hank became one of the gooey babies running amok in the candy aisle at Food Mart.

Hank walked in behind her, and he was telling her how he'd quit his job at the Chinese restaurant, an act of liberation from slavery and family exploitation that Liz applauded. I worried what Hank's dad would say about this latest move. There'd be an explosion, and not a pretty one. His father, a Calvinistic soul, bred in the rigid discipline of Saigon streets, was not one to be trifled with.

"I thought I'd surprise you," Liz said. "But obviously everyone else had the same idea."

And it was a surprise. As much as Liz and I had remained friends, our meetings were always for dinners, for lunches, even at her office. She'd been to my apartment a few times, usually running in, dropping something off, and then fleeing the iceberg that was her former husband. Her apartment was across town, an expensive condo, one of the sleek modern ones built to look like late Victorian houses, with wraparound front porches that no one ever sat on for fear that neighbors might think them working class.

Jimmy spoke. "I was in the neighborhood, too."

Liz gave him a peck on the cheek. "I knew there'd be pizza here. In the golden age of our marriage, in old little New York, there was always pizza and Chinese food in every corner of the apartment."

"And Nathan's hot dogs," I added.

Liz settled into my overstuffed sofa that had become even more threadbare since she last saw it. Hank allowed himself to be interrogated about his leaving his chop-chop job and his future life as a Connecticut state trooper.

"I will be the only Vietnamese state trooper," he declared. "That scares me."

Jimmy started spouting old cop wisdom and *Reader's Digest* advice for success and achievement, but Hank was more interested in the attention of Gracie and Liz, who both flattered and teased and generally made him feel like the only person in the room. For a second—and I hate to admit this—I was jealous of the rhapsodic attention thrown his way, but I squelched the pettiness, or I tried to. Good-looking, confident, happy with his life, Hank exuded a robust charm, a kind of unselfconscious manliness that I didn't think I'd ever had in my whole life. American-born, a male in a Vietnamese household, fully entitled to primacy in the world at home and abroad, Hank never for a second questioned his masculine power in the universe.

Liz was babbling to Gracie, "Can you imagine how great he's going to look in a Connecticut state trooper's uniform?"

Gracie was about to coo a sticky response, which I interrupted. "Can we end this meeting of the Hank Nguyen Fan Club?"

Jimmy looked at me with one of those chummy old-boy glances—narrowed eyes and slight jerking of the head—that suggested women were just plain nutty. Hank was a boy. Didn't they realize that there were two real men in the room? One experienced and a bit world-weary? The other a little untutored and raw-boned but nevertheless carrying a State of Connecticut private investigator's license.

Eventually the chat moved into the story of Mary, as I knew it would.

"Are you going to talk to the young Spanish kid who was shot in the leg?" Liz asked.

I shook my head. "I don't think I can take this out of the Vietnamese community. I'm still tracking Mary's movements. And getting nowhere."

"And besides," Jimmy declared even though he was gnawing on a chunk of pizza, "these kids don't even talk to the police."

"So you may never know," Gracie said, drawing the last of a beer, upturning the bottle.

"The secret is to get inside the mind of Mary on that last day," I concluded.

"So how do you do that?" From Liz.

"I'm gonna work my way through the kids. Maybe Danny. And Benny. But especially Molly. Mary was the most unlikely person to be murdered, but innocent people get murdered every day. The only thing that makes this out of the ordinary is the *place* she was shot."

"And that's why," emphasized Hank, "it has to be looked at."

"But logically she *could* have made a mistake," Jimmy said. "Goodwin Square is ten or so blocks from Little Saigon and Benny's market."

"Yet that's really a world away," said Liz. "You know how city neighborhoods are. The boundaries shift so quickly, good neighborhood to bad. Look at Manhattan."

"Why didn't she carry a cell phone?" Hank wondered.

Jimmy smirked. "Not everyone has phones, son. People of a certain age…"

Hank frowned. "Not so, Jimmy. Everyone has a cell phone."

"Look," I broke in, "we may never know why she was there. She gets dizzy, the sun in her eyes, she's tired, a car cuts her off and she has to turn down unknown streets that lead her away from where she was going, there's a detour off Main Street that you gotta know how to maneuver, she's feeling sick, she's—whatever. She may not have known the reputation of that square. There's no reason she'd have read those pieces in the *Courant*, even the one recently about the little girl murdered there. She's lost, she gets out of her car, and at that moment Los Solidos gang-turf enemies happen by and bang bang bang."

"Death by chance." From Hank.

Gracie had been listening quietly. "You know what I think? I think you gotta talk to the twin sister Molly some more. Twins got a bond that goes beyond words and space…."

Hank sat up. "Yeah, that flicker-of-the-eye thing you saw, Rick."

"Come on. I told you how she explained that away when I went back. She was frightened."

"Or something else?" Hank asked.

"Or maybe not." From Liz.

Gracie, again. "A psychic bond. Intuition. At the moment Mary was shot, Molly must have *felt* some tinge, some spasm, some—sensation. Twins are one person."

"That's bunk," Jimmy roared.

"Well," Gracie said, "it seems to me that if there is any reason that Mary was *intentionally* murdered, any reason, then Molly must have an inkling of it."

"Because of intuition?" From Jimmy, snidely.

"No, forget that." Gracie looked into his face. "These were sisters who talked all the time, I guess. Isn't it reasonable that if there was any trouble in Mary's world—money, kids, fear—she would have *told* her twin sister Molly? And wouldn't Molly have told *you*, Rick? Wouldn't she want you to *know*, so you could get at the truth?"

I nodded. "Not bad, Gracie. Not bad at all. Makes sense. But Molly had nothing to offer. She said there was nothing wrong in Mary's life. Mary was just going about her business."

Jimmy was nodding his head. "Except…"

"What?" I asked.

"Except for one thing. What if Molly doesn't *want* you to know something?"

"She's hiding something?"

Liz grinned. "The flicker of an eye."

"But what could that be?" I wondered out loud.

Collectively the group made an *aaahhh* sound, and it reminded me of a Perry Mason courtroom moment. I shrugged my shoulders. "We're all out of pizza."

"And beer." Gracie pointed to the empty bottles. "Good night. Lord, how did it get to be one in the morning?" She waved at us as she left the room.

Liz stood up. "Time to go home."

But she looked as though she wanted to stay, standing there, arms folded, rocking a bit. Jimmy sank deeper into the armchair, and Hank, excited by the turn of the conversation, was twisting and turning in his chair.

"Stay," I said to Liz. I'm not sure why.

She sat back down.

Hank's phone rang, and he reached for it. "Mom?"

The three of us stared at him as he started to chatter in Vietnamese, questioning his mother, not letting her speak. "Why are you calling *now*?" He sounded defensive, and I thought his father was tracking him down after he blew off work. Or that his father, drunk, was slapping his wife. But immediately the tone shifted. "What? What? What?" He lapsed into silence, his face caving in. "*Chua oi!*" Oh God.

"Hank." I got up. He waved me away.

I could hear the strident voice on the other end, but couldn't tell what his mother was saying—a little incoherent, and clearly crying. Vietnamese women, with that naturally rapid-paced, high-pitched speech, always struck me as weeping. A comment that says something about me, I'm the first to admit.

He ended the call and stared at us.

"What?" asked Liz.

When he spoke his voice was hollow, washed out. "Molly is dead," he blurted out. "She was murdered."

"Oh my God," whispered Liz. "What happened?"

Hank looked at her, then back to me. "She was shot around seven tonight. She drove to the same spot where Mary was shot. *That* square. Goodwin Square. And someone shot her."

"Oh my God." Liz again.

Jimmy turned to me. "Well, now it's a real case, Rick. Now you've got a case on your hands."

Chapter Thirteen

Detective Ardolino, standing inside the yellow tape and holding a Burger King coffee cup, a cigarette in the corner of his mouth, spotted me the minute I joined the crowd of onlookers gathered on the late-night street. Hank and I had driven there, mostly in silence, after saying good-bye to Liz and Jimmy. Liz looked dazed and Jimmy wiped out—he'd headed home to a couple more beers and bed. I parked my car in the lot of a closed Thai restaurant, walking two streets over. The murky corner was quiet now. The medical examiner had finished his work, the body removed, but the Hartford evidence crew was at work and would possibly be there until morning. A small crowd of locals and a few press jostled one another, almost wordlessly, waiting for something. Hank and I locked eyes. The cordoned-off corner was the same one where Mary had died.

A crew buzzed around a car. A Volvo. License plate: MOLLY2.

This just didn't make any sense.

"You!" From Detective Ardolino, as his trained cop eye scanned the crowd. "Come here."

Hank and I dipped under the tape. Ardolino stamped out his cigarette and used a crumpled handkerchief to wipe sweat from his brow. He looked tired. He'd been there awhile.

"I know you," he barked.

I reintroduced myself. "I gave you my card."

He narrowed his eyes. "Sorry. Don't have it with me. I had it framed and hung over my desk."

He nodded at Hank.

"Hank's mother called us."

He bit his lip. "So Batman and Robin come running over. Everybody was kung fu fighting."

"What?" From Hank.

"Nothing," Ardolino said. "Okay, what's this all about?"

I started into his face. "What?"

"What's with this sister act on this corner?" A few onlookers leaned in, noisy as hell. "And what the fuck is your problem?" he said to a woman who was bending over the tape, trying to listen. She backed off, cursed at him in Spanish. He mumbled something insulting back at her, also in Spanish.

"You and your boy wanna join me for a cup of coffee?" He motioned across the street to a Spanish café.

"He's not my boy," I said.

"Your *aide de cop*."

"That's better."

Detective Ardolino sat in a back booth, facing the street, muttering about a cockroach he'd seen in this very café two years back. "Drink the goddamned coffee," he advised. "Skip the *arroz con pollo*, if you know what I mean."

I ordered a bottle of spring water, Hank an Arizona Green Tea, and Ardolino looked at us as though we'd toppled off a Vegan-for-President truck. He slurped a cup of coffee so lightened by cream it might justifiably be called a glass of milk. He licked his lips, happy.

"So maybe I was wrong," he admitted, flat out. "But then again, maybe I wasn't."

"What does that mean?"

"I mean, maybe the first woman *was* the intended victim, especially since her sister bites the dust in the exact same spot two weeks later. Both sisters should be nowhere near this part of town."

"Hard to say." My eyes darted around the room.

"Yeah, sure. Let's believe that, okay. Sister number two got a little nuts thinking about dead sister number one, and she gets drawn down here to see what she could see. To lay some plastic

flowers on the sidewalk. And she got in the way of some badass
street business. Coincidence?"

"A little farfetched." From Hank.

"You bet, sonny. Sorry, I don't believe in coincidence."

"So what happened?" I asked.

"Same old, same old, to tell the truth. I get a call around
eight, some 911 anonymous from a phone booth, saying there's
a lady dead on the sidewalk, drive-by shooting that nobody, it
turns out, heard happen. Someone walks out of a bar, sees a
body lying on the sidewalk, with a cell phone in her hand, but
not turned on, how convenient. A nice, new Volvo is nearby,
still running. Very strange."

"How strange?"

"Someone leaves a Volvo running in this neighborhood, and
no one decides to take it for a joyride?"

"But there's a body nearby," I said. "Would you want to be
suspected of murder?"

"A joyride is a joyride. By the time we trace the car, the kids
are gone with the wind. All we'd find would be blurred fingerprints and a few burnt-out roaches in the ashtray."

"So when you got here, you saw it was Molly Torcelli."

"I seen it's an Asian lady, and suddenly the bells and whistles
start to clamor like it's fuckin' New Year's Eve in Times Square."
He sighed. "And I learn it's the wife of a prominent Hartford
businessman to boot. High class. That's real trouble, this one,
let me tell you."

In the hours since the police arrived, Ardolino said, a lot had
happened. The state forensics crew had joined the city team, and
the body had been removed to a morgue slab at the hospital in
Farmington. Ardolino had already visited Larry Torcelli, with the
chief of police and "other big-shit brass" in attendance, given the
weight of Torcelli's social standing. But Ardolino hadn't stayed
more than a few minutes, leaving, as he put it, "most of the
suck-ass brass apologizing for a murder they didn't do."

"What happened at the house?" I asked.

"It wasn't pretty. Well, it seems this Torcelli had been calling around, looking for her after he got home from work, pissed off 'cause she didn't leave a note like she always did when she had to go out at night. He usually worked late, he said. When we rang the doorbell, he thought it was an accident. He even asked about the car, which I thought was a little heartless. But that's me. I think of people first. When we told him she was dead—murdered, in fact, in the same spot where sister got it—well, he just didn't get it. He kept looking over my shoulder like this was a trick or a game. We had to repeat it over and over again."

"Were the kids there?"

"Not at first. Because of the squad cars and the living room filled with cops, they traipsed downstairs. Torcelli just stared at them, dumb, and so we had to tell them. Torcelli slid down his chair, crumpled up, but the two kids looked like they had just been told the family was out of ice cream."

"That's unfair," Hank blurted out. "Maybe they were in shock."

"Shock?" Ardolino said. "If so, they bounced back real fast, walking out of the room and heading upstairs. Torcelli starts to sob when he's told he got to come for identification. So he blabs something real strange—'You know, she's one of the beautiful Le sisters. She's the most beautiful woman I ever met.' Like she's still alive, and not on this slab of concrete with a sheet over her. I gotta admit, she is—*was*—a looker."

"So what's your thinking?" I asked.

"That's what I asked you first. Assuming there is some connection between the two murders, I'm gonna need your help here. The Asian angle. There's stuff here I don't know nothing about. Asians is one of them. They keep to themselves—you people do, I mean." He looked a little confused as to how to address Hank and me. "I mean, maybe I gotta rely on you, Mr. Rick Van Lam, for some help here. This double killing is gonna get ugly in the *Courant* and the chamber of fuckin' commerce. Nobody was on my back about a drive-by that winged a lowlife drug spic, and we wrote off the first sister as wrong place and wrong time, but two middle-aged, middle-class women, twin sisters, and one the wife of a super-rich car king, and, well, my ass in on the line. Christ Almighty man."

"Especially since you put a quick period on that first murder."

"Tell me about it. Who knew?"

Hank spoke up. "If Molly had died first, the rich one, it would have been a different matter. Then maybe there wouldn't have been a second murder."

"Hey, kid," Ardolino grumbled, "that's the way life is. Look around you."

Hank and I drove to the Torcelli estate, even though it was after three a.m., but the circular driveway was ringed with cars, the house ablaze with light, upstairs and down. Hank had called home and learned his mother and father were at Molly's, as well as other relatives. We rang the doorbell, and Hank's mother let us in. She was just leaving, she said, but come in for a minute.

The vast living room was like a funeral parlor, pockets of people tucked into chairs, clustered in groups, but no one was speaking. Who were all these folks? In the center of the sofa, sitting alone, was Larry Torcelli, and for a second I didn't recognize him. The slick business tycoon with his pressed dress shirt and expensive tie, with his costly haircut and steely eyes—none of that was in evidence. Instead, I saw a train wreck of a man, someone who'd just weathered a sharp blow to the head—shoulders bent, skin sallow, eyes cloudy and red, and trembling hands. That shocked me. A lit cigarette burned in an ashtray.

Hank and I decided not to talk to him, though he did look up as we entered the room.

Hank's mom whispered to me. "Come to my house, Rick. Please come." I nodded.

We were in the foyer when Jon came down the center staircase. Hank greeted him, but Jon just frowned, looked a little inconvenienced by the crowd in the house. I waited for him to join his father, but he glanced in, grimaced, and jangled his car keys.

"I can't stay here," he mumbled to Hank. "I'm going crazy. I gotta drive somewhere."

"Are you okay?" Hank asked.

Jon said too loudly, "Am I okay? Some asshole Rican murders my mother, and I'm supposed to be okay?"

"Jon," Hank started, "you don't know…"

"I really can't talk to anyone." He twisted around. "Not now. The last time I see my mother she's laughing about something, and then the police come and say she's dead."

"I'm sorry." Hank and I both spoke at the same moment. We looked at each other.

"This is one big fuckup," Jon sputtered.

Hank asked, "How's Kristen doing?"

"Well, no one knows. She's locked herself in her room and won't answer the door. Even good old Pop can't get her out of there—and she's his little baby girl, all three remaining brain cells and all." But he seemed to regret his cruel words, and stepped back, looking at the crowd.

"Your father's taking it bad," Hank said.

"Well, he's lost his trophy wife, Miss Saigon."

Hank, angry. "For God's sake, Jon, it's your mother."

Jon's upper lip trembled slightly, but he controlled himself. "My mother was the only one *ever* on my side." It was a strange, sudden declaration, and it hung in the air. He looked back into the room, staring at his father, who was rocking back and forth, eyes closed. Jon tightened his grip on his car keys.

Jon spoke at his father in a low, fierce voice. "Why wasn't it you?"

At Hank's home we sat around the kitchen table in the pale hours before dawn broke. Grandma was wrapped in her old bathrobe, her eyes bleary, refusing to go back to bed, despite the hour. She kept shushing her daughter who repeatedly said everything could wait until daybreak. But that was not the case. Everyone—even Hank's father and grandfather—sat with bowls of steaming jasmine tea before them, waiting, expectant.

Hank did the talking, succinctly filling in the tale of woe, as the family, particularly Grandma, sighed and shook her head. He summarized our talk with Ardolino.

Grandpa, always so silent and wary when I was in the house—a man who was generally uncomfortable with strangers—was actually talking rapidly, even glancing at me for agreement. I suddenly entertained the vagrant thought that someday he and I might actually have a conversation, that he would accept me.

"I don't like this," he stressed. "Someone is killing members of this family. *Your* family," he added, looking at his wife. Grandma sat there ashen and nervous.

Hank's mother spoke up. "This is getting dangerous." She looked pointedly at her son. "There must be a madman out there who is targeting Asians."

"Ma," Hank begged, helpless, "that's paranoia."

Grandma, yawning, spoke up. "Nobody's going after Asians."

"What?" From Hank's father, looking grumpy.

"No, this is the story of these two women. The two sisters. Twins. It has something to do with the worlds they lived in. The two of them. Asian, white man, no matter."

"Grandma, what are you saying?" Hank asked.

"I'm saying that they are sisters who lived in two different worlds—one white and one Vietnamese—but where the circles of their lives overlap, that's where the answer is."

I smiled. "The one is the other."

Grandma looked at me. "And the other is the answer." She sighed. "There is where you'll find the hunger, the thirst…the murderer."

Grandpa frowned. "What the hell are you two talking about? This is crazy." He stressed the words: *dien ro*. Madness.

"Buddha," I offered.

Hank's dad raised his eyes to his own heaven, good Catholic that he was. I thought how odd it must be for him as a Roman Catholic, married to a wife raised in the Buddhist tradition, especially with Grandma the resident dispenser of Buddha's fine wisdom. "Buddha has nothing to do with this," he informed us all.

Grandma winked at me.

"I don't think this has anything to do with being Vietnamese," Hank said.

"Why not?" his father asked.

"I feel it. Something else is going on here."

Everyone smiled. Grandma touched him on the shoulder lightly, affectionately, and he looked at her. "Am I talking like a Buddhist, Grandma?"

"No." She tapped his shoulder. "You're just talking like someone who is looking for answers where others say there can be no answers."

"And there are always answers?" Hank asked.

"If there's a question," I said, "there has to be an answer."

Grandma nodded at me. It was a blessing from her.

Chapter Fourteen

Hank told me that Jon Torcelli was an intern at a law office in Hartford, and took his lunch precisely at twelve-thirty every day at the Capital Grille. How Hank knew this I don't know, but as I walked into the packed, noisy cafeteria, I spotted Jon sitting by himself, head bent over a tray, a cell phone gripped in one hand. A paperback lay on the table.

"Jon." I startled him. He looked up.

"Oh my, the detective himself." He spoke in a deadpan voice, low and raspy. "I saw you watching me at Mom's funeral yesterday."

"I'm sorry about your mother." He nodded and bit his lower lip. He finished texting and pressed Send. I shook his hand. "I didn't want to bother you at the funeral or luncheon afterwards."

"So you bother me now."

"If I can."

"Well, why not?" He pointed. "Sit down."

"Your father is really taking this hard."

"Right now he's pissed because I returned to work the day after the funeral. Do you know what it's like to stay in that house with him?"

"He's suffering."

"My father used to tell us that only two things were important in his life—his vast money and his beautiful wife. Of course, he always forgot to mention his two adorable children."

"He was probably working some old joke."

"He is the old joke."

"That's kind of harsh."

A burst of thunder made him jump, and he glanced out the window. The long stretch of hot days had ended with steady rain showers. The huge plate-glass windows glistened with runny streaks. But the heat would return, despite the crackle of distant thunder and the spitfire lighting. Jon looked annoyed at the weather. He nibbled on his tuna-on-toast, chewing silently, his eyes on me.

"Well, I'm sorry."

"No, I don't think you are," I said.

He tucked his tongue into the corner of his mouth. "I don't know what you want me to say. I'm a little confused. You may have heard that some asshole murdered my mother. It hasn't put me in the best frame of mind."

"I'd like to talk about your mother."

He rolled his tongue into his cheek. "Oh, yes, the detective at work. I understand this is a pro bono endeavor of yours—for the love of the Vietnamese community."

"Which you're not happy to be a part of."

He looked surprised. "I'm *not* a part of it, Rick Van Lam, in case you haven't noticed. I live in a world where I can look out my bedroom window and see nothing but trees. And I can while away my life at Yale. You know you can stay there forever if you're rich."

"But you're half-Vietnamese."

"Like you." His tone was sharp. "Yes, living my life as a half-gook."

"I hate that word."

"Gook? Why it's a lovely American invention for us, don't you think? They'd already milked *chink* to death. Ah, being Vietnamese in good old America."

"But I don't mind it as much as you do."

He flinched. "It doesn't make my life easy."

"That's bullshit. You've had an easy life."

"Look at me."

I did: a tall, lanky man, with a creamy-toned oval face, eyes slanted as my own, but the beard stubble of a white father. His father's hazel eyes. A good-looking man, he looked like his dead mother, the face a little too soft, almost feminine. "You inherited your mother's good looks."

"Yes, and if you don't think that isn't a curse, you're a fool."

"How so?"

"Dad didn't want a son who looks Asian. The man's a bigot. I turned out to be pretty like Mom, not the he-boy he'd like to toss footballs to or wrestle to the ground—or bring to his cigar-smoking poker games. He wanted a son who looked like him. Swagger and spit and hairy chest."

"So that's why you don't like him?"

"One of the reasons. How much time have you got?" he snickered. "Mom used to quote a hideous Vietnamese saying when I bad-mouthed Dad. *An qua nho ke trong cay.*" I looked confused. He translated, "When eating the fruit, don't forget the man who planted the tree. So I was supposed to worship Dad."

"What about your sister?"

He snickered. "That's another scream, Rick Van Lam. Kristen takes after him. How ironic life can be. God does like his games, no? Sometimes people don't even *see* the Asian blood in her. She looks like Dad's younger cousin. See what I mean? Nature fucked things up. She was supposed to be a kewpie-doll replica of Mom, another Vietnamese princess, all frills and perfume and lipstick and silk dresses slit up the side like Anna May Wong in one of those black-and-white late night movies my Dad loves. But no, I'm the son who looks like a chorus boy from *Flower Drum Song.*"

I smiled. "You seem to have assimilated all the cultural references."

"You note I leave out *Miss Saigon*—too close to home."

"For both of us."

"I'm *bui doi*, like you, but Dad forbids us to use that term in the house."

"Too close an association with the Boat People?"

"You got it."

"So that's why your father dotes on your sister?"

"Yep. Even though he hates the fact that she's a vacuum cleaner, and I'm the whiz kid in the family."

"You're being cruel again."

"Have you met my sister? I mean, she's okay and all, but she's barely eligible to be a cabinet member in one of the now-historic Bush administrations."

I smiled again. "I would have thought you'd be a Republican."

"Think, Lam boy, think. If Daddy is a big Republican contributor in Connecticut political circles, would little plum blossom Jon follow suit? Oh, I don't think so."

"So you hate your father."

"Which has nothing to do with your half-assed investigation into the murder of Aunt Mary and Mom."

"If you say so."

"I can't help you out at all." He pushed his sandwich away, crumpled the napkin, looked around the room.

"What did you think of your Aunt Mary?"

He was surprised at the question. "You know, I never really gave her much thought. She'd be there—they'd all traipse over, the Benny Vu show—and I'd nod and leave the room. I'm sorry but I just don't hang around with Vietnamese people. How can you respect people who speak in monosyllables—and at a pitch that can shatter a glass?"

"But you went to prep school with Cindy and Tommy, your first cousins. Weren't you friendly with them?"

"We were *together*. That doesn't mean we were friends."

"No socializing?"

"A little. Of course. It was Chesterton, remember. I was a loner and had few friends—didn't want any. So I sat with Cindy and Tommy. It was better than sobbing into my book locker."

"You didn't like Cindy and Tommy?"

"You know, Rick, you are pretty dense. You're not picking up what I'm saying. I don't like Asians that much."

"And you don't like white people that much."

He grinned. "I just wanna be left alone. The only person I ever talked to was Mom, and now someone took *that* away from me."

"Why do you stay at home?"

"Because I don't have my own money. Daddy does. I stay there in the summer, but in a few days I'll be back at Yale, happy as a Whiffenpoof on a nubile coed."

We lapsed into silence. I was getting bothered by his mannered smugness. He was putting on a show.

He spoke first. "You know, if you want to see Dad's handiwork first hand, look at Cindy and Tommy."

"What do you mean?"

"You've seen them, Benny the Banal's progeny. Tommy, some punked out druggie with enough tattoos to qualify for membership in some Polynesian tribe. Cindy the New Age Lady Gaga clone, all feathers and exposed navel. Two great success stories that Daddy funded magnanimously."

"He wanted to give your cousins a good education at Chesterton."

"And it paid off. A dropout and a Disney cartoon character, Betty Boop meets Lady Gaga. What a waste of money. Dad just hurled those bucks left and right."

"Why?"

A long pause. "Well, I guess because Mom asked him to. She always felt sorry for Tommy and Cindy, the poor church mice of the family. And you know the Vietnamese and their love of knowledge. *Biet ro rang.* I think that's the phrase. It doesn't matter. A love of learning. Study, study more, study till your eyes fall out. *Hoc, hoc nua, hoc mai.*"

I smiled. "For someone who doesn't like his people, you remember the language."

"Not really. Some phrases have been beaten into my overly bright cranium."

"So your father can be a generous man."

"So my father will keep peace in the family. He doesn't like *scenes*, though he creates them all the time. One way of keeping people away from you is by throwing money at them."

"It works with you."

He smiled. "But some day I'll own the well."

"So you resent your cousins for not becoming success stories. If they had, would you be happy?"

"It's the *waste* of money that bothers me." He looked ready to leave, fidgeting in his chair, looking around, and drumming on the table. "I got to get back to my unpaid internship." But he didn't move. "You know, I never could satisfy Dad." A heartbeat. "I'm a Yale grad, mind you. But he never really *liked* me, and I started wanting him to go away—back when I was a boy, in fact."

"What would you like to do, Jon?" I asked.

He took the question very seriously, looking over my shoulder, pondering. "I'm still working on that. The models I've tried out—the ones I've inherited—just don't cut it for me."

I thought of something. "Your father paid for Danny Trinh to go to school."

I saw color rise in his face, a flash of anger in the eyes, and the tightening of the lips. "Another person I truly hate."

"Danny?"

"I hate him because he's the family success story, and he's not even family. Isn't that ironic?"

"What's to hate about him?"

"Have you met him?" The drumming on the table got louder.

"Yes. Very impressive."

He made a fake chuckling sound. "Impressive, indeed. He comes out of dirt poverty, some Vietnamese working class struggling in public housing, but lucky enough to be the son of our housekeeper…"

"But also bright and ambitious," I interrupted.

"That helps, especially in a world where no one else in the family seems to have more ambition than staying in bed, a la Tommy. You know, Danny is the son Dad always wished he'd had—handsome in some street-thug masculine way, athletic, charming, intelligent, a go-getter. One time Dad even joked that Danny is really his biological son, saying that in front of Mom and Susie and even Danny, and Mom starts to cry."

"Is it true?"

"You've seen Danny. There isn't a bit of Dad in him. My God, he looks like downtown Saigon."

"So that's why you don't like Danny?"

"Of course. He made something of his life. It helps starting out poor."

"He did have an episode of drugs in prep school."

"You mean that stupid thing with Tommy? A couple of dime bags doesn't translate into a drug problem, Rick Van Lam. It's just that they got caught. Daddy took care of it, at least Danny's end of it. But he gave Danny a warning. One more episode with the cops, and no dinero for scholarship boy. Danny knew which side his scholarship was buttered. He straightened up, became Mr. Prig, in fact, some horse's-ass sermonizer like Cotton Mather. A Vietnamese Dale Carnegie—How to Succeed in Business by Learning to be Obnoxious with Daddy's Money."

"You got a lot of resentments."

"Hey, I've earned them."

"You can't blame Danny for taking advantage of opportunity."

He bit his lips. "True enough. But I had to hear all about it when Danny was in school and then, of all places, Harvard. In Dad's mind Harvard is better than Yale."

"Why?"

"It's out of state, I guess. Dad's sort of simple that way. So Danny comes back and is now a rising star at Bank of America."

"But that makes your father proud."

"It makes his mommy proud. She's so grateful that she won't leave Dad's employ, even though Danny has demanded that she do so. Bankers don't have maids for mothers. You see, Danny isn't around much any more, now that he's on his own. Sure, there's the birthday gift for Dad and the Christmas gift of a box of cigars, but Danny has flown the coop, sort of."

"How does your father feel about that?"

"It's never come up in our conversations."

"Does he talk about Danny?"

"Not while I'm in the room."

"That's a smart-aleck response."

He smiled. "Haven't you been listening? All of my remarks are sassy. You bring out the best in people."

I breathed in. "Who do you think killed your mom?"

He didn't miss a beat. "I don't have a clue."

"No ideas?"

"The only person who sometimes resented her was her sister, Mary. And she was already dead."

"So what happens to you?" I asked.

"I stay at Yale for enough years to become student emeritus, then inherit Dad's bucks, so my beautiful bride—bought with inherited money—and I can honeymoon on Maui.

"Sounds to me like you have inherited your father's values already."

He shook his head. "No need to be cruel, Rick." He stood up. "Let's not talk again." He picked up his cell phone and walked away, leaving his tray on the table.

Chapter Fifteen

Late in the afternoon I sat in the Torcelli kitchen, drinking a cup of coffee while Susie polished silverware. I'd knocked on the back door when I'd discovered no one at home, but I already knew that. I'd made certain the house was empty. I knew Susie would be alone. "Mr. Larry is not home. Come back later."

I wanted to talk to her. "Maybe you can help me, Susie. I'm talking to anyone who knew Molly."

She let me in and immediately poured coffee.

"I always polish the silver when I am sad," she told me. "It helps me."

"These are sad days. For the family."

She stopped polishing the silver and wiped her hands. "What's gonna happen to Mr. Larry and the children? Miss Molly, well, she was the—the heart of the family. Mr. Larry is like a ghost, walking around, not speaking."

I sipped the coffee. "Two sisters murdered."

She looked at me, fiercely, right into my eyes. "You have to get the answer, right? Isn't that your job?" She had a thick accent, made heavier by her mood. "I cry and cry, and now I stop. Now I'm angry."

"But the police are stumped."

A dismissive sound broke from the back of her throat. "Oh, the police. They don't care. I know the police from when I lived in Hartford."

"But Molly is a rich woman, married to a prominent businessman...."

She thought about that. "Well, maybe. When it was a simple drive-by, then they could say the people deserve it. But Mr. Larry tells me the police don't know nothing. Nothing at all." She got up, wiped her hands, and reached into a cupboard for some sugar cookies. "I make these. Try one. I bring them for the house but nobody got an appetite. Mr. Larry sits and cries, then talks to the wall."

I bit into one of the cookies, savored the bite of sugar, and nodded my approval. Susie was watching me.

"So Molly had no enemies?"

She sat back down. "What enemies? Her and Miss Mary. Two good women, they don't bother no one."

"The big question is why they went to that dangerous square."

She threw her hands in the air and clicked her tongue. "I don't know. Mr. Larry says to me, over and over—tell me, why did she leave the house? What did she *say* to you? What can I say? I do my job, I leave, I catch the bus. I'm home watching TV when I get a phone call. Miss Molly is dead. I still can't believe it. How that man suffers now. How he needed her. A good, good man."

She went on extolling Larry's virtues, his spirit, his generosity. The more I tried to steer the conversation back to Molly, the more Susie circled back to Larry as savior. I suppose it made sense, what with his mentoring of her son. While she respected Molly—"She no yell at me and always smiling at me, we go shopping together, like friends"—it was Larry who owned her unrelieved allegiance. "He is a great man, that Mr. Larry."

"What did you think of Mary?"

"Very quiet. You know, I have trouble remembering her voice. Miss Molly did almost all the talking. It was like Miss Mary did not like the sound of her voice in these rooms. Like she didn't feel she belonged here."

"But she was always welcome?"

"Oh, yes, of course. Miss Molly seemed, well, crazy to have her come here, not like to show off or anything but to have her around. I think Miss Molly got a little lonely sometimes, the kids off in their world, Mr. Larry working, working, working all the time at the dealership, coming home midnight and tired."

Idly, she picked up a piece of silver, examined it, breathed on it, and then vigorously rubbed it with a soft cloth. She held it up to the light, seemed satisfied, and laid it in a velvet-lined wooden box. "Miss Molly demanded the silver look a certain way," she smiled thinly. "She watched Martha Stewart one night and said we did the silver all wrong. I tell her, I been polishing silver since I was a girl, but Miss Molly said Martha Stewart knew best."

I smiled. "You don't agree with Martha Stewart?"

"I don't know who Martha Stewart is until I see them dragging her off to jail."

I changed the subject. "You must be proud of your boy Danny."

Immediately, as though I'd switched on a hidden light, her eyes got bright, her chin rose.

"Of course. A mother's dream."

"You must be thankful to Larry."

"He gave my son a future. We had *nothing*."

"You must have been scared when—you know—that business of drugs in prep school?"

The question caught her off guard and wasn't welcome. I noticed her body stiffen, her eyes losing the dreaminess.

"That is old history."

"Well, prep school."

"What? Like eight years ago. You know how kids are in prep school. Try this, try that. I almost killed my Danny. I warned him about smoking weed. Is no big deal, I think, but Miss Molly was crazy about it. Her sister, too. Mary screaming and screaming. The walls of this house shook, let me tell you. I am so careful with my boy, sheltering him, hiding him from the world, but he likes to talk, get out, meet people, impress girls. High school boys. You know. But it is Miss Mary's son Tommy that is an awful boy. Back then a troublemaker."

"He got Danny into drugs?"

"What do you think? One time. Yes."

"They all went to Chesterton together."

She sighed. "A mistake, Mr. Larry paying for Miss Mary's kids. Cindy is a dizzy girl with too much rock music in her head. Tommy is lazy drug boy, a bum, all loud cars and crazy haircuts. Even now."

"So Tommy was behind it all?"

"Yes. Danny told me Tommy gave him the drugs. They smoke a little at home, but then they smoke in public."

"And they were arrested."

"I can't tell you how I slap my Danny in the face that night. And how he cried. How sorry he was. I told him to stay away from Tommy."

"And Larry took care of it with the police?"

"And for that I am always grateful. Always. That's why I work for him even now that Danny is making money. He bought me a small house, and he lives with me, a good son. He works hard every day at the bank—more and more responsibility. Always busy. Every Saturday morning at the gym down the street. Like clockwork. Discipline, he tells me. Discipline is the answer. Body and mind."

"And Danny hasn't touched drugs since?"

She stood. "My Danny went to Harvard." She walked to the refrigerator and poured herself some milk. Standing there, her back to the sink, she said triumphantly, "Danny will be rich some day. Trinh Xuan Duong." She used his Vietnamese names. "My joy."

I heard the front door open, listened as Kristen and a girl-friend chattered about something, then rushed up the stars. Susie and I were silent, both paying attention to the giggling, breathy girls, and I caught her eye. In that instance I realized how much she disliked Kristen.

Susie turned away. I asked her how Kristen and Jon were dealing with their mother's death, but she was noncommittal. "Okay, I guess. They don't talk much. I hear Kristen crying in her room." And then she closed up. I could see she wanted me to leave, but I lingered, reaching for another cookie, examining it as if I'd made a wonderful archeological find. Susie packed up the silver polish and cloths, even though I noticed she was not done with the work.

"How does Danny get along with Kristen and Jon?" I asked.

She didn't look happy. "Why you ask?"

"I mean, he's like a member of the family."

"When he was little, yes, playing with Jon, mainly."

"But not later?"

She hesitated. "He didn't care for Jon that much. Jon is, well, hard to be friends with."

"Jealousy?"

"Jealous of Danny's looks, intelligence…"

"But," I interrupted, "Jon has those things, too."

"Danny wanted to be just like Mr. Larry. You see, my own husband, Danny's father, he takes off to California, leaves me broke and living in a dump, when Danny was two or three. So Danny sees Mr. Larry as a father."

"And Jon didn't like that?"

She hesitated again. I thought she was going to say that Jon didn't like anybody, but she seemed to remember her position in the household, sitting there in the bright kitchen. "Jon is all right." She ended it.

"And Kristen?"

The corners of her mouth twisted slightly. "All the kids were friendly once. Kristen these days is into some boy at the country club. She is very pretty, you know. Boys chase her. She likes that."

"You don't."

"Is not my business," She turned away.

"Did Molly like Cindy and Tommy?"

"Let me tell you something," she confided. "I have no business telling family business and it's only because Mr. Larry tells me to cooperate with the police. And, I guess, with you, Mr. Investigator. But I don't like this."

"Say what makes you comfortable."

"None of this make me comfortable." She sighed. "Miss Molly put up with—yes, put up with—Cindy and Tommy because they were Miss Mary's kids. But she *hated* Tommy. Hated him. She felt sorry for Benny because everything he touched turned to dust—and Cindy, who was, well, just there, like a rock. But Tommy had brought drugs into the family, and she hated that."

"Did Mary know how much she hated Tommy?"

She ignored the question. "When the police arrested Tommy, Miss Mary sat in the kitchen with Miss Molly, and two of them crying and crying. They thought the family was in trouble. Miss Molly said one time that some relative back in Saigon years ago was ruined by opium, and it tore apart the family. A death that shattered the family—a beloved cousin. So the two sisters sat right there"—she pointed to the other side of the table—"while I poured coffee for them, and worried about their children."

"But that turned out to be nothing."

"How could they know that back then?"

"Well, let me ask you one last thing, and then I'll go." She was already rustling some baking tins in a cabinet. "If Molly hated Tommy for drugs, how did she feel about Danny, who was arrested with Tommy."

Silence in the room. She stood there, a stone block, impenetrable.

"Susie?"

She trembled. "That is a difficult question." I waited. "Miss Molly and my Danny always had a little difficult relationship, you know." She smiled a bit, but not happy. "I work for them for years, and little Danny, everybody knows and loves him. He is good boy. A favorite of Mr. Larry. And I don't think Miss Molly liked that too much. Mr. Larry likes Danny more than Jonny, she tells me once, when the boys are six or seven. I say no no no. Oh yes, she says, and she looks at me."

"Why?"

"Mr. Detective, I know you gotta hear the stupid stories, how Danny is Mr. Larry's son. Everybody jokes about that. A horrible story, not true. Danny looks like his father, who ran away. I got pictures I can show you. I start work here after Danny is born. Danny is dark, true, like Mr. Larry, but it don't matter if something is a lie sometimes…"

"Because people believe what they want to."

She nodded. "Yes."

"But Molly must have known the stories were false, especially after all these years."

"Yes, true, but, you know, women have doubts and those doubts go on and on."

"So Molly didn't like Danny?"

"I'm not saying she *disliked* him. But after the drug thing with Tommy, Miss Molly put her foot down, Mr. Larry give him a lecture, and Danny listens."

"But Molly still wondered?

"It sort of made her lose a little *respect* for him. He's always been the…the overachiever. Danny always flattered her, thanked her too much. Too many times. I tell him enough. People think you're sucking up. Keep quiet. But he was a boy, you know, and afraid all *this* would disappear." She waved her hand around the kitchen, as though she owned the place.

"Did she compare Danny with her own kids?"

"Not Kristen, of course."

"But to Jon?"

"I always felt that was a problem. Jon was bright, but Danny brighter. Jon good looking but Danny the heartthrob. Jon the loner but Danny charming, making friends. Danny was always one step ahead. The poor boy beating the rich in every race but one."

"But one?"

"Money," Susie said. "Jon always had more money than my Danny."

"Not any more, maybe."

Her smile was conspiratorial. "Not anymore."

Chapter Sixteen

Late Friday night, around ten, the crowd at Zeke's Olde Tavern shifted from the older Budweiser folks downing New England stew to groups of noisy, partying college kids, looking for love in exactly the wrong place. Hearing a burst of laughter, I turned to spot Kristen Torcelli tucked into an excited gaggle of young women, all talking on cell phones as they moved from the doorway to a booth. They made enough noise to make heads turn.

I'd never seen her at the Tavern. She wasn't a local, like me, possessive of the place and decidedly territorial, nor was she one of the fun-loving kids from Farmington College, a couple streets away, those junior-grade intellects with real or with fake IDs.

So we watched her topple into a booth and then blow a kiss at a college kid who glanced her way.

"I think she's a little drunk." Hank flicked his head toward her.

I pointed her out to Gracie, Liz, and Jimmy, who stared directly at the booth until I told them to stop. We'd just finished a late supper, and now, sated, we lounged and sipped beer and coffee, often in silence or talking about the weather, politics, and the lethargy our meal had created in us. Kristen's entrance, unheralded, had made us sit up.

"Go say hello, Hank." Liz nudged him.

"Maybe later." He wasn't happy.

Gracie frowned. "I guess the period of mourning ain't very long these days."

"When I was kid," Jimmy said, "for a whole year you had no music, dancing, partying. We grieved a whole goddamned year."

Gracie smiled. "Poor Jimmy. No 'Beer Barrel Polka' for a whole year."

Liz shook her head. "Well, the mall is open seven days a week now, Connecticut Blue Laws going the way of all flesh."

I was ready to leave. It had been a long day for me, sleeping late, jogging a bit, answering some overdue e-mail to old college friends, which took me all afternoon. And then the lazy evening with friends. I'd done no work on any of my investigations, including The Case. But as we talked, occasionally looking at Kristen who was whooping it up about something, Jimmy mentioned that a Hartford cop buddy of his worried about the resurgence of gang activity in Hartford.

"I used to be afraid to come into the city when I was a kid," Hank said. "All you'd see on TV was gang kids lined up by the police against a wall."

"And then the gangs were gone." Jimmy snapped his fingers.

"So what happened?" From Hank.

Jimmy sat back, took a swig of beer. "You know how gangs flourished a decade back or so, out of control. The Latin Kings, the Solidos, The Black Knights. The Nelson Court turf wars, drug sales, gun power, slaphappy preteens with assault rifles. For a while the city was held hostage by punks running wild in the housing projects and in the streets. Shoot 'em up time. Then two things happened. Two ten-year-old girls, walking home from school in the South End, got caught in some cross fire between two gangs, both shot. Broad daylight, with a school crossing guard just feet away. Good neighborhood folks organized committees. But what really got the goat of the local and state police was when Dan Rather or somebody famous interviewed some lowlife gangbangers on *60 Minutes*, a live feed directly from Hartford, and this one wacko kid brags that his gang ruled the city. Hartford, in a heartbeat, had become a national laughingstock, a disgrace."

"And the crackdown began." From Hank.

"Rounded up by the state police and tossed into prisons. And suddenly it was safe to walk around Hartford all day. Not everywhere, but at least in front of the State Legislative Building."

"So what happened?" Gracie asked.

"Well, think about it. People get out of prison. Five years, ten years. Time off for good behavior. You know how it is. So the pros are back on the street, not rehabilitated, and the young bucks are coming up, in need of guidance perhaps, but also not happy with sharing turf with old-timers."

"And the streets are at war again," Liz summed up.

"Bingo."

I spoke up. "But it seems this new crop of gangs took everyone by surprise."

"Yeah," said Jimmy. "All the brains in City Hall thought those drug education programs in school were helping. Hey, if you're poor and ain't got no future, well, there's always real estate on a street corner for small-time investors."

"But *why* Goodwin Square?" asked Hank. "How did that spot get so notorious?"

Jimmy tapped his fingers on the bottle he was holding. "That's just one of a number of the city's hot spots. You know, the police clean up a corner, the traffic drifts a few block over, just the way hookers do, and then back again. Goodwin Square has a special feature, though—it's right near the on-off ramps of I-91 and I-84. Easy on, easy off. Nice for the crack addicts from the suburbs. The thing is, everybody *knows* that square."

"Why?"

"The *Courant* did a couple pieces on it."

"And," I concluded, "if anyone wanted to set up a murder to look like a drive-by, that's the place."

"But *two* murders?" Liz asked.

"That's the problem," I said. "How do you get two skittish Vietnamese sisters to go to a corner that must have filled them with dread?"

"I can't connect the dots." Hank sounded helpless.

Jimmy yawned. "Got to get some sleep." He rose and tossed a twenty-dollar bill on the table. Liz and Gracie stood up to leave. Hank and I stayed. Kristen glanced over and spotted us saying our good-byes. Hank caught her eye and waved. She didn't look happy to see him, looking nervously toward her two girlfriends and then back at him, her lips pushed into a thin, disagreeable line.

After a few minutes, Hank whispered to me, "I'm on a scouting mission. Give me a few minutes and then wander over. Act natural."

"Hank, she's a blood relative of yours. I don't think you need all these KGB tactics."

"We'll see."

Kristen introduced Hank to her two girlfriends, who were obviously delighted with the handsome young man. But Kristen made it clear that Hank was off-limits. Whatever she was saying was done with a rigid, stony face, her mouth tight. Yet the girls tried to get Hank to sit at their booth, even sliding in for him. One even touched his forearm. Kristen would have none of it. She jumped out of the booth, nodded to her friends, and led Hank to a small, unoccupied table back by the restrooms. I waited for Hank to glance in my direction.

"Rick, join us," Hank called to me, so I walked to their new table, pulling up a chair. Kristen looked annoyed, but I suddenly realized that perhaps she had a repertoire of only four or five looks, petulance and annoyance high on the list.

"I was just asking Kristen if she came here a lot. I told her it's a hangout of mine."

Kristen shook her head, and the diamond studs in her ears caught the scant light of the dim room. She sparkled. "One of my girlfriends goes to Farmington College. I've never been here before." As she pointed back to the booth, she looked around. "It's a real dump."

"We like it," I said.

"Well, what?" She turned back to Hank.

Now he looked confused. "Well, what?"

"You said you wanted to talk to me." She looked back at her two girlfriends, who were staring at us, annoyed, their heads peering over the top of their booth.

"No, no," Hank spoke quickly. "I said I wanted to, you know, say hello. We didn't have time to talk at the funeral."

"The funeral? That was two days ago." She stated the fact as though she were imagining life in the Bronze Age.

"How's your dad doing?" I asked.

"He made me get out of the house. I was moping around. Getting on his nerves."

"It must be hard for you…"

She shrugged her shoulders. "What can I say?" Then, her words laced with melancholy, "I just don't know what to do."

She was not exactly dressed in funereal black. Instead, she sported a pink polka-dot halter top over tight tennis shorts, tennis sneakers with pink socks. I guessed those were real diamonds in her tennis bracelet and in the slender necklace she wore.

A heavy sigh. "You know, I wake up and miss Mom."

"I'm sorry," I said.

"She's always downstairs in the morning." She looked at Hank. "Your mother keeps dropping in."

"She's bringing food."

"But how many spring rolls can a human eat?" She smiled. "After a while they taste like rubber. They're piling up in the fridge like firewood."

I could see Hank getting peeved. "I'll tell her to stop." His tone was icy cold.

She went on. "My girlfriends think you're cute."

"I am cute."

"But they're not for you. I *told* them."

"Why not?"

"They, well, *screw* around."

Hank looked over at the booth.

At that moment a young man sitting at the bar, who'd been watching us, sauntered over, trying to look casual and off-the-cuff. "Kristen, remember me?"

She looked at him blankly. "No."

"From Chesterton. I sat behind you in English Lit. Jason. Jason Leibner. We sat together on that field trip to Mark Twain's house. But you dropped out…" He stopped.

She scarcely looked up at the nervous young man. He was dressed in creased chinos and a polo shirt, collar turned up, looking as he probably did in his class picture, a fresh-scrubbed, friendly boy. She looked away. "No, sorry." He started to say something, but she cut him off. "Can't you see I'm with people?" The young man, embarrassed, swiveled and fled back to the bar. Within minutes he tossed cash on the bar and left the tavern.

"I hate when boys come on to me."

"Some girls find it flattering."

She rolled her eyes, cartoon-like. "I don't need a *boy* in my life right now. I don't *need* one." She smiled, and I realized how beautiful a woman she was going to be—her father's striking Mediterranean looks with a dash of her mother's exquisiteness. Truly stunning.

She picked at the polish on a manicured nail and looked back at her friends. "I gotta get back."

"How's Jon doing?" I wanted to talk more.

She made a what-if shake of her head. "Jon? Lost in his own world. The ivy tower of Yale."

"This must be hard on him."

"Why?"

"To lose a mother."

"I guess so. He and Mom were *close*. It's just that Jon…well, I don't know what he thinks most of the time. He's the family *genius*, you know. He told me that once. He tells me all the time I'm the family space cadet."

"He said that?" Hank asked.

"Well, he's an ass. Everyone *knows* that. No friends. Not really. Let me tell you something. I got more street smarts on one finger than he's got in his whole body."

"Street smarts?"

She preened. "I can handle *people*. I'm not stupid, you know." She leaned forward and I smelled alcohol on her breath. "He's a rat fink. Always has been." She was irritated now, sitting upright, her right hand adjusting a loose stand of her hair. She rolled her tongue over carefully applied lipstick, and smiled. "I'll tell you a little secret, Hank. Do you know who snitched on Tommy and Danny back in prep school? Who let the cops know they were carrying? Jon *told* the headmaster, who called the cops. They picked up Danny and Tommy in downtown Hartford."

"Are you sure?"

"Yeah. the headmaster told Mom and I heard her tell Dad. But Mom and Dad never said a word to Jon."

"Did Tommy and Danny know?"

"Tommy suspected. He got mad and said he was going to kill Jon, especially after he got probation."

"But Danny got nothing."

"That's because of Mom and Dad."

"You like Danny?" I asked.

She stared at me vacantly, but I realized she was choosing her words carefully. "He's all right—never did me any harm. Him and his mother Susie are like family. Sort of. I mean, well, his mother's the *help* and all."

"What does Jon think of Danny?"

"Hates him. Better looking, smarter. You've seen Danny, right? Dreamboat."

Something curious was happening as Kristen spoke. Her body relaxed, her face softened, her eyes got cloudy. Her smile was silly. She was a different girl from the tight, brassy girl of moments before. Hank was looking at me, charting the metamorphosis, and I wondered suddenly about Danny and Kristen. Was there something going on?

"Have you ever dated Danny?" I asked her.

She roared with delight and hit the table with her hand. "You are something else. Danny is, well, family. And besides my father would *kill* me, just *kill* me."

"But Danny is like a son to him."

"*Like* a son. You're right."

"Then what's the problem?"

She looked at me as though I were dense. "Haven't you noticed? He's Susie's son. His mother is a *servant*."

She got up and returned to her booth, where I could hear her repeating the line about Danny's mom being a servant. The other two girls screamed in unison.

Chapter Seventeen

I didn't believe Kristen. Neither did Hank. On Saturday morning I called the Torcelli home, looking for Susie, but Jon told me she was at her own home.

"Why her?" Jon asked.

"Loose ends," I explained, but I could tell Jon wasn't really interested. He hung up without saying good-bye.

Susie's Cape Cod was on a side street off New Britain Avenue in Elmwood, a few houses down from a busy Mobil gas station and a Dunkin' Donuts. I sat nursing an iced coffee, watching the intersection, and eventually I saw Danny's car. Susie had mentioned his ritualistic workout on Saturday mornings, and I didn't want him around when I talked to her. I trailed him down the street to the Power Gym, watched him park, and then circled back to Susie's home. She was in the front yard as I stopped in front of the chain link gate. She'd been working in a flower bed, bent over, weeding zinnias and marigolds, a shock of color against the drab gray clapboard house. She stopped what she was doing, stood up, took off her garden gloves, and waited. I waved, and she motioned me through the gate.

"Mr. Lam," she yelled, friendly, "is everything all right?"

"Good morning. Spare me a minute?"

She nodded. "You still investigating?"

"That's what I do." I smiled.

"I don't know what I can tell you, but come on in. It's too hot outside." She was wearing an old housedress torn at the shoulder, with a sagging hem. Her hair was tucked under a straw hat, the rim tattered. "Excuse my appearance. I wasn't expecting visitors." She looked toward the street. "You just missed my Danny. The gym, you know."

"You look like you enjoy your flowers."

She studied the lush, dense bed of flowers, a riot of crimson and orange and white. "Someday I'd like to have the whole front yard filled with flowers, from the door to the sidewalk. No grass. Just flowers. Years ago I had a window box in the projects, one little plastic box hanging off the window, inside the iron bars they put up to stop thieves, and my flowers always started out good, but then the pollution made them puny. So I stopped doing it. Now," she pointed to her beds, "now I am the best gardener on the street."

Inside we sat in an immaculate kitchen, the appliances polished, the cabinets gleaming, the floor glistening. I noticed calendars from local Asian markets, and the obligatory shrine on a wall shelf, with incense, candles, and a statue of the Virgin Mary. On the counter sat a tray of chocolate-chip cookies, cooling. Nearby a loaf of fragrant homemade bread, obviously fresh from the oven. A bowl of fresh fruit rested in the center of the round table, apples and pears surrounding a pineapple, and I noticed that even the fruit looked fake: polished, sparkling, crisp. "Can I get you something?" she asked.

I said no, but she poured some fresh Vietnamese-style lemonade into two glasses, and set one in front of me. In the hot, un-air-conditioned room—she did switch on a small little fan near the stove—the utterly cold drink was invigorating. "Very good," I complimented her.

"I make my lemonade for Mr. Larry and Miss Molly…" She suddenly lowered her voice. "I'm sorry."

"It's hard to get used to her death, isn't it?"

She sighed. "Life there ain't never gonna be the same."

"I bumped into Kristen last night at a bar I go to." I watched her face.

She frowned. "The day after the funeral she went out, romping around like a whore." She bit her tongue, regretting her words. "You know," she continued, "it is only Mr. Larry I worry about, and I shouldn't say that. Sometimes Jon and Kristen act like little children." She smiled. "I always speak my mind, Mr. Lam."

"You talk like this to Larry?"

She deliberated. "I've been there so long I can say anything. Well, almost anything." A thin smile. "I think. Mr. Larry and I—and even Miss Molly—talked about Kristen and Jon like they were somebody else's kids. They ask me what I think."

"I can see Kristen is bothered by Molly's death, but I don't think she knows how to deal with it."

In a clipped voice, "Well, she's a woman now. Grief is all around now. *Find* a way."

"You're hard on her."

She sipped lemonade. "I no like empty lives."

"And hers is?"

"How many prep schools did she drop out of years ago? And since then—nothing. Sitting in front of her mirror. Going to the country club. Mr. Larry just wants her married because she's too pretty and also she's not too bright, always wandering around. He's always trying to fix her up with some business guy, son of a business friend, that kind of thing, but she's too flighty, dizzy. No one is good enough for her." She paused. "One time Jon said she's like ice cream— great when you get it but you don't think about it a hour later."

"That's a horrible thing to say about a sister."

She waved her hand in the air, took a sip of lemonade. "I'm just repeating…"

"Did she ever date your Danny?"

The question was met with a stony stare, her face locking up. Her two hands gripped the sweaty glass, and the ice cubes clinked. "What?"

"Well, they're all the same age. Both real good-looking kids."

"No," she said, emphatic.

"That seems strange. In prep school they were around each other a lot."

"It never happened, Mr. Lam. And you know why? Danny's no fool. You think he'd risk *everything* to have a—a fling with her? It would fall apart, they all do, and who suffers? Danny."

"Would Larry fight it?"

She stood up. "I no like this conversation." She faced the counter. I could see a ridge of sweat on the back of her neck.

"It's just that Kristen, last night, when Danny's name came up, seemed a little intoxicated with him."

She turned to face me. "Get out."

I sat there.

She raised her voice. "You gotta leave now. This ain't proper. Danny and I are good Catholics, churchgoers. You think my son would touch her like that…"

I stood up. "She speaks about him with…"

A harsh, flat voice. "Get out of my house."

"I mean…"

"Out now." She gripped the counter, her knuckles white. She was trembling. I mumbled good-bye and left.

I sat in the parking lot of the Power Gym on New Britain Avenue, a few cars away from Danny's Mercedes, talking to Hank on my phone, waiting. Eventually I spotted him leaving, the gym shorts and a tank top over a muscular body, pumped up now. He stopped to joke with a very healthy-looking woman who tried to get him to go somewhere, smiling broadly, but he smiled, waved, and headed to his car, tossing his gym bag into the trunk. He looked freshly showered, with the swagger of a young man on the move. For a second he stopped, read a text message on his phone, frowned, then shoved the phone into a pocket.

I got out of my car. "Danny."

He didn't look surprised. "Hey, Rick, what are you doing here?"

"Your mother told me you were here. I stopped in to see her."

He smiled. "Every Saturday morning, faithfully. And two nights a week." He showed me an impressive bicep.

"I thought bankers were scrawny, pasty guys."

He didn't answer. "What can I do you for?"

"Buy you lunch?"

He seemed ready to say no, but said, "Sure, why not? "But quick. Got a lot to do. Day off."

I chose a small Vietnamese restaurant up the street, Café Ba Le, a mom-and-pop place with little kids scampering underfoot, wobbly tables, wallpaper peeling, linoleum cracked, and mismatched chairs and tables. And the best Vietnamese pancakes in Connecticut. *Banh xeo*, sizzling egg crepes filled with shrimp, bean sprouts, veggies, and topped with fish sauce. Danny, it turned out, had never been there. "I never think to come here. Mom feeds me enough Old Country food to last a lifetime," he explained, looking around. He followed my lead and got the pancake, with *nuoc mia*, a sugar cane cold drink. We split some fresh-made summer rolls, dipped in aromatic sauce. He loved the crispy pancakes. "As good as Mom's." He swallowed a chunk of spiced chicken. "Hearty, too. I put bean sprouts in everything."

"So," he said finally, "why were you visiting my mother?"

I detected an edge to his voice. We'd been making small talk until then, though I'd seen wariness in his eyes. But the wide, toothsome smile—had Larry paid for those gleaming, perfect teeth?—never disappeared for more than a second.

"I don't really know." I shrugged. "I'm talking to everyone. All roads lead nowhere."

"I find it amazing. Two sisters, dead. Like that. Makes no sense."

"No, it doesn't. But there has to be some logic behind it."

He locked eyes with mine. "Good luck." He tilted his head.. "But what can my mother tell you?" He smiled. "And, I suppose, me, considering this little lunch."

"I wanted to talk about Molly's relationship with Mary and Benny…"

He broke in. "Molly had too much money. It made her uncomfortable."

"Meaning?"

"As the wife of Larry, you know, she had to be on boards, clubs, garden projects, charity functions, dinners, balls. And I don't think she ever *really* felt comfortable in those roles. She put on a show. She liked the money, yes, she did, but not the social butterfly stuff that came with a marriage to a guy like Larry."

"She started out poor."

Danny's eyes kept moving. They followed a girl walking by. She smiled back at him. He looked back at me. "She brought a lot of baggage with her, let me tell you."

"Like what?"

"She saw what poverty did to Mary and Benny, struggling, missing mortgage payments, the tough neighborhood."

"How'd you get on with her?"

He shook his head. "I wasn't Molly's favorite person. Tommy and I got caught smoking pot in prep school. But I'm guessing that you already heard that story from everyone. *Everyone* talks of it." He smiled. "The family still talks about it. It was nothing. We got—careless. Stupid school kids. But, my God, World War Three broke out, especially for Molly and Mary. And, of course for my own mother. Drugs to them was—opium. A head filled with nightmares. Back to Saigon streets. Some dead relative. Messy. Larry threatened to take me out of Chesterton, send me to public school. Mom cried and cried."

"You were born in Hartford?"

"Right in Dutch Point, down by the river. Ramshackle project housing, broken windows, rats, wild dogs, broken doors, empty kids hanging out all day. Lucky we got out when I was a little boy, so I don't remember much. One of two Vietnamese families placed there by Catholic Charities. My dad quit when I was a baby, headed to California. I never knew him, though his brother's still around. Mom worked temp jobs until Molly took over. Larry saved our lives. He found Mom an apartment in Elmwood, on a bus line to Farmington because Mom won't drive a car, and I grew up there." He smirked. "My life in a nutshell."

"You know, there's rumors you're Larry's kid."

A wide grin covered his face. "You know, that old story drove Mom and Molly to distraction. Larry found it funny. So did I."

"Not true."

"Do I look like I got white blood?"

"It's possible."

"No, it isn't. I don't look like my mother, true, but I don't look like Larry. I look like my father's brother, who's in Hartford."

"What about Kristen?"

He didn't miss a beat. "Kristen? Kristen's a sweet girl, pretty."

"She's not a go-getter. Like you."

"Well, Kristen has other things going for her..."

"Drop-dead looks?"

"Yeah, well, a stunner. But I mean, well, a kind heart, too. She's *sweet*."

I downed the last of my drink. "You close to her?"

"I don't see any of the kids much any more."

"Jon?"

Sarcastic: "Yeah, sure."

"Last night, talking to Kirsten who was out with some girl-friends, she had nice things to say about you."

"We always got along." Hesitation in his voice.

"In fact, the only time she lit up was at the mention of your name."

He said nothing. I called for the check. Henry, the owner, walked over. We knew each other to nod to, so I greeted him. *Chao ong*. We shook hands. I thanked him for the delicious lunch, and he walked away. Danny hadn't taken his eyes off my face.

I looked into his face. "She said Larry would kill her if she went out with you."

He frowned. "This is a nonsubject with me. I can't answer that."

"Why not?"

"Larry's not like that. He's like a father..."

"But Kristen seems to have a warm spot for you."

"I can't help that." Then, slyly, "What are you getting at?"

"I'm wondering if you ever had a relationship with her?"

"You think that we screwed?"

"Why not? Two good-looking kids. Not related. Always in each other's company."

His words were clipped now, humorless. "What did she say?" I didn't answer. "God, I wish she had a brain cell sometimes." He laughed. "All right, then, we *did* fool around a while back."

"A while back?" I waited. "Kristen is a little too intoxicated with you…"

"Man to man, I tell you, okay. We see each other now and then, a quickie. I suppose she hinted *that* to you. No one knows. She hinted about it on her Facebook page one time—I stopped that quick. Larry would kill her. And *me*. He thinks I'm a player, so he has to protect her. Nobody has to know, right?"

"Did Molly know?"

"God, no. Kristen knew better."

"Why are you telling me?"

He reached into his wallet and threw a twenty-dollar bill on the table. "Because I think you already know."

"I am the detective."

"We're over twenty-one and single."

"When's the last time you two were together?"

He actually blushed and looked away. "The night Molly was murdered."

"I guess that explains why she's still glowing."

He stood up. "I have that effect on women."

Chapter Eighteen

Hank and I cornered Tommy at his father's grocery in Little Saigon. He was alone, sitting on a stool, playing a video game on his smartphone. "You looking for Pop? He's gone to the bank."

We told him we'd stopped in to say hello, despite the fact that we'd sat in the car until we'd spotted Benny leaving the grocery and getting into his car. He never looked around him, head down, purposeful, unlocking the old Chevy, sliding in, glancing at traffic on the street, and driving away. Here was a man with little connection to the world around him.

"Yeah?" Tommy eyed us.

"What?" From Hank.

"I don't think you two are here to buy a fifty-pound bag of Thai rice."

"I'm looking for one of those yummy cold-cut grinders," Hank told him. "One of your famous *banh mi*." The familiar sandwich usually made with French bread, pâté, chicken, ginger, and onions.

Tommy yawned. "We're all out. I ate the last one."

"How's your father doing?" Hank was looking around the room.

Tommy shrugged. "Moping around. He's lost interest in the store. I don't think he cares anymore."

"And you?" Hank asked.

"Well, I didn't care shit to begin with. Look around you, man. This is my life. Partner in Daddy's rice hovel. Can't you smell the decay in the walls?"

The place was a shambles: a tiny corner store with Asian products strewn around haphazardly, some still in half-opened cardboard boxes piled in aisles. Cartons of canned soy milk. Bags of rice nearly blocked the front aisle, and the floor hadn't been swept in days. It had a funky smell. According to Hank, few folks shopped there, except some old buddies, loyal friends from the early days of his arrival in Hartford. As the Vietnamese community thrived, the area that came to be called, romantically, Little Saigon by the chamber of commerce witnessed an influx of entrepreneurial spirits, sons and daughters with degrees in Business Administration from the University of Connecticut. Soon glitzy bright stores opened on the strip, American style, with wide aisles, cruel florescent lighting, and zip-a-dee-doo-dah scanners at the registers. On Saturday you couldn't move in the parking lots. Cars with Rhode Island and Massachusetts license plates lined up, and the young professionals parked their red BMWs diagonally in two parking spots so that their cars and lives wouldn't risk dents. And at Benny's grocery, Vu Pham Market, an hour would pass, and an old woman would come in for *che ba mau*, a tricolor pudding that Mary used to make and sell. Or a neighbor would run in, in need of a tin of soy milk or a few sticks of lemongrass or a single piece of some fruit, like *du du* or *xoai*, papaya or mango.

"Your father works hard," Hank grumbled, a little angry.

"Yeah, I suppose so."

"Why do you work here?" I asked.

Tommy stared back, defiant, running his fingers over the gel-stiff Mohawk, today a mint green. "It's the closest I can get to getting free cigarettes and beer money, and not have to go to a real job."

"Noble," I said.

"And your snooping job is more noble?"

I didn't answer.

"Come on," Hank pleaded. "We're here to help…"

"What does that mean?"

"It means," I went on, "I'm looking into your relationship with Molly's kids."

"Kristen? Does she know the world exists outside her mirror?"

"I'm thinking about Jon."

Tommy lit a cigarette and blew smoke at us. "I could give a fuck about him."

"Didn't you threaten him once?"

Surprise in his voice. "How?"

"You suspected he ratted on you about drugs."

Tommy laughed loudly, then started to choke. "One fucking moment in school, a couple of rolled joints, and a puff at a dance club—and Christ, I'm branded for life. Why is that coming up now? Who's talking about it?"

"Kristen, for one."

"Yeah? What she say?"

"That Jon ratted on you and Danny."

"Hey, everyone knew that—at least Kristen told everyone then. In secrecy."

"And you wanted to hurt him?"

"Yeah, but what the hell. That was years ago. We were dumb kids."

"Why would Jon rat on you?"

"You're not that bright, Rick Van Lam. Think about it. It had nothing to do with *me*. Don't you see? It was Danny he wanted to get at. Danny the wonder boy, Danny the great yellow hope. Get Danny in trouble—the hell with me, blood cousin. He and I actually got along. Neither of us liked anybody around us, and so we sort of found each other. But Danny got in the way."

Hank shook his head. "But Danny got away with it. Nothing happened to him."

"And I got probation, thanks to Fresh-Off-the-Boat daddy and mommy. Scare little Tommy into manhood. Well, it wasn't fun going to juvenile court, talking to the lawyers, afraid of being sent to Long Lane Detention. The whole shit. Thanks, Mommy and Daddy."

"That wasn't Danny's fault."

Again, the artificial laugh. "Everything is Danny's fault."

"What does that mean?"

"You don't seem to realize how Danny fits into the life of the Torcelli-Vu community. Not that he did anything to make us hate him, but his *presence* alone. His *being* there. Don't you see? Handsome, charming, super intelligent, slick, athletic, you name it. He walks through a room, and the Torcelli-Vu world goes apeshit. Molly was afraid of him, Larry adores him like the son he never had, Jon hates him because he can never be as good, and Kristen throws goo-goo eyes at him and moistens her panties. And that's just the Torcellis. In the Benny Vu world"—he half-bowed—"of which I'm the shining example, he's the poor boy—like *me*, get it—who got the chance to shine. Unlike me, he did it. Honor student, future banker of America—the example of what me and my little New Age crystal-jingling sister can never be. And everyone keeps saying, 'Look at Danny.'" His face got hard. "Look at Danny all right. Do you see why I don't give a rat's ass about him?"

"He paid a condolence call to you after your mom died."

"Yes, Danny has a way of stopping in to remind us of what we are, driving up in a Mercedes and looking around my apartment like he's a social worker who's thinking of changing his job."

"You used to be buddies."

"I 'used to be' a lot of things. I mean, we still talk and all. Facebook each other nonsense. 'I'm going to Starbucks now.'" He laughed. "We don't come to blows."

"What does he think of you?"

"You gotta ask him that. He stops in at the store now and then. Even at the house. We gab about…I don't know…music. Sports. Nonsense." He looked around. "Now, if you'll excuse me, I have to get ready for the Boat People who'll be here to buy scratch-off lottery tickets. The thing that keeps us afloat. As if coming to America wasn't a big enough gamble."

"Tommy…"

"I don't see how any of this connects to the murder of my mother."

"Maybe it doesn't."

"Then it's over."

◇◇◇

Early that evening as the sun started to go down, the air still humid and sticky, Hank and I went for a jog. I tried to jog every other day, usually early morning, followed by a swim at the college pool. But lately I'd been sleeping later and later. This morning I'd got up late, sloshed through too much coffee, worked on my other cases—my tedious insurance fraud cases. I scribbled note cards on Tommy, Kristen, Jon, and, new to my pegboard, Danny. So when Hank called and said he wanted to jog around the West Hartford Reservoir—a lazy mile of water and pine and meandering collies and schnauzers—I said yes, come over. I thought I needed a run to clear my head.

The path was largely deserted at the supper hour, a few stragglers loping along with tired, panting dogs. It was sweltering out, and within seconds my T-shirt was plastered to my chest, my ankles ached, my sides burned. But eventually I caught my stride, and Hank and I cruised along, not fast not slow, comfortable enough to talk.

"I'm thinking Danny is somehow in this mix," I told him. "But maybe unwittingly."

"Meaning?"

"Meaning everyone reacts to him. He's like the eye of a hurricane, there in the center, doing whatever he does, and all around him swim anger and jealousy and distrust."

"But how do family squabbles lead to double murder?"

For a while we jogged without talking. Suddenly everything I'd been doing the past couple of weeks—all the conversations with family members, all the voyeuristic delving into their conventional pasts, even the pathetic rehashing of that simple marijuana bust almost a decade ago—seemed folly, a waste of everyone's time. I told Hank this.

"I know," he said. "These kids do have a lot of baggage with each other, but it's all in the past. Prep school was their battleground."

"But that incident in school keeps popping up. It's like it's not history, but something that happened yesterday. Which leads me to believe that maybe that story is still somehow relevant *now*."

Back at the apartment Hank showered and dressed in clothes he'd brought with him. While I showered, he cranked up my stereo—I expected Gracie to bang on the ceiling with a broom—and drank a beer. Sprawled in a chair, I relaxed, feeling good, listening to the pleasant strains of Alicia Keyes.

"I was thinking about the kids while I was showering," I told him. "Maybe something happened with them like the thing with Tommy and Danny, and of course that immediately involves the two sisters. That's what happened in prep school. The Tommy incident became warfare for everyone, mainly the grown-ups. Mary and Molly react for years to what their American kids are up to. They don't understand, and they overreact."

"So you're saying maybe Mary and Molly found out something."

"Maybe."

"And it involved one or more of the kids."

"Or maybe Danny."

Hank bit his lip. "Probably not Benny or Larry. Both seem out of the loop. It's the mothers who maybe found something out."

"So if there's an answer, it might lie in the kids. Maybe we're just not looking at this the right way."

Hank nodded. "Maybe."

"If I may quote Buddha: 'If the glass appears empty, it is just because you have failed to observe its contents.'"

Hank shook his head. "I'll never understand half of what you tell me."

Chapter Nineteen

The one person we hadn't paid much attention to was Tommy's younger sister Cindy, and Hank offered a reason—she hid in her eccentric clothing and her stark makeup. "She's created a caricature that keeps people away," he summed up. "Her brother Tommy is a freak with his dark Goth clothing and chains. Jon is the Yalie with an attitude, and Kristen is the prom queen standing in front of a mirror, trying to remember her name."

"But to hide what?"

We were sitting in my apartment, early afternoon, drinking iced coffee. Hank was chomping on a bag of chocolate-chip cookies he'd bought with him.

"You know, of all the kids, she's the one whose gene pool got fucked up. I mean her *looks*. Kristen used to taunt her, calling her moon face because her face is so round and flat and puffy."

"That explains the makeup," I noted.

"I don't know her that good, but she always struck me as unhappy. The other three are moody, careless, sometimes boisterous, always running with friends. Off to the mall. That kind of thing. Cindy—her real name is Hanh but she never uses it—had to invent her own world."

"But at least she stayed in school. Unlike Kristen and Tommy."

"Kristen is sadly dumb. Cindy is sadly intelligent."

"I wonder how she looks at her aunt's murder."

Hank grinned. "Maybe a lot, but none of it she'll share with you."

"Call her up, Hank. See if she's home. Does she work?"

"She works at a Burger King on Farmington Avenue in Hartford."

But it turned out Cindy was at her father's house. "Taking the day off," Hank told me. "She called out because she felt drained."

"Drained of what?"

"She didn't say. But she said it was okay to stop in. She's bored, she said."

I hadn't been back to Benny's home in East Hartford since right after Mary's murder. The difference now was staggering. Newspapers and magazines littered the floor, video game sleeves and CD cases were stacked on the coffee table, someone had left a dirty footprint on the living room floor, and a hazy pall of dust covered the tables and chairs. Clothing lay in bunches in corners, as though the wearers, entering the warm rooms, simply shed them as they moved through the house.

She was sitting in the tiny living room, leafing through an issue of *People*, and she tossed it onto the floor, her foot nudging it away. Her head was bobbing to some music, but she slipped off the ear buds, dropping them onto a table. Her cell phone beeped, but she frowned at it. She'd colored her hair a brilliant scarlet, spiked it so that it mimicked a porcupine, and the filmy white lacy blouse, designed to expose her navel, reminded me of Stevie Nicks—Cindy'd probably never heard of her. But she was antsy, her left hand picking at the crimson lacquer of a nail on her right hand. Finally she bit off part of the nail, working it with a feverish dedication of a beaver on a river log.

"To what do I owe the pleasure," she sang out, and then giggled at her own words.

Hank began, "Well, Cindy, we'd like to talk to the kids about your mother and aunt."

She frowned. "The kids. We haven't been *kids* for years. I'm twenty-three now."

Hank grinned. "To me, we'll always be the kids."

Cindy narrowed her eyes. "You were never part of our group. You didn't go to Chesterton."

"I didn't have Larry paying for my education." Hank's tone was a little too sharp.

I stepped in. "Cindy, you know I've been asked to look into the murders."

"Isn't that why police get paid?"

"But sometimes people say things to relatives"—I pointed at Hank—"and to friends of the family, like me, that they would never tell a cop."

"I wouldn't tell a cop a damn thing."

"Well, that's my point."

"But I got nothing to tell you either." She was still picking at that aberrant nail, and some of the glossy red polish broke free.

"I'm trying to get a picture of how your mother and her sister socialized. Maybe there was *somebody* they met together. Somebody they didn't like."

She spoke in a flat monotone. "Mom went from this crummy house to the crummy store, and then sometimes to Aunt Molly's. She didn't *know* anyone…"

"And yet she was killed," I interrupted.

She shrugged her shoulders. "You know, I keep asking myself why. I come up with nothing. Mom never went into Hartford. Outside of Little Saigon, I mean."

"But she did that day." From Hank.

"You know, Mom was a lady who was, well, just there. Like I never really thought about her having a life away from the house and Pop. Nothing. She didn't have any, you know, adventures."

"Adventures?"

"Like, you know, excitement. She cooked for us. Cleaned." She closed her eyes, sighed. For a moment I detected melancholy, real sadness. "She was good to us. She never bothered anyone. Nobody should die like that." Nervously, she bit at that nail, attacking it.

"But someone killed her," I said.

Suddenly angry, like a child: "Tell me why?" She yelled out the words.

"I don't know."

Then she retreated back into her shell, tucking her chin into her chest. She looked up, staring from Hank to me as though waking up from a sleep, her eyes wide, unblinking. "My mother did something stupid." Her voice was flat, low. "And that's why she's dead."

"Stupid?" I asked.

Cindy kept rolling her tongue over her lips, moistening them. "She always did dumb things."

"Tell me."

"She was always trying to make everybody happy. That's why she died. If someone asked her for five bucks, she'd hand it over. Someone says drive me to Motor Vehicles, she does it. Mom the coolie. She never wanted to say no to anyone. If she got herself killed, it was because she didn't *think* about what she was doing."

"I don't understand."

She looked at me as if I were stupid. "She never *thought*. Don't you get it? She wasn't a *thinker*. She just smiled and smiled and apologized and begged forgiveness for things she didn't do. She didn't *choose* to go to that spot by herself. That's not the way she was. Somebody drove her there."

I waited, patient. She twisted around, nervous. "But the police found her car there. No one drove her there."

"No, you fool. I mean she drove herself and all, but somebody *told* her to go there. Somebody said—get into that car, lady, and go to *this* address."

"So you don't believe she went there by accident?"

She paused. "Maybe. But I think she drove there for a reason. Think about it—it's not like she's driving to Alaska. Pop's store is a dozen blocks over, not that far away. She wasn't a moron."

"What if she got dizzy or something?" From Hank.

"She never got dizzy any other time. Why there? Why all of a sudden?"

"Who would tell her to go there?"

"I dunno, but she was trying to make somebody happy. That's what she did. She didn't want to be on Molly's fucking charity but she couldn't say no. I had to hear about that all the time.

All I'm saying is that, if she went there by herself, she was going there because it would make somebody *else* happy. Not her."

As she was speaking, she sank deeper into the sofa, wilting, and I noticed, as she extended her legs, that her black nylons, tucked into high boots, were torn at the seams. Absently, she picked at the tears, exaggerating them.

Hank leaned forward in his chair. "Would Tommy have told her to go there?"

She chuckled. "Yeah, like she'd listen to Tommy."

"What about her sister?"

"Aunt Molly? Maybe, but for what reason, for God's sake?"

"What about Danny, Susie's son?"

She waited a second before answering, then started to pull her body up on the sofa, wrapping her hands around her knees. "Why Danny?"

"He used to be close to Tommy." From Hank.

"Not really. Not close. They hung out together in school, more than any of us. He's around now and then, you know, I've seen him slicking by in that car of his, blowing the horn. He pulls over and chats me up. Shows me his latest high-tech gadget—like I care."

"You don't like him?"

"He's all right. Just a little too taken with himself. Pretty boy."

I looked at Hank, who was staring intently into her ghostly face. "Did you two ever go out?"

She tightened her lips, her voice thick with emotion. "Look at me. The ugly duckling. Miss Plain-as-can-be. Look at me."

"But Danny has a way…"

"You better believe it. A way. He should be *put* away. He's scum with girls. In school he had to have *everyone*, and the ones who said no were the ones he had to have most. He's a charmer, hands all over your neck and back and arms…"

"So you did go out with him?" I broke in.

She laughed. "A curious expression—go out with him. No, not really. I was there for the fucking. A hookup. One time.

Almost charity, a pity fuck. Look, Danny, look. See girl there. Fuck girl, fuck."

"And then he left you?"

"Listen to you. 'Left you.' There was nothing to leave, Rick Van Lam. I was an after-dinner mint. A booty call. Next day he's back to being buddies with me, joking, teasing. Like it never happened. And to him it didn't."

"But it's something you can't forget."

She laughed again. "Not the sex. You can always forget sex." A long pause. "You can't forget the humiliation."

"I'm sorry," Hank said.

"Everyone gets a crush on Danny sooner or later." She turned to the side, retrieved a diet Pepsi off a table, slurped half of it. "Christ, my own mother had a crush way back when. When we'd come here from school. He'd flatter her, talk to her, bat those wide brown eyes, lean in to kiss her hello or good-bye, woo her like she was Miss Universe, sing Vietnamese songs to her. She'd get silly, and I'd want to gag. One time I told him, for Christ's sake, Danny, she's my mother. Do you know what he said? That she's a woman, and women love him. My own mother. Of course, after the pot bust he got on her shit list pretty fast. She didn't want him around, afraid of his influence on Tommy, the boy blunder."

"Did your Aunt Molly have an infatuation with him?" I asked.

That surprised her. "Well, no, I don't think she ever really *liked* him. She was polite and all, but no, she thought he was too slick for TV. But I'll tell you who also had a crush on him. Uncle Larry, Mr. Money Bags."

Hank asked, "Gay?"

"No, no, not like a sexual thing. But he was taken with the boy because Danny flattered, batted those eyes, praised, and asked for advice. 'Oh Mr. Money Bags, I wanna be just like you—rich and powerful. Oh oh oh. Mr. Larry, *sir*.' And Uncle Larry fell for it. Danny this, Danny that. Danny's handsome, so bright, so top of the heap. One time Jon, disgusted, told his father he was acting like a fag, and Larry recoiled. I thought he'd hit Jon."

"What happened?"

"Larry cooled it, and Danny sort of read the signs, drifting away. It's just that Danny is turned on by ambition. For him it's like some magic potion." She finished the Pepsi, stared at the can, then idly dropped it to the floor, where it rolled a few feet into the leg of a table. We all watched its short journey.

"Ambition, huh?" I asked.

Cindy looked at the table clock and actually pointed at it, miming the gestures of I've-gotta-go-sorry. "Ambition," she echoed me. "Danny has enough for a whole fucking army."

Chapter Twenty

Benny Vu struck me as a man so simple there was no way anyone might see him as a mystery. Which was why he intrigued me. Hank made a comment on the phone that got me thinking about the quiet, grieving widower. Actually he was questioning me, the way he often did, hurling back my random Buddhist-infused aphorisms, my loose translations, and my own brand of American-tinged Asian wisdom. "Remember," he was talking about his own father, "what you always say. 'Sometimes in the silence is the greatest noise.'"

His father had stopped talking to him. They'd been having a running battle after he quit the Chinese restaurant but also his sudden interest in a Vietnamese girl who happened to be the granddaughter of a North Vietnamese soldier. His father rarely liked Hank's girlfriends, mostly white girls. But there usually was something wrong with the Asian girls he brought home—mixed blood, *bui doi*, lowlife parents, too giggly, too skinny, too timid, and now, the ultimate horror, a Vietnamese-American from the Commie North. Uncle Ho's army. Viet Cong mon amour.

"Are you listening to me?" Hank spoke into the silence.

"I'm sorry. What you said made me thinking of Benny Vu."

"My father?"

"No, the silence. The quiet man who doesn't talk. The unassuming grocery man, lost in the bags of Thai rice and stalks of lemongrass and mint."

"Sounds like you're composing a haiku. But why Benny?"

"Because we never think about him, other than to express sympathy over his loss."

"Maybe that's all he is, Rick."

"I'm gonna check him out, Hank. By myself."

The next afternoon I found Benny alone in the grocery. Of course, there were no customers, so Benny sat on a stool, reading a Vietnamese newspaper published in one of the colonies in California. Tommy wasn't working. Benny looked up, didn't look surprised, nodded a faint greeting, and shook my hand. The guest in his house. The stranger at the door. His thin smile was laced with the smallest hint of wariness.

I apologized for interrupting and asked if I could visit. Is it okay? Yes, he said. *Da.* But I knew that Vietnamese men and women would often agree, say yes when they meant no. I'd have to read him carefully.

"*Ban co thích uong gì khong?*" Did I want something to drink? he asked. He knew I was not a customer.

I accepted a can of soy milk. It tasted metallic to me, or how I imagine aluminum might taste on the tongue. He offered a cigarette, which I accepted. To do otherwise would be an insult.

I expressed my sympathy again, which was customary, and he nodded gratefully. Looking at him, I saw a humorless man with a tiny coconut head set on a skinny, bony frame. And the clothing he wore—like today's faded blue dress shirt and the baggy, rolled-up jeans over shoes cracked at the seams—looked hand-me-down.

"I saw Cindy at your home." I told him something he probably already knew. "And I've seen Tommy, too."

He made a thick, heavy sound and jerked his hand in the air. "American-born children."

I joked. "Typical American kids, these days."

"Look around you. This is the American civilization that everyone wants. Money and makeup and babies born in the street."

Hank had told me that Benny Vu was the world's last moralist, and the most melancholic. Here was a man who compartmentalized the world into black and white and refused any gray areas. Looking at him, I realized that he could be unyielding, unforgiving. A man with a code.

"You know," I countered, "America gives everyone a lot of choices."

He looked into my face, searching for meaning. "Which can be a blessing. But to choose bad is not to choose well."

"True," I agreed, "but what's the truth?" Intro to Philosophy 101, I thought, grinning. A B-plus grade at Columbia College.

"If you don't know now, you never will." Then he smiled that humorless smile. "But you didn't come here to discuss philosophy."

"It's safer than a lot of topics."

"And more interesting perhaps."

"But there are no answers there."

"And you're looking for answers to my Mary's murder." He said the line so matter-of-factly, but the words hung in the air. I waited.

"And Molly's," I added.

He nodded. But mentioning his wife's name seemed to have some effect on him, softening the corners. "Come." He nodded behind him. "I will make good tea for us." I thought he'd hang a "Closed" sign in front, but he didn't. We walked into a small back storeroom with a tiny stove and refrigerator, almost lost among boxes and boxes of canned and paper goods. "In the afternoon I drink a root tea I buy in Chinatown. It takes away worries and loss." He pointed to a chair. "Sit, please, sir."

Neither of us said a word as we waited for the water to boil. Meticulously he spooned dried herbs into a tea caddy, poured steaming water on them, and the two of us waited. The acrid smell of dried autumn chrysanthemum and old weathered wood permeated the small space, not pleasant or tempting. With the cups steeping before us, he finally nodded, and I picked mine up. The taste was amazingly soothing, a little tart, a hint of old dried flowers and the sweet mildew of an attic space. But in the hot, steaming back room, sweat on my brow, the liquid calmed me down, settled me, and, in fact, cooled me like a window fan.

"I sense you're a good man, Rick Van Lam." He watched me closely. "This awful pursuit my family—Hank's mother—has set upon you. It's an honorable journey but maybe an empty one. Maybe the answer is some misguided Spanish boy in Hartford we'll never meet." He didn't speak with any acrimony, just a low-key statement of fact. "I don't sense murderers in the aisles of my store or on the green lawns of Larry Torcelli."

"It's something I have to do now."

"As I said, a good man. Loyal to his people. To a country far away. But what do you find?"

"So far I seem to be collecting studies of the family, bits and pieces of lifetimes."

"These are character sketches, not clues."

"Exactly."

"But let me tell you—that is the only way to do this. I don't understand American investigation. I can't watch the TV police shows because they are all microscopes and fingerprints and red flashing lights and…DNA."

I laughed. "That works."

"If you say so." His tiny face was animated now. "But I think you are hard on yourself because you believe you are *not* listening to the white part of your soul, Rick Van Lam. The American self that is good and perhaps logical and fine. You are listening to the Asian part of your soul, the part that uses the mind to draw pictures of each person you meet. Snapshots in a book. Have more faith in the way you are doing things. If there is a story behind the faces, then you'll find it. Do you know why?"

I waited. "No."

"Of course you do. You're being polite. It's because when you look into one of our faces you see yourself, and in the act of looking you understand your heart. All the parts of your heart that are black are the parts that let you see the evil in others. The less-than-good in people that you call evil."

"I thought we weren't gonna talk about philosophy." I sipped the tea. The afternoon seemed dreamy, suspended.

He almost smiled. "This is not philosophy. This is conversation over tea on a hot, hot afternoon."

I was starting to like this man.

We sat back, sipped the tea, which seemed to put him into a trance. "You are too much in this country to remember the old Vietnamese saying." Then he quoted: "*Khi than vang mat khong co la tri nuong tuong.*"

I had trouble translating. "I don't know—something like— When God is away, imagination can't come about."

"Roughly." He looked at me. "You have a difficult job, despite your talent. God has chosen to ignore the world. I have told no one how much my wife meant to me." I stared at him, uncomfortable. "I love my boy and girl, though I don't understand them, but Mary was my life. Now there's this empty store and an empty home. The best part of me is gone." But there was no sadness in his voice, not even bitterness. A plain statement of fact—there, out there, presented to me, a virtual stranger he somehow felt comfortable with.

"I'm sorry."

He waved the comment away. "Of course. We had nothing but everything we needed."

I drank the tea and felt like napping, my eyes lazy with the mixture of coolness and heat.

"Now I can grow old watching the mountain of disappointment in my own children."

"They're all right." I tried to say something, but my words sounded too American, even in my stilted Vietnamese. So I said in English, "They're all right."

A weak smile. "A little right."

I nodded.

"Tommy is weak, so unusual for a Vietnamese man. He lacks the spunk of a king."

"How weak?"

He thought about it. "A couple weeks ago he's working here

and Danny is on the phone. Tommy is saying he has to work, but then he tells me he'll be right back. He doesn't come back until closing."

That surprised me. "Danny? I didn't think they were friends—spent time together."

Benny looked at me. "They are not friends. They haven't been friends for years."

"But you said he called…"

"I didn't say he wasn't around."

"He comes around?"

"Now and then, running in with his fancy suit and his fancy car, bowing and scraping to me. All slicked over like an oiled road."

"But if they're not friends…"

"Tommy tells me he can't stand Danny."

"But…"

Benny threw his hands in the air, as though the contradiction was trivial. "Danny stops in to say hello now and then, to talk to Tommy, to me, to Cindy. It's like a rich person visiting a poor person—some charity. There's nothing friendly in their talk, not when I'm here listening. In English: 'Hi, how are you? Nice to see you. How's the job? How's the car?' Strangers on a city bus."

I had to digest this new information. I'd been lied to, it seemed. Danny, indeed, was more a presence in Tommy's life than I'd been led to believe.

"You don't like Danny?"

He didn't hesitate. "I'm indifferent to him. To *dislike* him is to, well, value him too highly. He's a violator of what's good in life because he's too hungry."

"Hungry?"

"He is someone else's success story."

"Larry?"

What was Benny talking about?

"Danny has no influence on my Tommy now. He once did. A bad influence. Trouble with the law. Some drugs. But that is over. Now he's just a reminder of how some people make it and some don't."

"But you don't trust his success."

"I don't really think about it."

"Did Mary like him?"

"At first, yes. But that changed. She thought he was dangerous around the impressionable Tommy. But once he became a banker out of Harvard, well, he charmed her again. He wooed her, praised her cooking."

"But still around." I was talking to myself.

"Not around. Running in, running out. Months go by, and then the visit. We need to stop and honor him."

"Are you bitter?"

"I told you—indifferent. Bitterness takes too much energy."

But then I noticed cloudiness in his eyes, dullness. "What?"

"I was just thinking of his last visits to the store and once to the home."

"Like what?"

"Well, I mean, he was the same, all that swagger. But I think he could no longer charm my wife. She got quiet when he showed up at the house that one time. Tommy was staying there because of the fire at his building. But she frowned at him."

"Did she say anything?"

"No, just closed up. It was strange, though."

"How so?

"She wouldn't leave the room when he came. Like she was guarding Tommy *from* him. I know it made Tommy angry, but Danny just chatted and flattered. But she stared at him. Hard."

"Could he have offended her?"

"He was never around long enough. Quick visits, hello and out the door. Blowing the horn on the fancy car." Benny stopped to prepare us a second cup of tea. I waited.

"He ever let Tommy drive his car?"

"Once, I think. That's all Tommy could talk about. But Danny said never again. Tommy came close to running over an old woman. Danny joked about it, but he never tossed the keys to Tommy again. If they went off for a spin, Danny drove."

"They did go places?"

"Up the street to get food. For a slice of pizza or a hamburger."

"But you didn't want him around?"

"Tommy doesn't have many friends. Danny has a flashy car and bucks for food."

"When was the last time you saw Danny?"

"A while back. Later I heard Tommy on his phone, and he was not happy about something."

"Why?"

"I couldn't catch the words but he called Danny an ass. Tommy calls everyone—including me—an ass, but this time he was sputtering, he was so mad."

"Do you know what happened?"

Another surprised look. "Do you think he'd tell me? Tommy yells at everyone who gets in his way. Sooner or later Danny gets on his nerves."

His eyes were closing so I knew it was time to leave. I thanked him for the tea and conversation, and we shook hands.

As he walked me out, back through the empty store, and ushered me onto the hot sidewalk, he shook my hand again. "You are important here," he whispered. "*Gio thoi la choi troi.*" When the wind blows, it is God's broom.

I started to say something, but he stopped me. "You know, in the war, many dead soldiers and civilians were buried in unmarked graves or left rotting in the fields. Their bodies were untouched. In Vietnam we believe the ghost of these people will wander, lost and afraid, seeking proper burial, homage, respect. At night I think about Mary's murder. Her violent end. And I think her ghost is wandering now, somehow stunned, shattered, wanting retribution. There is no world without justice, you know. She—her ghost demands it."

I must have looked confused because he tapped me affectionately on the chest. "It is up to you, Rick Van Lam."

I nodded, and thanked him again.

He touched my sleeve. "*Ban la mot nguoi ban tot.*"

He considered me a good friend.

Chapter Twenty-one

On Saturday night I met school friends Vinnie and Marcie for Chinese food at the Joy Luck Palace in Avon. My best friends on campus, they were away for the summer at their cottage in the White Mountains of New Hampshire, but they'd come back for the weekend. I'd missed them, Vinnie the conservative and Marcie the firebrand liberal—Republican and Democrat—entangled in a long, talky marriage. When Vinnie had called on Friday, I'd filled him in on the double murder case, and Vinnie and Marcie wanted to know everything. He told me his old college roommate taught English at Chesterton, and he'd make a phone call. I hoped to get a better picture of the five kids at the upscale prep school in the woods of Simsbury.

Marcie and Vinnie looked tanned, relaxed, at peace. Summers, they always said, were terms of necessary truce: no partisan politics, no elaborate social entanglements, no wrangling over the world's precarious condition. Boating, swimming, barbecuing, they said. The trinity of escape that led to long, blissful nights of sleep.

"All right. I'm jealous."

"Come back with us," they pleaded.

Last summer I'd gone for two weeks, and had a good time. But this year I'd gotten lethargic, content with jogging and local friends, even teaching that one-night-a-week course at the college, which I'd just completed, turning in the final grades the previous morning. I'd paid it so little mind, but now it was over. And then there was…The Case that ate away the last days of August.

The three of us sat with a bottle of merlot, sharing salt-battered shrimp, moo goo gai pan, and Chinese broccoli sautéed in garlic sauce. We caught up on each other's lives. They knew Hank, of course—he'd been a student in both their classes—as well as Liz, Jimmy, and Gracie.

The talk turned to the murders. "We read about it in the *Courant*," Marcie told me, "since we get the paper delivered, a day late."

Vinnie spoke. "We should have known you'd be involved."

Marcie grinned. "Two deaths in the Vietnamese community. And rich, rich Farmington money. Come on. Staying away from that drama is like Vinnie avoiding french fries at McDonald's."

"Well, at first I was just trying to find out why Mary went to Goodwin Square. That was all. Then, of course, it mushroomed."

"How's Hank doing?"

"He's okay. Hank was never close to that part of the family. His affection is more for his grandma and mother, and their concern."

"We had lunch with my friend from Chesterton today," Vinnie told me. "When I called, he was free, so we met. We'd been roommates at Brown my senior year. I haven't seen him in a couple of years. He's divorced now, and restless."

Marcie winced. "Midlife crisis, I fear. Who else would leave a good, stable marriage?" She turned to Vinnie. "Don't get ideas."

He teased her. "I run all my ideas past you, Marcie." He got serious. "His name is Joel Riley, has been there for years. Likes teaching among the bright and moneyed, though he says the scholarship kids are often the ones worthy of real attention."

"And?" I prodded.

"Joel remembers them, and he says he's been thinking about them after reading of the murders in the paper. A couple were a little out of focus—like Kristen, there for so short a time—but he talked to someone after my phone call, and a lot of it came back. He even brought a yearbook to show me." Vinnie reached into a folder and extracted some papers. "I've made notes, Rick."

"The memory is going," Marcie said.

"I know how you like *exact* quotation."

"Anything scandalous?"

"My, my, so impatient. Of course. Why else would I be taking my sweet time here?"

"Kristen," I began. "What about her?"

"The least memorable because she dropped out early. Flunked out. Never his student, but known to him. Part of the problem was her looks—just too movie starlet to fit into the obligatory school uniform which hid, but not well, the curves and dips of outrageous adolescence."

"He said she was stupid," Marcie added. "But manipulative—cagey."

"That, too. I mean you get a lot of rich kids there who don't have much brainpower, but she stood out. Because she didn't even *try*. She just looked pretty, said vacuous things, answered the instructors back, sassy as hell, and seemed to rely on her being her Daddy's little favorite. The teachers were in uproar, but her grades and some foul language directed at a fellow student meant that she had to disappear. Fast."

Marcie added, "Daddy's money notwithstanding."

"I don't think she was there the whole year," Vinnie noted.

"Barely," I said. "What about her brother Jon?"

"The spy in the house of love," Vinnie laughed.

"What does that mean?"

"Jon was good looking, very bright, but he always seemed to be—Joel's word—'lurking.' A tattletale. He'd be friendly with his cousins, with the other kids, but a lot of the kids didn't trust him. Someone called him a moral prig—he didn't like the sexual escapades of his friends. The parties, even the drugs. Girls came on to him because he was so good looking, rich, but his relationships always ended. He found fault with them—too shallow, too fat, too bony, too clinging. Worse, too promiscuous."

"So he probably didn't lose his virginity there?"

"Maybe not. Joel said he had a steady girlfriend for a year or so, a prim and proper young thing from Brookline, Massachusetts, supposedly a descendant of John Adams, who took her lineage way too seriously. She had chronic back illness—even an operation—so I don't think they *did* it. They were always together, and then her father transferred her to Rosemary Hall Choate in Wallingford. They didn't like Jon's attention. He told a teacher it was because he was half-Vietnamese. The girl's uncle had been a helicopter pilot at the My Lai massacre. Too many psychiatric-couch dilemmas there."

"Then nothing?"

"Then Jon went back to his studies and his solitude."

"Good student, right?"

"The best. But Joel said he hated it when he raised his hand in class. He loved finding any mistake a teacher made—a wrong date, a lapse in grammar, a random aside that Jon thought egregious and therefore unacceptable in an institution like Chesterton."

I laughed. "Thank God most of my students in Criminal Justice just want to fire their revolvers at me."

"As for Benny and Mary's kids, Cindy and Tommy, there's a lot that Joel can recall. Both were his students. Tommy was belligerent from the start, balked at the school uniform, developed this strident counterculture manifesto he proclaimed at any chance, and let it be known he despised the uptight, asshole school. His friends were kids he met in town, not classmates. No one was surprised when he dropped out, but they were surprised he lasted almost to the end. He actually handed out a flyer he'd run off in which he described the school as 'a penitentiary for the petit bourgeois on the road to trust fund perpetuity.' Folks there still bandy around that phase, delighted."

"He hasn't changed much. More tattoos, more leather, more chains."

"And Cindy, the homely, gum-clacking girl, seemed not to know where she was but would surprise Joel with keen, insightful essays about her shitty life. He remembered her well. She resented being a poor girl at a rich school. The other girls avoided her. Even then she'd violate school rules by accentuating the uniform, trying to give herself a punkish look. She was always being told to tone down the clown makeup, but it only got worse. And, on top of that, instructors felt sorry for her, the dark side of a family that held Jon, Kristen, and even Tommy, three good-looking kids, lucky as hell. Joel said she looked like the lost child at a county fair, waiting for someone to find her."

"Poor kid," Marcie mumbled.

"Poor kid, indeed. Now and then she'd lose it, going off into hysterics and tantrums. She'd be out of school for days, rushing back home to mommy and daddy, who didn't know what was going on."

"And what about Danny Trinh, the quintessential scholarship boy?"

"Yeah," Vinnie said, "I was wondering why you'd included the housekeeper's son. At first. But, as it turned out, Danny is the most interesting of the lot, in my opinion. And in Joel's."

"How so?"

"Well, by the third year he had become the poster boy for the school. In the age of social gospel, he was the face on the postage stamp. Chesterton did a public service promotional deal, a multipage PR spread. You know, recruiting students, telling the community how generous and liberal they were, impressing the alumni, situating themselves firmly in the ranks of the American Dream. They used Danny's welcome picture to promote the school. Not some predictable bleached-blond Aryan ski bum, shot from the loins of the CEO of Aetna, no, no. They'd found the all-in-one champion of prep school success story."

Marcie interrupted. "To cut to the chase, Danny was gleaming boy staring out from the display ad in the *Courant* and elsewhere. The boy, I must admit, is photogenic, if I can judge from the yearbook picture: that square-jawed face, that shock of deep-black hair. My, my, my. And an honor student, as well. Straight A's. Athletic. Lacrosse, swimming, field hockey, you name it. Harvard, Princeton, Yale, all banging at the door."

"But I feel you're leading to something not so savory here."

"Bingo." From Marcie.

"It seems," Vinnie continued, again scanning his notes, "Danny was having his biggest love affair with himself, though he managed to charm a dozen ladies along the way. One pregnancy scare. No big deal there, but it seems in his senior year he started to coast, a little lazy, not cracking the books the way he should, using charm to keep the As on the old transcript. Later on a teacher said she'd heard he got through Harvard all right, but just got by, smoothed through, as it were, the sloppiness nodded at, until they handed him the coveted BA in Finance."

"He lost steam? You think he learned how to work it?"

"Probably a little of both," Vinnie said. "But he never lost his ambition, Joel said. They were surprised when he came back to Hartford."

"Why?"

"He had an in-demand internship at John Hancock during his junior year. But he chose to move back here. They offered him everything, but he took an offer from Bank of America."

"Danny had a sense of his destiny all along."

"But Joel didn't like him. Too cocky. And then the notorious scandal."

"I knew it." I pounded the table.

"It seems a young male teacher made a couple of passes at him, acting a little foolish around the pretty boy. And someone reported it to the headmaster. The guy lost his job."

"Who reported it?" I asked. "Wait. Was it Jon, the snoop?"

"Don't know," Vinnie said. "But the rumor was that Danny had actually encouraged the overtures, not because he was interested, but because he liked the *power* he had over the man. He'd hang out in the guy's office. He was pissed off when the guy disappeared from campus."

"Did Joel say anything about drug activity?"

"Of course. There's always lots of drugs on campus—pot, cocaine, Ecstasy, that stuff. Party drugs. These kids have money and absent parents. Many times they keep it under wraps, but sometimes it gets out in the school. That's what happened with Tommy. That arrest. He thinks that why he dropped out of school near the end of his senior year."

"Danny?"

"No, he was specific about that. Danny's name never surfaced in any talk about drugs, though Tommy told someone that Danny was involved. Joel thinks the headmaster kept it quiet. Larry's money."

The evening wound down, the last of the wine gone. Sleepy, Vinnie yawned, looked for the waitress.

"I met Molly Torcelli once," Marcie said, surprising me.

"And?"

"Well, nothing. It was at a charity function held at the Farmington Country Club. I was moderator of a silent auction. She was introduced to me as *the* Mrs. Larry Torcelli, of Torcelli Motor Works fame, and I was supposed to bow."

"Any impression of her?"

"It happened so fast. I remember being surprised that she was Asian, and thought that she was incredibly beautiful. But she also looked a little uncomfortable, but in the few words she spoke, I didn't like her."

"Why not?"

"Well," Marcie breathed in, "she seemed too snobbish. Someone nearby nodded to her, that kind of Queen Elizabeth nod rich women effect, and Mrs. Torcelli just turned away, whispering to a woman at her side, 'And just who does she think she is?' But she was smiling. It was a beautiful mixture of insecurity and arrogance wrapped up in a real strange lady."

Chapter Twenty-two

I hate the surveillance part of my job. There's nothing romantic about it. You sit as inconspicuously as possible, watching, watching. Nothing ever happens. You get hot, you get cold. You get hungry, you have to pee. People spot you sitting longer than they think you should and they dial 911. Cops rap on your window, expecting to haul in a pervert. A little cocky, you show them your ID. They still want to drag you in.

But on Saturday I made up my mind—the day belonged to Danny Trinh.

I borrowed Gracie's car, a decades-old Ford, so I'd be less visible, leaving her my decade-old BMW. Gracie never drives, but believes she needs a car for emergencies. The men in her home take care of her. We squire her to doctor's appointments, to church suppers, to the bus station in Farmington so she can catch a Greyhound to the Indian casino at Foxwoods. On Sunday she walks down the street to Catholic Mass. The tenant on the top floor services her car on schedule, tunes it up, makes it hum like a happy pet, and I have it washed and keep the tags current. It's what we do for her. Sometimes she lets me use her car. Like now.

I figured Danny would be at the gym near his home, and I was right. I spotted the Mercedes, freshly washed, parked near the street, away from the other cars. I tucked Gracie's car in between a male-dominant Hummer and an SUV that was supposedly good for rigorous mountain trails it would never come near. Gracie's rusty Ford nosed out from both vehicles, with me slumped in the seat, windows open to catch what little air there was, nursing an iced tea and croissant from Dunkin' Donuts.

Eventually Danny strode out of the gym with the same cocksure strut he'd shown the last time I met him there, this time with low-slung chino shorts and the neon-blue muscle shirt. He paid no attention to anyone around him, hurling his gym bag into the trunk, and then driving out of the lot. I was close enough to hear the pumped-up stereo. It was a CD by Bruno Mars. That should have made me like him.

As expected, he pulled his car into the garage at his mother's house, and disappeared inside. I circled the block, dallied at the corner, tucked the car behind a Dumpster at the Mobil station at the corner, and generally tried to appear as inconspicuous as possible. I had a clear view of his house. The car sat in the garage, the overhead door down, and the street was quiet. I nearly dozed off.

But then the side kitchen door opened and Danny, dressed now in a baggy jeans and a white polo shirt, as well as a Boston Red Sox baseball cap pulled backward on his head, strolled out, looked at the flower beds, and said something to his mother, who stood in the doorway. He pointed to the shock of color, and she made an it's-nothing gesture. In a tender moment, he strode back, gave her a quick peck on the cheek, and walked down the small driveway onto the sidewalk, opening the gate of the chain link fence.

To my horror, he seemed to be walking to the end of the street, to the Mobil station. There was his house, the other two Cape Cods, and then the station. I ducked down in the seat, my head concealed, as he strolled within ten yards of me, and I could hear him whistling. Within seconds I heard an ignition start, and, sliding up as surreptitiously as I could, I spotted him in the next lot over, a used car lot, pulling onto New Britain Avenue in a nondescript gray Honda. Quickly, I turned onto the Avenue, trailing five or six cars behind him. So, I thought, he keeps another car for city use, leaving the Mercedes home. Not unusual, I thought, but, well—intriguing.

I had little trouble following him. He was in no hurry, slinking long, idling long at stop signs, seemingly enjoying the day. He was headed into Hartford.

For a moment I thought he might be heading to Goodwin Square, but he cruised through side streets leading to another seedy part of town, a street of shabby three-families, a few buildings boarded up, one burned out, others surrounded by dirt yards and little Spanish kids playing in the spray of a fire hydrant.

He pulled in front of a bodega, parking the car in a handicapped zone, and rushed in, emerging seconds later with a pack of cigarettes. I'm not sure why I thought that strange, other than his recent dedication to the gym and his body, but he flipped off the cellophane and tapped out a cigarette, lit it, paused for a second to inhale the smoke. His eyes scanned the street. He looked like he was at home on the littered, broken sidewalk. Back in his car, he chatted on his phone, then headed off, turning at the next corner, and suddenly, with me three cars behind, turned into the driveway of a three-family. The car disappeared into the backyard, out of sight. I drove past, craned my neck, but the other houses blocked my view.

I circled, hid behind parked cars, did my surveillance dance, but two hours later, he still hadn't come out. Enough, I told myself. Time to go home. But I was armed with a new license plate number as well as a new house and street address.

Back at home I did some research on the web, found the listing for the current residents of 97-98 Hartt Street, Hartford, the three-family house. Owner, current occupants. Cross-referenced with online phone records. I learned that the resident on the second floor was Duong Xuan Trinh, age twenty-five. Danny himself. An unlisted land phone, but a call to Liz got me the information under the name Duong Xuan Trinh. Occupation: banker. She also made a call to someone with access to motor vehicle records, and I learned that the car he was driving was registered to none other than—Duong Xuan Trinh.

"What does this mean?" Liz asked.

"I don't know. But our boy Danny seems to have carved a second life for himself, one a little bit under the radar."

"Maybe he just needs a place away from Mommy."

"Still and all…"

"A little too spy who came in from the cold?"

"This could be nothing, but Danny needs more looking into."

Liz laughed. "You know what Jimmy would say."

I smiled to myself. "Yeah, money."

"Banker, Money. Think about it."

I called Jimmy and filled him in on what I'd learned. "The second car bothers me. But I keep telling myself that I'm looking at him funny because he comes off as so perfect, so charmed, so—well, heroic."

"Nobody likes a hero these days."

"That's because there aren't any," I told him. "You know, I should be applauding a guy like Danny, pulling himself out of poverty, but…"

"But what?"

"I don't know how to fill in the rest of that sentence."

"I think it's time for me to call in some chips," Jimmy said.

"Meaning?"

"A few phone calls. The money trail. Let me use my network…" He paused. "Expect a call within the week."

I grinned. "Very mysterious." He hung up.

Gaddy Associates, largely doing fraud investigations in the world of Hartford insurance, had ways of penetrating the often obtuse machinations of financial worlds. Jimmy had avenues I couldn't even begin to imagine.

Then I called Hank and told him the same story. I picked him up, and we drove to Hartt Street. From a phone booth we called Danny's apartment, got a message that was curt—"Not in. Leave number"—click. But clearly Danny's voice. And by pulling into the back lot of another three-family house, we saw that his old Honda was now gone.

"Let's check it out." From Hank.

"There's nothing to check out. What do you want to do—break in?"

"Sure."

"And you want to be a state trooper?"

"In class my instructor said sometimes the best cops were once the best crooks."

I frowned. "Too much education for you."

"I think it was you who said it."

"I was probably thinking moments like this."

But cruising by the house, we noticed an old Asian guy dragging out trash bins to the curb, sweating under the late-afternoon heat. "Pull over," Hank insisted.

The guy eyed us warily, waiting. He was three or four feet away. "Yeah?" I started to say something, but stopped. "You cops?"

"No, we're looking for someone."

"If he's a friend, you should know where to find him."

Hank leaned over. "You know a guy named Harry Vinh? Vietnamese guy. I thought he lived in your building."

"No."

"Never mind," I said to his back.

The man swiveled around, faced me. "Around here people get nervous when strangers ask questions."

Hank spoke. "We're not asking questions. We're looking for someone."

"That's a question." He walked away.

"That wasn't good," I said, driving away. "It was real stupid."

"Why?"

"Well, if he's buddies with Danny and something is up, he might mention the two Asian guys who came nosing around. He's a little too suspicious."

"Comes with the neighborhood, I think," Hank said.

"Makes you wonder why a guy like Danny keeps an apartment here. This is not a place to leave from in the morning dressed in an Armani suit and tooling a Mercedes."

"He pays the rent here. He *needs* this place."

"The question is, what for?"

In the rearview mirror I saw the old man, standing by the trash bins, arms folded, staring at us as we drove away.

No, I thought: this was a stupid move. But maybe not. Sometimes stupid moves kicked in action that proved all to the good. Everything was too static. Maybe it was good to stir things up.

Chapter Twenty-three

Detective Ardolino had left two messages on my machine, one telling me to call him at home. Neither message was pleasant. When I called him back, reaching him at his house, he was eating. He was chewing on something, and he gulped so loudly I had to hold the phone away from my ear. "That good?"

"The wife's barbecue ribs. Nothing like it. If I liked you, I'd invite you over."

"I'm not the one leaving frantic messages on my machine,"

A pause, then a chuckle. "I've never been frantic in my life."

"So?"

"I thought it was time to get an update from you." He waited. "You were supposed to share info."

"What makes you think I have any?"

"Well, I've been talking to some of the same folks you have, and we seem to be covering the same tired ground."

"Then you know what I know."

"Maybe you see things a little different. Maybe your people tell you things they don't tell me, an officer of the law."

"Okay, here's what I know." I gladly filled him in on my investigation, the saga of the Torcelli-Vu children, the jealousies and temperaments. Even the pot bust back in prep school.

"Yeah," Ardolino said, "a bunch of freaks, if you ask me. The parents hold that pot bust over Vu's kid like he fucked the pope's daughter. Problem is—a couple of kids got money to burn and they fuck it up. And they all seem to hate each other."

"But none of this translates into murder."

"Who knows?"

We talked about Larry Torcelli and Benny Vu. He grunted. "Torcelli's a self-serving money bag, real proud of himself and his little gasoline-powered world. Pissed that someone took his beautiful wife away because he lost a thing of great beauty, like she's a statue in the fucking Athenaeum. And Benny Vu, that cipher, sitting there nodding at me like a skinny Buddha, agreeing with everything I say, and then telling me nothing. Nothing."

"He's a philosopher."

"A what? Are you nuts? He sells jars of stuff I can't even identify and probably illegal in the good old US of A. I picked up a jar and he tells me it's toad skin. Another one's powdered deer bone. We should raid the place. I tell you I got a headache from his nonanswers. And he gives me a gift when I leave. Tiger balm."

I smiled. *"Dau cu la con Cop.* Rub it on your temples."

"Haven't you people heard of Vick's Vapor Rub?"

"Try it."

"Give the man a scratch-off lottery ticket, and you've made his day."

"That's not fair." I wanted to defend Benny Vu. "He's a simple man who lost his wife…"

"And don't know where to find her." He chuckled.

"I don't think the Anti-Defamation League is gonna be naming you Citizen of the Year."

"My job is to catch murderers, not talk pretty." He sighed. "Look, Rick Van Lam, we're at the same dead end here. The punk Rican that got winged in the first murder is in jail, won't talk, but, I'll tell you, he seems like small potatoes here. I've checked all the snitches, from the North End to Frog Hollow, and let me tell you, the word on the street is that the two murders ain't got no connection to anything going on. Increased gang activity, but everybody laying low. You know the Mayor's civic crackdown, with cops all over the place for pictures in the *Courant*. Well, that good-time-Charlie feeling is still going on. As I said, right now everybody's laying low. What I mean is that the drug lords—not the pipsqueaks on the street corners—don't want no major shit coming down right now. They know the game—wait for the mayor to fall in love with preschool programs for AIDS-infected, drug-addicted mommies and for the *Courant* to rediscover the joys of gubernatorial corruption—and then the drug kings will kill each other." He stopped suddenly, almost out of breath.

"So it comes back to something to do with Mary and Molly."

"Or, and this I don't believe, there are new, higher-up players on the scene, trying to take over the territory. But that don't make sense."

I agreed. I asked him about Danny Trinh. He seemed surprised. "That fellow?"

"You talk to him?"

"Of course. And his I'm-so-happy-I'm-the-American-Dream mama. Neither one likes talking to cops, and the mama complained about you, but she wouldn't tell me why."

"I asked her if Danny was screwing Kristen."

Ardolino cracked up, choked, and ended up with a hacking smoker's cough. "You did? Fucking fantastic. Man, I may actually grow to like you."

"Don't try too hard."

"What'd she do?"

"She kicked me out of the house."

"Don't blame her. But you know I sort of liked Trinh. Didn't have much to say. Like everyone he's baffled by the 'turn of events,' as he put it, speaking in better English than the President. Just seems to be a little too edgy, ambitious." He paused. "But you obviously don't like Trinh as much as I do."

"How do you know that?"

"You forget I'm a detective. Years of experience."

"In fact, I don't." I told him about Danny's being a player through the years, a cad. A sexual hotshot. I told him how he used Cindy. But I also told him about the old Honda and the apartment on Hartt Street in Frog Hollow.

Silence. "Thanks for saving that thunderbolt until the end." A long pause. "What's with that?"

I told him what I'd found out.

"You gotta be careful running around that neighborhood," he said. "Lots of crime there."

"It's my job."

"No, it's *my* job."

"I'm helping you."

"Yeah, I forgot. I'm the one who called you."

"I was gathering my thoughts."

"I'll call you back. I gotta check this address out."

"For what?"

"I'll call you back."

And he did, an hour later. "Guess what I learned? That house is *owned* by the guy on the first floor. Binh Ky Trinh. Lives there with his wife and a hundred children and grandchildren. He's sixty-three, one of the Boat People. And he's a cousin of Danny's mom's ex-husband. The third floor is another cousin. And Duong, a.k.a Danny, has been living there for three years, since moving back to Hartford. All in the family."

"I wonder if his mother knows."

"The ex-husband walked out on her, but I learned he'd been around town, off and on. Out to San Jose, back here. Dead now, five years. But Danny—Duong—knew him to say hello to. The guy uses the place to chill, most likely. I guess the stress of Mama Susie and Bank of America and Larry Torcelli's vision of greatness can get to a man."

I was impressed. "How did you find all this out so fast?"

"I told you. I'm a goddamned good detective." I heard him belch and cough.

"So all this could be nothing."

"Yeah. Or something. I'm having background checks done on the whole house."

"But you still like Danny," I said.

"Hey, the guy has to have a place to bang girls, no? You can't do it with Mama Susie in the next room, blessing herself and saying the Rosary." He sighed. "Keep in touch." He hung up.

◇◇◇

The next afternoon I stopped at Hank's house only to find him out with his mother and grandmother. The crusty grandfather was annoyed when I knocked on the door. He watched me through the screen door, saying nothing, looking as though I woke him from a nap. Did he know when they'd return? He didn't answer. Would he tell Hank I'd stopped in? He didn't answer. I felt foolish, just standing there, so I turned to leave. Behind me, I heard a dismissive grunt. Exiled in a strange land he could never understand, the man would never like me, I knew, blaming me for the death of his serene life in the old homeland, the American soldiers as destroyers of national identity, these same soldiers who brought about the bastardization of his Vietnamese people. And I was one of the bastards.

So I drove back to my apartment, did some paper work, went for a run down past Miss Porter's School, and then returned for a bracing shower. It was a good afternoon for running. Another rainstorm had made the air pleasant.

At six I met Liz at the police station and we drove to a Thai restaurant on South Whitney Street, near downtown Hartford. I stopped at a liquor store so I could pick up a six-pack of Sam Adams, and we sat at the tiny, out-of-the-way restaurant, eating hot basil shrimp and red-curry chicken, the cool beer accenting the spicy food. Liz had on her work clothes, very professional in a light-blue cotton dress and sandals, her hair pulled back so that her prominent cheekbones were even more dramatic. A slight trace of peach lipstick. Pink nails. Toenails. A late summer confection. A beautiful woman, I had to admit. And once my wife.

"You look good." I toasted her with a glass of beer.

"You always say that." A heartbeat. "You look tired."

"I am."

"It's summer and you should have a tan."

Liz had news for me. "Listen to this. Mary made a phone call to the to the Hartford police three days before she was murdered. She identified herself as Mary Le Vu, and asked to speak with Detective Eric Smolski."

I looked blank. "And?"

"Well, Eric Smolski retired three years back. There was no way she could have known that. And when she was referred to someone else, she said she'd call back."

"Did she say what she wanted?"

"No," Liz said. "I just discovered this by talking to Detective Ferguson, who got her transferred call. He wrote down her name in a log, but she said she'd call back. She never did."

"Christ, what does this mean?"

"Well, Ferguson said she didn't sound anxious or anything, so far as he could recall. It was brief. Wanting to talk to Smolski. When she learned he'd retired, she sighed, said good-bye. So all he had was her name in his log book, but nothing else."

"Why didn't this come up before? After all, she was murdered."

"He's been on family emergency leave, out of state for a month. Mom dying of cancer in Rochester. He returned to work, caught up on the life of crime he'd missed, and spotted the name Vu. It caught his attention. He remembered the call. He told the chief. I got a call out of Hartford from my friend, who put me through to Ferguson. Ardolino also knows about it now."

I sat back. "So she wanted to talk to a Hartford detective."

"Not just any detective. Eric Smolski."

"Why him?"

"Simple," said Liz. "He's the detective who handled her son Tommy's drug bust back eight or so years ago. He was probably the only detective she knew."

"Something is up."

"It brings us right back to that pot bust."

"Which no one seems to have forgotten."

"But why Smolski? After all this time."

"Mary wasn't just placing a friendly call to Smolski. She needed help," I said.

"And three days later she's dead."

"And she didn't tell anyone about it. Not even her husband Benny. He would have told me. I don't think he's hiding anything."

"Maybe she was scared."

"Or maybe she *did* tell someone."

"Who?"

"Maybe she told her sister Molly." I tapped the table. "That makes sense, the two conspiratorial sisters."

"Which meant Molly had to die, too."

"But," I added, "if that's the case, why didn't Molly tell the police—or even me—when I talked to her after Mary's death? If she *knew* something involving Mary's murder, why would she keep silent?"

"Maybe she didn't believe Mary."

I remembered the flicker of an eye in Molly's eye when I first spoke to her, "Or maybe she was too scared."

"And then she was dead," Liz spoke softly.

"And she took that fear with her."

Chapter Twenty-four

Hank and I sat in my living room reviewing my note cards, juxtaposing one family member against another. He looked up. "Mary knew something that scared her. Okay? And she must have told Molly. She didn't tell the kids or Benny. And Molly didn't tell Larry. She was scared of something—or someone."

I nodded. "And when Mary got killed, Molly *did* have an idea what happened."

"But," Hank went on, "maybe Molly didn't think the matter a big deal until Mary died. Then she got scared."

"But even then she wasn't scared enough to tell anyone, least of all the cops. She went to that square looking for something."

"The same thing that Mary was looking for."

Hank and I looked at each other. "What's there?" I wondered. "You go there for drugs."

"But that's impossible." Hank pursed his brow. "The two sisters weren't buying drugs."

"Then they were looking for a person who had an *answer* they could only find there."

"The kids?"

"Which kid?" I asked.

"One or more of the kids may have an answer."

"Why not the husbands?"

"True," said Hank. "But that's farfetched."

"So where are we?"

"Well, the murders are tied into the family. That's why Molly wouldn't speak up."

"What about Danny?"

"He's family, of sorts."

"Family, but still an outsider."

He nodded. "But an outsider with a secret life. That apartment in Frog Hollow."

I sighed. "Maybe it was only a secret to us. Maybe it was the most natural thing in the world for him to want his own space."

"Still, it's unusual." Hank flipped the cards as if he were dealing a game of poker.

"But Molly didn't like him. If Danny was involved, wouldn't Molly have spoken up after Mary talked to her? She had no reason to *protect* Danny. Larry liked him. She didn't."

"Or maybe Danny was connected to one of her kids. Like Kristen," Hank said.

I breathed in, sat back, closing my eyes for a moment. "A lot of this hinges on what Mary said to Molly. That must have been some visit."

"Or phone call. I'm calling Benny now."

"Hank, it's late."

Hank dialed the phone, sitting on the edge of the chair. I got the extension from my bedroom. Hank spoke in rapid-pace Vietnamese. I understood most of what he said, but my Vietnamese was slipping. Certain phrases, sentences, words flew by me, unknown.

Benny Vu wasn't happy, but he agreed to talk. And to me, too, because I spoke into the phone, letting him know I was on the line.

"Uncle Benny," Hank began, differentially, "did Mary tell Molly anything out of the ordinary on the day before she died?"

"They talked all the time, Hank."

"But were you around—did you ever hear her say anything unusual in their conversations?"

A pause. "They talked of family, mostly. Let me think. They talked mainly of how they feel, the children, a charity Molly had put Mary on."

"How did Mary feel about that?"

"Mary just wanted to stay home. She wasn't a public lady, you know."

"But Molly insisted?"

"Yes, Mary told me she did it because Molly wanted her to, but her heart wasn't in it. She didn't like the company of strange women."

"But she did it."

"Of course. Family. The only thing important to Mary was family. You know that."

Hank took a breath. "Then could family be a reason she was murdered?"

A long silence. "I thought about that." Benny's high-pitched Vietnamese was gravelly and raw. "But why? These are simple families, ours."

"Did you know that Aunt Mary tried to reach a detective a few days before she died. She called Detective Smolski."

He was surprised. "Smolski? From years ago?"

"Yes."

"Why?"

"She didn't say. But he's retired and she hung up."

The news surprised him. I could hear his breathing getting heavier, shorter. "She didn't tell me."

"No idea what she wanted to ask him?" Hank asked.

"Or tell him," I interrupted.

Again, the contemplative thinking. Finally, slowly, "No. This bothers me. We had no secrets, the two of us."

"Maybe she was afraid to tell you something."

Hank added, "Maybe something happened to—well, maybe Molly told *her* something."

Benny's voice was getting raspy, agitated. This was not going well. But finally he remembered something. "Mary did say Molly was a little different lately."

"Like what?"

I could almost hear him shrugging. "I didn't pay attention. Molly always unloaded her *troubles* on Mary. The hard life of the rich. After a while, I couldn't listen. Mary said Molly was depressed about Kristen, who was doing nothing with her life. But they'd had that conversation before, I know. Over and over. Molly complained about Kristen lately—and how Larry indulged the vain and silly girl."

"So this wasn't something new?"

There was a long, long silence. Then Benny recalled scraps of overheard talk. "They had one conversation that left Mary depressed. I know she started to talk about it, but I didn't like hearing about Molly's world because Molly world's was always more important than anyone else's. And Mary usually felt the same way. I mean, she'd listen to Molly's whining—or bragging and celebrating something—and then, when she put down the phone, she'd forget about it. Sort of like—oh that Molly! But there was one time recently Mary *did* want to talk about it, and I shut her out." A pause. "That was a mistake."

"So you don't have any idea what Molly said?"

"Oh, but I do. It had to do with Kristen again. It was always Kristen lately."

"What this time?" Hank asked.

"Drugs." Benny's voice got low. "Molly got it into her head that Kristen was experimenting with drugs. But I thought it was just Molly's—well, craziness."

"My God," I said into the phone. "That's probably why Mary tried to reach Detective Smolski."

Hank added, "The detective who arrested Tommy."

Benny interrupted. "Mary would not intrude on Molly's life that way. Molly would be furious."

"But what if Molly *asked* her to?"

"What? Arrest Kristen?"

"No, maybe get information. Mary didn't know—and Molly, too—where to turn to. Mary saw Smolski as a help line. He'd been a decent guy way back when."

"But wouldn't she tell me she was calling him?" Benny asked.

He'd just admitted to closing Mary out, refusing to hear yet another Molly complaint, but I kept my mouth shut.

"So it comes back to drugs," Hank said.

I asked Benny, "Do you remember why Molly thought Kristen was on drugs?"

No answer. Then, "I never asked." He sighed. "I turned away from her."

Hank spoke to me. "Nobody pays attention to Kristen because she's dumb."

"Except Daddy, who treats her like a little girl."

"Which," Hank concluded, "could be why no one noticed anything about her."

"Except Molly."

"Who then told Mary."

"And Mary," I went on, "had a special hatred of drugs, given what happened to Tommy. As did Molly—her worst fear."

"So," Hank ended, "if this is true, you have two women who didn't understand what was happening, trying to solve a problem they couldn't fathom."

Benny's voice came over the line, tinny now, sad. "And maybe that's why they're now dead."

Quietly, he hung up the phone.

Chapter Twenty-five

Drugs, I thought. *She* thought. Molly thought.

Drugs and Kristen. But not Kristen alone. I couldn't imagine her maneuvering the mean streets of Hartford to cop a nickel bag. Not in a hundred years. But, admittedly long ago, that had not been a problem for one of the children.

I knocked on Tommy's door, surprising him. It was midmorning, but he was waking up. One of his roommates, a scraggly man in his late twenties, was leaving for work. Dressed in baggy shorts, no shirt, and flip-flops.

"Are you a lifeguard?" I asked him.

"No," he mumbled, "I work at a carnival."

He walked out, nodding at Tommy who was sitting in boxer shorts that had seen better days, a bottle of Pepsi in his hand. His punk hairdo—that careful construction of Mohawk and fade—hadn't yet met his morning mirror. He looked like a hayfield after a hailstorm.

"Now what?" The departing roommate had let me in, unceremoniously.

"I'm bothering you."

He shrugged his shoulders. "Whatever."

"I'm still trying to help find your mom's killer." A beat. "You interested in that?"

"I don't think talking to me is gonna do the trick."

"Yeah, but you might have some answers to some questions."

"Hey, I doubt it." He pulled his legs up under him, inclined his body. He sipped from the soda bottle, smacked his lips noisily, and frowned at me.

"Can I be the judge of that?" I said.

"Well, you're the detective. So detect."

"I just have a couple of questions."

He cleared his throat and ran his fingers over his nose, back and forth, like he was trying to stop a sneeze. "Shoot."

"Did you know that your Aunt Molly was concerned that Kristen was into drugs?"

He stared at me, wide eyed, and then burst out laughing, almost rolling off the sofa. I waited, but he laughed and laughed. "That's a good one. Real rich."

"What's so funny?"

"Where did Molly get that idea?"

"I'm asking you."

"Look." He sat up, angry now. "Just because I had that bum probation shit over a couple of joints doesn't make me the family authority on drug use among the rich and stupid."

"She's your cousin."

"Who lives in another world from me."

"So you don't think it's true?"

"I mean, maybe Kristen tokes a joint or two at some party now and then—for Christ's sake it's pot, not crack or heroin— but do you know how little contact I have with Kristen and Jon? Almost nothing. Now and then, some family function that nobody wants to be at. Viet Cong New Year's or something. The Tet Really Offensive. But now that the beautiful Le sisters are no more, maybe that will finally stop."

"You don't miss your mother?"

A bit of a pause. "What do you think? Of course I do. Every day. Mom was, well, *my* Mom."

"I'm sorry."

"It's just that, well, there's not a damn thing I can do about it now."

"You can help me by giving me information."

Tommy stood up, pulling up his sagging shorts, and walked to look out the front window. He looked back at me. "If I could, I would." I could see he was sweating, but then so was I. The tight, close room was baking.

"That's why I asked you about Kristen, Tommy. I'm not trying to harp on your past. As far as I'm concerned, that was nothing but a teenage moment. But I thought you might know something."

He sat back down. "I'll tell you something, Rick." His tone now was confidential, almost intimate. "Yeah, Kristen smoked a little dope back in prep school, but if she does it now it ain't much. You know. Recreational. You mean to tell me you never smoked?" He waited.

"Yes, I did, back in college."

He feigned a hopped-up gesture. "But you didn't go on to become a frenzied heroic addict, did you? Reefer madman."

"Something I did with friends in a dorm room. Now and then."

"Still do it?"

"No."

He looked at me. "Well, if you wanna know, I'll tell you something. I *still* smoke. Recreational use. But that doesn't make me a druggie, for Christ's sake. And it certainly has nothing to do with Mom's death. That just makes no sense."

"You didn't stop after prep school arrest?"

"Yeah, for a year or so. But, you know, you hang out with friends—they smoke. But they're cool. But never with Kristen and Jon. Jon? That uptight asshole. Kristen, well, I think the only thing she puts in her mouth these days is diet soda."

"You sure?"

"No, I'm not. All I'm saying is that this drug shit is just that—a lot of noise about nothing. So I don't know where you're going with this. You know, we get a bag of good chronic every month or so. That's all."

"We?" I asked. "Cindy?"

He laughed. "No, she's happy in her dance club with Ecstasy. Who knew?"

"But you said 'we.'"

He hesitated. "Danny and me."

"Danny?"

"We go in for halves on an ounce of real good stuff every so often. Hey, we don't sell, and we're careful. I told you, it's for recreation."

"Who buys it?"

"Danny gets it from a guy he knows. I give him the money and he gives me half. It ain't a big deal. Some good weed he knows where to find. That's all."

"You smoke with Danny?"

"No, I buy it from him. It's cool."

"He sells?"

"Christ, man, you ain't listening. Danny has a real job, a real life. He just picks some up for partying, and I'm in on it. I trust him and he trusts me. You can't be too careful."

"You think Danny gives Kristen any drugs?"

"How would I know?"

"Are they sleeping together?"

He laughed. "Nothing would surprise me with Danny. But who cares?"

"But Molly suspected Kristen of using drugs…"

"I didn't think it had anything to do with Kristen."

"What do you mean?"

"I thought it all started with Mom."

"I'm not following you, Tommy."

He chose his words carefully. "You know how Mom felt about drugs. If I had to hear one more time about the cousin who died of opium in Vietnam and how his wife suffered and the kids starved…Man alive. After I got arrested, she spent years asking me, over and over, 'Are you on drugs?' It got to be almost a dumb joke between us. I told her over and over that I was clean, but sometimes she looked at me weird. You know, given the way I choose to look, haircut and all. But I didn't want her to know. To worry. Because she didn't understand drugs. A single joint late at night listening to garage bands—or Danny lighting up for a night of sex, since he told me he loves pot for sex alone—couldn't be explained to Mom. Or to Molly. Drugs was, you know, some freak screaming on TV. And commercials about this-is-your-brain-on-drugs. Addicts."

"So big an issue?"

"It was their big fear. Christ, I grew up with stories of the beloved cousin who became a raving lunatic on opium back in Saigon—destroyed his life, his family. It's one of our childhood fairy tales. So, yeah, drugs—any drugs. A hint of drugs would send Mom and Molly into orbit. So I couldn't sit down and say, 'Hey Mom, pot's recreational. Like a glass of wine you have.'"

"I'm still not following what you're saying."

"Well, lately Mom was watching me more closely. One time I caught her fiddling with my phone, for Christ's sake, but she only fucked it up. Another time when Danny stopped in, she caught us going out back. He was giving me the stuff. She didn't see, but, you know, mother eye and all…"

"I still don't understand why Danny would risk his job at the bank."

"Risk what? The man likes a puff now and then. If every banker in America stopped lighting up, you'd have a lot of grumpy souls in expensive suits."

"So your mother worried you were back on drugs?"

"Yeah."

"But Molly, I guess, suspected Kristen was on drugs."

"Mom never mentioned that, but she did tell me Molly had told her drug use was on the rise—like it was a news flash that just hit her. I mean, she was on this antidrug charity or something. So, I guess, yeah, if she thought Kristen was using, she'd think it was Danny. Or me. Especially me. She'd call Mom about me and whine."

"What would Molly say?"

He smiled. "Keep an eye on Tommy and Danny." He paused, seemed to be thinking about something. "You know, that's what she did, in fact. Kept an eye on me, mainly. I saw Mom watching me real close. Mom told me Molly was on her high horse. But Mom never mentioned Kristen."

"You told me you rarely saw Danny anymore."

He grinned. "I lied. Well, not really. I don't see him. He ain't a friend. It's just because we go way back. In this matter I trust him, and he trusts me."

"Convenient."

He smirked. "Way back when, I knew Mom was listening to Molly's crap. She thought drugs would be the end of me."

"You know she called Detective Smolski?"

Surprise: "Why?"

"I don't know. For advice?"

"What did he say?"

"He's retired, and she hung up."

"Maybe she wanted to turn me in." He grinned. "Round two."

"She was worried about you."

"I always told her not to worry. Yeah, you know, when she told me Molly called about that antidrug charity, she looked at me suspiciously. When Danny was in the room, she stayed with us…wouldn't leave." He thought of something. "I think Molly poisoned her against Danny all over again."

"Did Danny know Molly had warned your mother to keep an eye on you and him?"

"Yeah, I told him Molly and Mom were on their antidrug crusade again. Keep a low profile."

"You did? Why?"

He shrugged. "Conversation."

"Was Danny bothered that Molly suspected him?"

"No, he laughed, in fact. Said it was no big deal. 'I'm not gonna lose sleep over a dime bag,' he said."

"You know, I thought you didn't like Danny."

He drew his lips into a tight, bloodless line. "I hate Danny."

"And yet…"

"I told you—Danny and I go way back. I share a bag with him now and then. Infrequent. He Facebooks me—I get back to him. No big deal. But he knows I hate his guts."

"But you still have contact with him?"

"I'm not his favorite person either. I'm a waste-of-space boy, the squanderer of opportunity. You know, we don't travel in the same social circles, that's for sure. Rick, we don't have to *like* each other."

I stood up, ready to leave.

"But," Tommy also stood, "I don't see how this has to do with Mom's murder. Come on, think about it. Me and Danny smoking a bowl, each in our separate worlds, I gotta tell you, 'cuz we never do that together. It's just party-time crap. Nobody gonna get killed over a nickel or dime bag."

"Where does Danny get the stuff?"

"It's like a network. He gets his off a claims officer whiz kid at the Hartford Insurance Group."

"Not on the street?"

"You mean like that square where Mom got shot? Come on. That's one world. Danny lives in a white-collar world. Pot passes next to the water cooler. There's enough shared drugs in that world to pay off the Connecticut state deficit."

"But your Mom suspected drugs. Molly probably got her going on it. She wouldn't understand how it is distributed."

"But she's certainly not gonna drive to some wild-west corner in Hartford looking for *me*," Tommy said. "Look, Mom told me not to use drugs, and I told her I wouldn't. Mom believed what I told her—at least until Molly started flapping her mouth."

"She believed you?"

"I've always lied to Mom. It's an art form."

"A charmer like Danny."

"No, he got it down to a science. But Molly was working her magic on Mom, I guess."

"What do you mean?"

"She bad-mouthed Danny. Mom mentioned that Molly didn't like having Danny around. I thought it was the old story… you know, Molly angry over the dumb rumors that Danny was Larry's son. That's what I thought it was about. Danny was… cocky. A bad influence."

"She wanted you to stay away from him?"

"I'm telling you, we didn't hang. He did me a *favor*. A little bit of guilt maybe—for the old days when I took the rap and he walked off into the sunshine."

"So your mother didn't know anything."

"She never did." He paused. "At least about my shit. But maybe she did. About other things. She knew *something*, maybe. She must've."

"Why?"

"Like it got her killed."

Chapter Twenty-six

Detective Ardolino called me on my cell phone. "Why am I always the one calling you?"

"What's up?"

I could hear the clacking of computer keys and the constant buzz of phones. Worse, I could hear him eating. "I gotta finish this. You let McDonald's shit sit, it's like eating sawdust." He described opening a packet of ketchup, squeezing the feeble contents onto the fries. Three fries slipped to the grimy floor. I heard a creaky chair shift.

"Did you pick them up?"

"Hell, no. We got a cleaning crew, you know."

"What's up?" I asked again.

"I'm gonna play the good guy and lay info on you. Mainly because you provided the first info."

"What are we talking about?"

"You told me that Danny Trinh—real name Trinh Xuan Duong—was renting that happy apartment in Frog Hollow. Somehow that information, well, *eluded* me." He stressed the word, humorously. "I know you got a bug up your ass about Danny, seeing him as somehow dirty. Based, I know, on nothing but Fu Manchu instinct."

"Detective…"

"No lectures, okay? I checked out priors on that beehive of losers. The owner, the gent on floor one, relative of a.k.a. Duong, is a two-bit hood, but small potatoes, picked up a half dozen times—with his wife, no less—for welfare fraud, shoplifting, domestic battery, a string of shit a mile long."

"No dope sales?"

"None. But he's a low-rent, small-business type."

"I was hoping there was a drug connection."

"They're probably all smoking, even the three-year-old, but nobody hawking wares outta that building."

I told him about Molly's worries about Kristen, as well as Molly's and Mary's eagle eyes on Tommy and Danny. Ardolino wasn't surprised and told me what I already knew—Mary's call to Smolski. "Everybody smokes," he summed up.

"Tommy said Danny got his pot from a guy at the Hartford."

Ardolino started to choke on his food. "Thanks for that good news. That's my insurance company."

"You're one lucky man."

He grunted. "Fuck." A pause. "I just got ketchup on my pants. Now I gotta wash them. Thought I could get another week outta them."

I smiled. "Tell people it's blood. Say you were in a shootout."

"I only exchange gunfire with the missus.'

"Tell them she's getting closer to her real target."

"Funny man. Hey, by the way," he added, "your boy Danny a.k.a. Duong has a heavy foot."

"Meaning?"

"Past year three speeding tickets across the border in New York. On the Saw Mill and I-684. Headed to the city and back. Last one recently, morning after Mary Vu's funeral. In White Plains. That boy is always in a hurry. Boys with their fancy cars don't believe the law is for them."

"He pay the fine?"

"You bet."

I smiled. "Good citizen."

"Yeah, the best. The first time he appealed the fine. Claimed he was stopped because he's young, Asian, and driving a Mercedes."

"What did the judge do?"

"Probably wet his pants laughing so hard."

"Danny pay?"

"Yeah, I told you. As you said, a solid citizen."

Liz met me outside her office and handed me a stack of printouts. "I can't stay. Too many meetings. But these should interest you."

I leafed through them: phone records, not only for Susie's home, but, more importantly, calls in and out of his secret apartment in Frog Hollow. And also the records for Benny Vu's home and store, for Larry Torcelli's mansion, for Tommy's phone. Kristen had her own phone. "You have me doing illegal acts. Police channels." She tapped the sheets. "And not for the first time."

Back at my apartment, Hank was waiting, having used his key to let himself in. He was sitting by the front window, headphones on, and the base line of some song punctuated the air. He didn't even hear me come in. I tapped him on the shoulder, and he jumped, then laughed. I waved the pile of printouts in front of him. "What's that?" he said.

"I am always dependent on the kindness of Liz." I fanned the printouts in front of me. "These are phone logs for a week before Mary was killed, up to the day of Molly's murder."

He was interested. "Cell phones?"

"We'll see."

"Anything good?"

"That's what you and I will be finding out this afternoon." I waved the sheets in front of him.

And intimidating it was. What Liz in her thoroughness had procured was formidable. So Hank and I sat with pen and pad and shifted through—a waste of time, perhaps, because most of the numbers called were not identified. Not that I could complain. Liz had dutifully and beautifully labeled all the prime players in the drama. The only problem, I told Hank, was that the unidentified calls could be the ones that were crucial—a number possibly appearing *one* time only—impossible to identify it. But we started. As expected, there were lots of calls from

Susie's home to Molly's home, but not many going the other way: Susie calling in for whatever reason.

"Or," Hank reasoned, "Danny calling the house."

"Maybe for Kristen." I checked Kristen's phone. The girl talked on the phone constantly, it seemed. "But in that period she made three calls to Danny's cell phone. All late at night."

Hank pointed to another sheet. "The calls between Mary and Molly's home, including to Benny's store, are all over the place."

We went back and forth, making notes, but it was obvious that these people were all involved with one another and liked to use the phone. Nothing stood out, other than Danny and Kristen's brief late-night communication. "Well," Hank noted, "he did admit to sleeping with her."

"Let's look at Tommy." I made a notation on my pad. "He clearly believes his cell shouldn't be separated from his ear lobe. We cross-referenced calls to the store, to his mother's home, but none to the Torcelli household."

"This is crazy," Hank said.

"What we need to do is look at the day Mary died and the day Molly died."

"Makes more sense," Hank agreed.

"In the morning someone from the Torcelli house called Mary at home. A couple calls back. But all real short—maybe just a message on the machine."

"Look at this," Hank pointed out. "At six o'clock the day Mary died, Danny called Tommy, but it's a brief call, just seconds, maybe to leave a message. But then he called Benny's store, also a brief call."

"Looking for Tommy."

"But," Hank went on, "he later called Benny's home phone, and that call lasted nearly ten minutes."

"Why would he be calling Mary?" I wondered out loud.

"Maybe he was still looking for Tommy."

"So three calls to get to Tommy."

"But," Hank said, "he ended up talking to whoever answered the phone there."

"It had to be Mary. Or Cindy? But she told us she'd had a fight with her mother that morning and stormed out. Well, it wasn't Tommy. He told us he didn't see his mother that day. He told us he saw her the day before at the store."

"Unless he's lying."

"And he *is* a liar," I said.

"But let's say Danny did talk to Mary."

"But it could have been idle chitchat."

"Ten minutes?" Hank was shaking his head.

"Two hours later she's dead."

"I wonder if he ever reached Tommy, after all."

Hank suggested another call to Benny Vu, who sounded groggy when he answered the phone. No, he told Hank, he couldn't remember who called the store that afternoon. This person called, that person called. "Did Danny call looking for Tommy?" Hank asked.

A pause. "No, I don't think so. I can't remember."

"Around six o'clock? Danny. We know he called the store."

Another pause. "Maybe. I don't know. How can I remember? Danny did call one afternoon, but I don't know what day."

"Looking for Tommy?"

"I guess so," Benny answered. "Yes, what else could it be? He's called Tommy before at work. I frown on that."

"Was Tommy working?"

"No. Not that day."

"Danny called your home that day."

"Maybe he thought Tommy was there. I don't know."

"But Mary didn't tell you he called."

A long, painful pause. "I never spoke to her again."

"Oh." Hank turned red.

"Is that all?"

Hank apologized for the call and hung up the phone.

"So," he stressed, "Danny was looking for Tommy, calling three places late that day."

"And never seems to have reached him."

"But he did talk to Mary, most likely." Hank was excited.

"He had to. Because Tommy said he didn't see his mother that day."

"Unless Mary wasn't home and Tommy *was* there. She could have been headed into Hartford."

"And what does that tell us? Just that Danny was anxious to reach Tommy."

"Or maybe Danny was the last person to speak to Mary alive."

Chapter Twenty-seven

When I pulled into the back lot of my apartment, headed to my spot next to Gracie's, I noticed my spot taken by an ice-blue Mercedes. Leaning against it, arms folded, was Danny Trinh, himself ice-blue in bright white chinos and a cobalt-blue muscle shirt that said: Tina Turner Farewell Tour. He wasn't moving. I couldn't see his eyes, hidden behind dark sunglasses. But his lean, muscular body told me quite a bit—anger, frustration, resentment. You name it.

I parked my car and got out. "You waiting to see me?"

"No, I'm here to pose for animal crackers."

I grinned. "If you came back as an animal, which one would it be?"

For a second I could see him simmer. "A fly," he snarled. "That way it's easy to track down a piece of shit like you."

"Not bad. I'd be a…" I paused, thinking.

He jumped in. "Man, I don't care what the fuck you'd come back as because in this life you're just a big asshole."

"So we have a problem. Wanna come upstairs?"

"Look, man, I just wanna know what you're trying to pin on me."

I leaned against my own car, the two of us perhaps ten feet apart, adversaries, arms folded, both in dark sunglasses, both dressed for a reunion of *Beach Blanket Bingo*. Frankie Avalon. I used to watch late-night TV when I couldn't sleep, especially during my college days. The Americanization of the Viet boy. Now, standing there, Danny and I looked like two grim CIA agents slumming in South Beach.

"I'm not trying to pin anything on you. I'm just talking to anybody who knew Mary and Molly."

The old charming Danny was gone now—in its place a cool, defiant anger, the words spaced out with deliberate care. "And that involves following me?"

"I followed you?"

"How else did you find my apartment in Frog Hollow?" He bit his lower lip. "Which has nothing to do with anything."

"Then why did you keep it a secret?"

He made a mocking laugh. "Maybe a secret to you, but not to my family. *They* know I live there."

"Your mother?"

"Well, no. She wants nothing to do with my father's family. As I grew up, his relatives were around. Not so much him, but an uncle, an aunt, some cousins."

"And your father's cousin gave you a place to stay?"

"I love my mother, but she can be a little nosy sometimes. Hey, I'm a young man. My mother spends her time talking to the Virgin Mary. Right now she tells me she needs me to live with her. For now. My cousin lets me rent the second floor. I pay him rent, I handle the mortgage and finances through the bank, and I have a little space to myself…"

"But *that* neighborhood?"

"It's my family, you know." He sneered. "You're talking about my family."

"Your mother doesn't suspect?"

"Enough questions. I'm here to tell you to back off."

"Why?"

"For one, I've done nothing wrong—as you've discovered—and, two, you'll screw things up with my mother. You're gonna make me into a bad guy. I've already talked too much to you."

"I'm just asking questions."

"No," he yelled, pounding his fist on the fender. "Enough. My cousin Binh tells me you and Hank are sneaking around. He spots you in front of the house, spying. Asking questions. Of course, he calls me. Tells me. 'Are you in trouble?' he says. No, but I gotta worry."

"Why the old Honda?" I asked.

He took off his sunglasses and glared at me. "I don't wanna leave the Mercedes in the back lot there. It's dangerous, as you pointed out. Even with an alarm. It's my baby. The old clunker, well, I feel safe with it there." He walked so close to me I could see a prominent vein throbbing the left side of his neck. "How does any of this relate to Mary and Molly's murders? Tell me how." He yelled the last sentence.

"I'm asking questions around..."

"Fuck you. You're ruining my life. I built a successful life. I'm respected, I got a future, and this negative chatter—this nasty innuendo—if it gets out, to the bank, it's gonna kill everything I built up. You're fucking with my future."

"Then I'm fucking with everyone's futures. Kristen's and Jon's and Tommy's and Cindy's. Because I'm asking the same questions of them."

He laughed that phony laugh. "The only problem is, they really don't *have* futures."

"And you do?"

"Haven't you been paying attention?"

"You know, Danny, I'd think you'd want to help."

"And you don't think I don't. I've talked to you—even the police at my door. That asshole Ardolino—that grade-school Neanderthal—knocks on my door, looks at me like I'm every lowlife he's ever hauled in for spitting on a sidewalk, and what am I supposed to think? And it all comes back to you."

"As I said, interviews..."

"Oh, that's right. Interviews. You're trying to pin an impossible murder on me because you don't want it to be one of the family."

I started to walk away. "You wanna come inside. It's hot out here."

He shook his head, but I noticed he backed up, into the shade of an old oak at the edge of the property. I stood in the blazing sunlight. "No, I'm not staying here long. Just long enough to tell you to lay off. I answer every question and still you track me down. My life is an open book, Rick. I work for a bank. You think they don't monitor my life, even my private life. And you'd think I'd jeopardize the life I've worked hard to build. You got to be crazy."

"Could you answer one question?"

He looked ready to say no, fishing his key out of his pocket, then moved closer, almost three feet away. I could smell his after-shave: pungent, almost sweet. "If it'll end this nonsense, shoot."

"On the night Mary Vu was murdered, around six p.m., you called her at her home."

He looked surprised. "You sure?"

"Yes, I am."

"I don't think I did. Why would I call her at home?"

"You called Tommy, then talked to Benny at the store, and then you…"

He breathed in, confident. "Oh, God, yes. I was supposed to meet up with Tommy for something, but his cell phone went to message. I had to change the time. I couldn't meet him. We were supposed to meet later that night. So I called Benny and, I guess, I called Mary. Though I can't remember that. Looking for Tommy." He finished dramatically, emphasizing the word *Tommy*. He looked happy.

"Did you talk to Mary?"

"I guess so. I don't remember. If Tommy wasn't there, I probably said hello or something and hung up."

"You talked for ten minutes."

"I don't know. The woman always made me nervous. I probably yapped about nonsense. How are you? What's new? This or that. Nonsense. I don't even remember making that call, but I probably did."

"Did you ever reach Tommy?"

"No," he said. "And plans sort of went out the window when we learned his mother was dead."

"Who told you?"

He hesitated. "I think it was my mother, calling from Molly's home."

"What did you think?"

"Like everyone, I thought—how dumb. Mary? Who'd wanna kill her? She was, well, just there. Like you never really thought about her."

I moved into the shade and forced him to turn to face me. I was sweating and I mopped my forehead with a handkerchief.

"Did you know that Molly warned Mary about you?"

"Yeah, I knew. Tommy told me."

"Did you know that Molly suspected Kristen was on drugs?"

"Yeah, she told me her mother was on the warpath. She found a goddamn joint. Look. Kristen leaves a fuckin' joint on the bureau in her room or something. So Molly finds it. The Opium Wars Revisited."

"Molly probably thought it was your influence."

"Yeah, I'd be the first person she'd think of. That fucking prep school arrest. My God, one little mistake and I'm branded *capo de drugi* on the Eastern Seaboard."

"Mary was keeping an eye on Tommy."

"Because Mary was nuts about drugs and always was afraid Tommy would get back in trouble. It kept her awake nights." He drew his lips into a thin line. "God, what a simple, simple woman."

"She'd been worrying since the prep school days."

"But we're all in our midtwenties now. Perhaps the mothers could take the drug-abuse hotline off speed dial."

"But you're still using," I said. "Tommy told me the two of you share a bag now and then."

He looked angry. "Big fucking mouth on him. That's why I didn't say anything about Kristen. Kristen herself thought it *funny*." Then he laughed. "Yeah, so what? Like you don't? Come on."

"Did you give that joint to Kristen?" I asked.

"No, but she took it from me. We'd smoke before sex. There's nothing like sex with good weed—it makes good sex, well, wonderful. But Kristen was too unstable for me to let her run around the house with grass. I think she probably took it from my cigarette case. It wasn't the first time, but I warned her. Seriously warned her. She thinks I never see her stealing joints. God knows what she does with them."

"Solitary pleasure?"

"I don't know. For a pretty but simple girl, she can be a little—wily."

"But Molly assumed drugs had reentered *all* your worlds—not knowing it had never stopped—and now Kristen was in. And she blamed you."

"No one said anything to me," Danny said.

"But Molly talked to Mary about it. And Mary worried, not about you, but Tommy."

"You know," Danny sighed, "this drug business is infantile—so unimportant. But I sensed a change in Mary." He smiled. "She'd recently quit my fan club. When I called the house or stopped in, I'd get the old arctic freeze from her. I guess Molly was, well, on my case."

"She suspected your affair with Kristen?"

He laughed. "Affair? That's quite a word for it. Makes me think of French movies in black and white."

"How would you define it?"

"Availability. Kristen is available."

"That's cruel."

"She knows the way I am."

"Are you sure?"

"We talk of it. I *told* her—don't expect a thing from me, except a good time."

"But did Molly *know*?"

He scratched the side of his nose. "No, of course not. Kristen knew how bad it would be otherwise. It would ruin a good thing—for *her*. And I got to worry about…"

"I know, I know—your image as a banker."

He didn't like that. "Fuck you," he sneered. "Kristen did say her mother might have suspected, a little bit, maybe. I mean, Molly would ask her what we talked about when I visited.

'Danny's a good-looking boy, isn't he? Right?' They were all fishing expeditions."

"But why would she mind?"

"I told you. Because Molly didn't trust me since prep school. And she made it clear that she saw me as, well, a player. Too many girls, you know. They don't want that for sweet little Kristen."

"You *are* a player."

"But top it off with Molly's worries about my friendship with Larry—he loved me like a second son—and her own husband's dislike for his own son Jon, her own blood—and, well, you got yourself a problem. And then there was the old wives tale that I was Larry's son."

"So I've heard."

"As tired a story as you can find." He straightened up, lifted his chin. "Finding that joint in Kristen's room probably moved Molly into overdrive."

"And Mary as well."

"True."

"Who else knew about the joint?"

"No one. I told Kristen to shut up. It would blow over."

"But it didn't."

"Well, I never thought it would be an issue."

"But," I said, "was Mary curt to you when you called her at home?"

Frustrated: "I told you, I don't even remember the *call*. How am I supposed to remember the *context*?"

He opened the door to his car and slid into the driver's seat.

"Tell me this. Would Larry mind if you married Kristen?"

"I'm not gonna marry Kristen."

"That's not my question."

He paused, thinking about it. "Like Molly, he's branded me as a womanizer, which he sort of likes. My fault because I used to regale him with stories of my teenage conquests. That was a mistake. He loves me, but doesn't think I'd stay with Kristen very long. There's always another girl on the next corner."

"So the answer is yes—he would mind."

"It's not an issue. But I do know he'd agree with me on one thing, though."

"What's that?"

"That I could easily do a lot better than his special-ed daughter."

Chapter Twenty-eight

Hank and I sat with Cindy and Tommy in Tommy's apartment. Tommy took a phone call from Danny, right after our parking-lot talk, and he'd called me, angry, spitting out the words so fast he had to start again. "Come over now. We gotta talk. Now. Cindy's here, too. We need to talk this shit out. Get the hell over here."

They were waiting for us, the two of them, sitting next to each other on the shabby sofa, cans of Pepsi gripped tightly, cell phones in their laps.

"Just what the hell's going on?" Tommy spat out the minute we sat down. Cindy grumbled. Humorless, jaws set, hands folded over chests, they looked like they'd practiced this particular posture especially for our mandated visit.

Cindy's voice was squeaky, nervous. "You trying to pin Mom's murder on Tommy? If you are…"

I broke in. "Is that what Danny told you?"

"Why are you hounding my brother?"

Hank looked from one to the other. "Nobody's hounding anybody, Cindy."

"Just what did Danny tell you?" I asked.

Tommy looked ready for another outburst, but he changed his mind, answering me calmly. "He said you're trailing him around, even to the apartment he keeps in Frog Hollow…"

"You know about that?" Hank interrupted.

Tommy frowned. "Everybody does. I've been there." But

then he looked as though he'd misspoke, and backtracked. "I watched a Super Bowl game there. His Mom doesn't like sports."

The look Cindy gave him told him to shut up.

I noted, "For someone everyone seems to dislike, you all seem to spend a lot of time with dear old Danny."

"What you don't understand is that he's one of us, but that doesn't mean we see him a lot. He's around now and then."

"So why did he call you now?"

"Because you put him on the spot—for that apartment, but also because of the fact we buy a little weed together."

"And?"

He looked exasperated. "A little weed, man. A little. We don't even think about it any more. It's like we buy toothpaste when we run out." He liked his own analogy because he smiled, looked appreciatively at Cindy, who wore a blank look on her face.

I stared into his face. "You know, I bring up drugs, and all you kids run amok."

"That's because you're trying to somehow connect it to Mom and Aunt Molly's murders."

"Preposterous," Cindy yelled loudly. "My brother would never kill our own mother. Do you know how stupid that sounds?"

"I never said he did."

"Danny said…"

"Tell me exactly what Danny *says* I said." I looked at Tommy.

"He mentioned that Molly found a joint in Kristen's room…"

Cindy scoffed, "Barbie goes to pot."

Tommy glared at her. "And Molly blamed Danny. The way she blamed him for everything. I mean Danny can be an asshole and all, but, like, Kristen is a twenty-something girl. She can buy her own shit."

"But what if Danny did give it to her?" Hank said.

"So what? A joint. Do you people hear yourselves? She's not hiding the whereabouts of weapons of mass destruction, for Christ's sake."

"But Molly called your mother, and you know how your mother got crazy over drugs."

"I know, I know," Tommy grumbled. "Do I have to hear it again?"

Cindy looked at me. "But I don't understand how this connects to murder. You don't kill people over a joint in someone's purse. The fact that Tommy and Danny smoke a bit—and me too if you gotta know, why don't you lock me up in your loony bin?—has nothing to do with murder."

"I never said it did."

"Then why are you asking the questions?"

"I'm asking *every* question I can think of. I'm hoping something will fall in place."

"That's a helleva way to do a job," Tommy snickered. Cindy smiled.

"So Danny told you I thought the drugs were connected to the murders?" I asked.

"Not in so many words. He said you were on him and me for smoking, and because Molly was losing it over the *idea* of her little kiddy smoking a little cannabis, *you* thought somehow that we had to kill them."

"Kill them," Cindy echoed.

It did sound—to use Cindy's word—preposterous, but somewhere deep within me, in that hollowness where I listen to my own quiet, I felt there was something going on here. And in that moment, just like at other times in my life, I remembered the Buddha quotations from that tattered phrase book my mother tucked into my breast pocket. *The smallest moment is the shadow of the greatest. The greatest is a shadow of the smallest.* In the tiniest moment, in the most irrelevant anecdote, there lurked, somehow, the larger picture, the sun spot that came to dominate the sky.

"Sometimes," I translated, "by talking about something like this trivial stick of pot on Kristen's bureau, sometimes, maybe, there's another story behind it."

Both Tommy and Cindy yelled. "There you go again," Tommy screamed. "What you're saying is that we're…like hiding something."

"No," I rushed in, "I'm saying that there may be a part of the story that *you* both don't understand because you don't have all the pieces."

"And you do?'

"No. Not yet."

"But Danny…"

"Tommy, the phone call from Danny was meant to scare you. He's pissed off at me, and he wants *everyone* pissed off at me."

"It worked." From Tommy.

"I don't get it." From Cindy.

"Look." Tommy looked first at Hank, then at me. "I wouldn't kill Mom. She was…my Mom. And I wouldn't kill Molly, even though she got on my nerves. This isn't news to us, you know."

Cindy drew her lips into a tight line. "Aunt Molly was a troublemaker."

"You know," Tommy said, "yeah, it was funny how Mom kept *asking* me if I was doing drugs just recently." We all waited. "I told her no." A pause. "You know something? One time she even asked me if Danny did drugs. Opium, no less. Sometimes we joked—you know, okay it's time to relive the Opium Wars again. Shit, who the hell sees opium? I thought that was strange, after all this time, but I figured that was Molly's doing." He sighed. "You know, sometimes like we're all eating together—like when she made *mi ga* on Sunday morning—I see her just staring at me, hard and long. Once, stoned out of my gourd, I told her how good her *mi ga* was, and she smiled at me."

Hank spoke up, "But your mother was getting worried. She'd even put in that call to Detective Smolski."

"I know," Tommy said. "Rick told me. I don't have a clue what that was about."

"What it suggests is that she *did* believe you were back on drugs."

He nodded. "I guess so. Unless—unless she believed me, and was calling *for* Molly. After all, Mom had lots of contact with Smolski back when. She *liked* him. Maybe she was helping Molly deal with Kristen."

"Huh!" Cindy roared, again melodramatically. "Kristen, the drug fiend."

"You don't like her?" I asked.

"What's to like? It's like asking my opinion of an air bubble."

Tommy grinned. "Cindy, that's cold."

"Kristen likes only herself."

"And Danny," Hank added.

Cindy sat up. "I *assumed* that. One dirt bag fucking another."

"Cindy." Tommy put his hand on her wrist. "Stop it."

She stood up and left the room. I could hear her rattling around in the cluttered kitchen, forks and spoons banging against a drawer.

"Your mother was afraid you'd go to jail," I told him. "She didn't understand how insignificant the prep school arrest was."

Cindy came back into the room and sat down.

"Danny talked to your mom shortly before she died," I told them.

"Yeah," Tommy said, "I know. He told me. He was trying to reach me. To change plans."

"He never got you?"

"I was planning on blowing him off anyway. Sometimes when I knew he'd be calling, I turned off my cell. Blocked his texts."

"What did you do together?"

"Not much. Like a couple times a year…you know…go to get a hamburger in his Mercedes and drive around. Maybe stop at Hooters or a strip club."

"Smoking dope?"

"I swear, we never did that together. I didn't want to—with him. It would bum me out."

"He must have been angry that Molly suspected him of giving drugs to Kristen." I looked at Hank.

Tommy answered. "I don't know. I told Danny that Mom *suspected* something, but he said, 'Your mom loves me to death. She won't believe anything bad about me.'"

Cindy echoed, "'Your mom loves me to death.' Sure got that one right."

◇◇◇

Driving back to my place, Hank and I were quiet. The united forces of Cindy and Tommy, two lost siblings on a decrepit sofa, bothered me. And, I think, their blood relative Hank. Finally, he mumbled, "The only comfort I got this afternoon is that Cindy has become Tommy's biggest advocate."

"Loyalty."

"It seems to be a novelty in my family," he said grimly.

My phone rang. "Where are you?" From Liz.

"With Hank, back from Cindy and Tommy's."

"Family reunion?"

"Of course."

"I just got back from Bank of America." Humor in her voice.

"Holding it up?"

"No, just protecting my cherished assets. No, I wanted to take a look at your boy, Danny Trinh."

"Why?"

"My being a world famous Farmington psychologist and all. I asked for information on my statement, an answer I had all along, being a financial whiz. I had to wait until he was free of the swooning women who encircled him like he's the last cupcake at the church bazaar."

"And?"

"Well, I hoped he'd topple the inkwell so I could get hints to his psyche, a la Rorschach—just what do you see, Banker Trinh? A dead rabbit? A coiled snake? But no, all I could manage was a good moment of chitchat."

"And?"

"You keep saying that word with such expectation. *And* I was very taken with him. He's quite the looker. And the way he looked at me, it was clear he liked what he saw." She waited.

"I didn't ask you to date him."

"A smooth talker, he is. Quite the work of art. Those dark brooding looks, Heathcliff meets Saigon. My, my, my. But the line of his female acolytes was bustling behind me, and you know how such women are. Full-force tsunami love. I had to thank him for ending my abysmal ignorance, and he flashed those brilliant ornaments the rest of us simply call teeth."

"Liz, for God's sake. Isn't there a car wash nearby you can walk through?" She laughed. "So what do you think?"

"I think that Danny could get a woman to do almost anything he wants."

"I hope you're not one of them."

"Alas, no." She sighed melodramatically. "I was once married to a good-looking guy. Hot actually. I've forgotten his name though. Sounded foreign. He had one of those smiles, too. Made a simple city girl like me dizzy. But that was a long time ago, in a faraway kingdom by the Rivers Hudson and East. That girl is no more. Once, to disappoint Jacqueline Susann, is definitely enough."

When I hung up the phone, I found myself smiling.

Chapter Twenty-nine

Jon Torcelli had moved back into his apartment in New Haven, getting ready for Yale grad school. When he answered the door, he didn't seem surprised to see Hank and me. This was not exactly typical student housing, I realized, one of those familiar, tumbledown apartments that looked used and thrown together, no matter how hard the new tenants tried to decorate it. True, it was a second-floor walk-up on Chapel Street, near the art gallery, but these rooms were nicely furnished, very tasteful, I thought, some cookie-cutter assembly out of *Architectural Digest*. He may have moved in the day before, but there wasn't a cardboard box in sight.

"It doesn't look like you just moved in."

"Yes and no. Yes, I moved in yesterday. No, because I've had this apartment since undergrad school and never gave it up." His hand swept the room. "This is my real world. My music, my games, my books, my sofa. My world."

"Why do you go home during the summer?"

"I go back and forth. But my mother insisted I come home for the summer. Be part of the family, dysfunctional though it might be."

"And your father pays for this apartment?"

He smiled. "Why do you think I have to spend time at home? But when Mom was alive, we talked. I *was* happy to talk to her. Dad never came home until late. Mom got lonely. And Kristen is, well, not that good at conversation."

Inside the living room we sat on IKEA furniture, and sipped iced tea in the ice-cold room. "I like it cold." He smiled. "I'm not paying for it."

"Great apartment."

"Women like it."

Hank probed, "You got a girlfriend?"

"Is that why Batman and his Robin have flown down I-91? To question my sexuality?"

"No," I said, "but I want to ask you some questions."

"About what? I don't know a fucking thing."

"We were talking to Cindy and Tommy yesterday, and the talk was all about Danny—and drugs." His eyebrows went up in a here-we-go-again look. "I wanted to hear what you have to say about that."

"About drugs?"

"Well, it seems to have been a big deal with your Mom and your aunt."

"Big deal? They were *consumed* by it. I always assumed the tale of the cousin's opium death was the only Vietnamese folk tale carried over on the plane."

"But why lately?"

He shrugged his shoulders. "I really think it's generational— and a little ethnic maybe. Old school. Fresh off the boat. I don't know. They watch too much TV maybe. A hundred years ago Nancy Reagan was their homeland security goddess."

"You're being flippant."

"It's what I like doing."

"It's a way of avoiding answering questions."

"Or, in fact, answering those questions in an interesting manner."

"What does that mean?" From Hank.

Jon looked at him. "Figure it out. You're a college grad. You went to that bastion of intellectuality called Farmington College."

Hank shut up, but I could see he was fuming.

I went on. "In their last days, Molly and Mary were afraid Tommy and Danny were back to using."

"*Back*? Like they ever left?"

"But they didn't know that. They were in the dark for years."

"But what's the big deal? It was nickel-and-dime level pot. They weren't importing brick kilos from Colombia, for heaven's sake."

"But how did it come up?" I asked.

"What come up?"

"How did drugs suddenly become an obsession with the sisters?"

"How am I supposed to know?"

I leaned in. "Frankly, I think you're the one who started to poison the well. You poisoned your mother against Danny..."

"That happened years back."

"But you made it a big deal now, to use your words."

"Bullshit."

"Did your mother tell you she found a joint in Kristen's room?"

He waited a second. "Actually, yes."

"And what did you tell her?"

He laughed. "She thought Kristen was a goddamned drug addict. Because of one joint."

"And what did you tell her?"

"I told her Danny gave it to her. How could I resist the moment?"

"Why connect Danny with drugs in your mother's mind?"

"Well, the idea was already there from years back. And Asians, like elephants, have long and simple memories. It was the perfect opportunity to, well, *campaign* against Danny, my nemesis. The other dark meat. One afternoon he was sitting in the driveway, waiting for Susie to come out. He picked her up on days she worked late. He was on his cell phone, yapping away, and I think I surprised him, coming around the side. Danny was saying something about profit or percentage or some banker lingo, but he jumped when he saw me, hung up the phone, and looked guilty. I chided him, 'You breaking some federal laws?' He didn't laugh. So I thought—wouldn't it be nice to get him in trouble?"

"But you didn't."

"He's too squeaky clean, that puppy, let me tell you. But then I bumped into Kristen inside, and she's all a-titter, with that giddy I've-been-fucked glow, and I think she's just made it with Lover Man, probably in the back seat of the Mercedes. Real classy."

"Where are you going with this?" Hank asked.

"She was high, giggly and stupid, and I followed her into the kitchen and asked her. She never said no, but when she went to the bathroom I looked through her purse and found that joint."

"*You* found it?" Hank asked.

"True confessions, I'm afraid."

I understood. "And you planted it where your mother could…"

"Horribly, painfully, dramatically, mournfully—find it! Voila!"

"And that's how you got the ball rolling."

"I'm good." He sat back, smug.

"A little evil," Hank said.

"It wasn't like I was making anything up." Jon locked eyes with me. "I started to tell Dad that Danny was feeding Kristen drugs, but I got no further than, 'Hello, Dad.' We don't talk much. He looks right through me, in fact. I *am* the other son. So I knew he couldn't be shaken from his ivory-tower view of Danny. But Mom was a different story. She went nuts finding the joint. I told her Danny was to blame, and all hell broke out."

"She called Mary."

"To warn her to look out for Tommy. To watch Tommy *and* Danny. To check for needle tracks in the arms, for excessive sweating, for hallucinations, for whatever. Unfortunately it got back to Danny."

"How do you know that?"

"I heard him protesting his innocence to his mother and Dad in the kitchen, My mother blamed him, and so Dad asked him. Danny lied, saying Kristen got the pot from Tommy. Tommy! I'm sure Daddy told Mommy who then told Mary, who then started a twenty-four-seven surveillance on poor Tommy."

"You knew it would get back to Mary."

"Hell, Mary was a busybody, crazy in her own simple way. I knew she'd fuck up Danny."

"But it backfired, didn't it?" Hank said.

"Sort of. Mary flipped out, Mom flipped out, Tommy got blamed, and Danny, as usual, gets off like a knight in shining armor. Dad actually told me how *heroic*—that was his word—Danny was, trying to straighten things out. I almost hit him."

"Who? Your dad?"

"Actually either one would do," he said. "So now you know. I was the joint-bearer in this medieval chanson."

"All because you don't like Danny."

His voice hardened. "Dad was talking of bringing him into some family business. That's a no no."

"And your father doesn't want you to be a part of the business."

"Dad prefers that I smile and keep out of the way. I don't really *like* the man. Mom—she I liked. Well…loved."

"But the incident of the joint blew over, no?"

"Unfortunately."

I caught his eye. "So you must have done something…"

He held up his hand. "Clever, you are. A few words in Mom's ear—like 'Search her room!' It did wonders. It seems Kristen squirreled away an envelope of stolen joy—doubtless taken from Lover Boy Danny. Mom lost it—ran to me. Wept out of control. I had to calm her down. 'I'll talk to Kristen,' I promised her." He laughed. "I actually said to Mom, 'Kristen may already be an addict. Check her Facebook, her e-mails.' But that went nowhere with Mom, of course. And then I mentioned Danny. Inspired. Truly inspired."

"Fiendish." From Hank.

"It is what it is." He shrugged. "She ran to call Mary. Another day of opium nightmares."

"Did she tell your father?"

"I don't know."

I leaned back, watching him, realizing he was a little bit nervous. A line of sweat beaded on his forehead.

"What do you remember the night of Mary's murder?" I asked.

"Why?"

"Humor me."

"Well, I wasn't home that afternoon. In fact, I was in this apartment, but I drove home later. I called to see if there was going to be dinner, but no one answered. I got back about seven, and the house was empty. Later on I heard Mom's car in the driveway. Anyway, she comes flying in, and she's rattled. I asked her where she'd been, and she said she got lost at West Farms Mall. Okay, I said, what does that mean? She kept saying, 'I was rushing around because I was late.' For some reason, she blamed it on Kristen. Anyway, I'm trying to talk to her, and she wants to know if I want dinner." Jon paused. "You know what she said? 'I've been to the mall a thousand times, and I got lost.' She went on and on, and I walked away."

"Why?" I asked.

"I went to watch the news on the set in the kitchen. And she came into the kitchen and started taking stuff out of the freezer."

"What did she say?"

"'I hate making mistakes,' she said. I remember that. 'I was late.' Then she looked nervous. 'Has Kristen come back yet? Just like her to mix things up.' I remember because I said Kristen wasn't home and asked *what* was typical. 'She's spacey. I'm worried about her,' she said. I figured it had to do with the drug nonsense…you know, tracking her down."

"And then?"

"And then the two of us made dinner together. I poured her a glass of wine and she relaxed. When I was clearing the dishes, I noticed her reading a slip of paper she took from her pocket."

"What did it say?"

"I didn't pay attention. She tore it up into little bits and threw them into the trash."

"She didn't add anything?"

She said she needed a good social secretary. And she laughed. 'I ended up in the wrong place. So I came home.' She said she wasted her time."

"That's it."

"I was on my computer and heard the phone ring. The news that Aunt Mary was dead. And Mom collapsed in my arms. And that took care of the rest of that evening."

Chapter Thirty

"What was Molly late for?" I said to Hank as we drove back to Farmington.

"She was going somewhere at the mall. Some store? Maybe to meet someone? Kristen, perhaps. She'd written down an address, but she was late."

"But could Molly going to the mall have anything to do with Mary's murder?"

"Well," Hank said, "it got her out of the house."

I dialed the Torcelli home. No answer. I reached for a folder on the back seat. "Hank," I slid him the folder, "look up Susie's home number."

Susie, it turned out, was home, her day off. Her voice was cool and guarded. "What do you want?"

I mentioned how Molly had gone to the mall the day Mary was murdered. She seemed to have an appointment, but somehow things got mixed up.

"Yes," Susie said. "I remember. She told me the next day. She was running late, and then she blamed herself for going to the wrong place."

"Where was she going?"

"She'd gone to pick up Kristen somewhere, then do some shopping for a dress, but they got their signals crossed. Miss Molly went to the wrong place, I think. Or, I don't know, she was late. I can't remember."

I thanked her and hung up. "She was going to pick up Kristen, but..."

The phone rang, Jimmy calling.

"I got the stuff I promised you. I got financial information. The money-talks information. I don't know if it means anything, but you gotta hear it."

I told him that Hank and I were headed back to the area, planning to meet Liz for lunch in West Hartford center, at the Blue Back Café. He could join us.

"Isn't that place pricey?"

"I'll treat."

"You better."

Hank spoke when I hung up the phone. "What if that note Molly tore up was *left* for her? What if she didn't write it herself?"

I nodded. "That's a possibility. There may have been wrong information on that note."

"And she tore it up."

"In frustration."

Hank and I sat on the roof garden of the Blue Back Café, tucked under spacious, cooling umbrellas and munching on bread sticks. We stared down at the sidewalk shoppers. Liz arrived, and then Jimmy, who wasn't happy. "I don't like eating outdoors."

"And why is that?" Liz asked.

"Reminds me of Vietnam. In battle, in trenches, flies all over you, bullets whizzing, wet food, dysentery."

Hank grunted, "They don't allow flies in West Hartford."

Jimmy glared. "No, just pests."

Hank and I summed up our conversations with Tommy and Cindy and earlier that morning with Jon. I told Jimmy, "Liz went to Bank of America to look at Danny."

"He's gorgeous." She fanned herself.

Jimmy frowned. "Studies have shown that women never believe a man is guilty of anything if he's good looking."

"Makes sense to me," Liz agreed. "If you're good looking, you don't need to commit a crime."

"Hey," Jimmy grunted. "I'm wasting my time here. Sex has nothing to do with this case. I came with information."

While the waiter hovered and we gave our sandwich orders, Jimmy pulled out a wrinkled stack of sheets from his back pocket. Jimmy believed in taking notes the old-fashioned way, sitting in the business section of the Hartford Public Library, hours at a time, digesting year-end reports, news clippings, sheets of statistics, stock indices. In the process he'd made enviable contacts in metropolitan Hartford over the years, a man whom people gladly talked to. I can whiz through computer search engines, but Jimmy can still find stuff I miss. His practiced eye can sift through pages and pages of aimless jargon and corporate dreck, culling the nugget of wisdom buried deep inside.

We waited, sipping sodas, while he took his sweet time, organizing the papers. Jimmy had to perform on his own stage with his own rhythm.

"I checked whatever financial histories I could find, believing, as I do, that money…"

I interrupted. "Is the source of all crime."

He smiled. "You learn well. Anyway, I had to call in a few favors because some of this ain't public information. It helps to know people."

"So you're saying you got this information illegally," Hank wondered.

Jimmy ignored him, clearing his throat.

"First of all, the life and financial times of Benny and Mary Vu. The store barely makes a living, just enough to pay the mortgage on the little house in East Hartford. But the guy knows how to stretch a buck, let me tell you. I think they live on rice and more rice. Anyway, there's no money there. Even the cars are old and clunky. Except a year back or so Benny deposited ten grand into his saving account, and pretty quickly used it to pay overdue bills, get a little ahead in the mortgage, that sort of thing."

"Ten thousand in one payment?" I asked.

Jimmy smiled. "That took a little probing. It turns out he won it at the Indian casino at Mohegan Sun. He plays blackjack and, according to my sources, is real lousy. Make a hundred here, lose a hundred, lose another hundred, and lose another hundred. Lots of the debt he has is due to losing at the casino. But he hit it big one night—you gotta sign papers if you win over ten grand—and he came home with piles of wampum."

"Did Mary gamble?" Liz asked.

"Dunno, but she was there that night. They both claimed the money."

"Any left?"

"Not much. Used a buck to bury Mary, I'm afraid. The rest went to house taxes, that stuff. Right now he's clear—no big bills. That won't last long."

"Why not?" I asked.

"Because he can't stay away from the gaming halls."

"How about the kids?"

"Cindy and Tommy? Pittance, low rollers through life. Working at this half-assed job and that. Minimum wage kids. Tommy probably siphoning a few extra bucks from daddy's till but there's not that much to siphon off. Cindy lives at home but seems to hide in her room, I guess. He lives with two buddies in Elmwood and the rent is dirt cheap. They got enough to buy cigarettes, CDs, and condoms. The essentials."

I laughed. "Wasn't that an FDR New Deal project? CCC?"

"FDR wouldn't put up with this shit."

"What shit?"

"Like eating on a roof in the middle of August." He sighed. "A good man, that FDR." But he kept going. "Neither kid has ever come close to a savings account."

The waiter placed platters of sandwiches on the table, and for a few minutes we ate, giving our attention to the food. Jimmy nodded his approval and signaled the waiter for another soda. "Not bad for expensive bread with a slice of bologna inside." He was smiling.

"And then," I said dramatically, putting down my sandwich, "we go to the other end of the world, the Torcelli money."

"Big, big money," Jimmy roared, smiling. "The kind of money people would *kill* for."

"Uh oh." Liz in a stage whisper. "Editorializing from Jimmy."

"I'm just presenting the facts," he explained. "Larry Torcelli inherited his motorized empire from his father, who made the first money. It seems his father, however, was brighter and swifter when it came to bucks. Over the years Larry has had a rush of dips in his fortune, almost declaring bankruptcy many, many years back. The problem has to do with ambition. He keeps expanding the empire. His dad left two dealerships, and millions. Larry now has five. The last one—in Greenwich—was added two years back. What I'm saying is he has constant cash flow problems, but he has no trouble getting backing, elsewhere. He's *stable*."

"Stable?" I asked.

"The business community sees him as a rock."

"Despite the fluctuations?"

"You know, even Donald Trump sinks and then rises. That is, part of the empire goes bust, then he recoups."

"And the last dip?"

"Well, the new dealership required megabucks. It's Greenwich, the Gold Coast. So he throws a lot of cash into it, and then the economy tanks, the stock market starts to slip, and he can't pay creditors. He wasn't worried, but he had to shuffle funds around."

"Where are you going with this?"

Jimmy fidgeted. "Don't be impatient. All I'm saying is that Larry likes to take chances. He's a little like Benny, in some way, a gambler. And when you're a gambler in the business world, you can get yourself in trouble. Last year he came close to the edge."

"But he's okay now?" Hank asked.

"Now the Ferris wheel is on the rise again. Lots of money. The place in Greenwich is solvent. He actually has *more* money than before. *That* gamble paid off."

"Sounds about right." From Hank.

"Things are good. Molly and Larry bought a cottage in Stonington, right on the water, in sight of Fort Trumbull."

"That's pricey," said Liz.

"That's four mil." Jimmy held up four fingers. "It's a rich man's cottage. At one point they even thought of buying Katherine Hepburn's old estate at Fenwick, but Molly balked. Too much repair needed, she said."

"I'd buy it for the memories." From Liz.

"The kids?"

"Kristen has a savings account, no checking. Not much. Jon has both, and plenty of money when he turns thirty—a trust fund from his grandfather when the old man died, earmarked for number one son. Kristen didn't get any."

"And what about Danny and Susie?"

"Susie has the house, in her son's name by the way, and modest savings. Torcelli pays her well. A little too much, but she has been with the family for years. Danny is interesting. No college debt, since the scholarship and Larry covered that. His job at the bank is fast track to big money, but he's new at it, young. A decent salary. Larry gave him an allowance through school. But his savings account is pretty average, maybe a little above average. The only problem is that he occasionally drops in lump sums of a thousand or so into it. I can't find out where the money is coming from. Not big change, to be sure, but sort of regular, and odd."

"Embezzling from the bank?" From Hank

"Not likely. He's real careful at the bank."

"So everything is what it's supposed to be?"

"At least on the surface," Jimmy said.

"Let me ask you this," I jumped in. "What bank handles the Torcelli moneys, personal and business?"

"Bank of America," Jimmy said. And then, with a smile, "I was saving that piece of news for last. Guess who's in charge of those massive accounts?"

"Danny!" I hit my fist on the table.

"Bingo. It's a little unusual, but maybe not. Someone on Danny's level would never handle such large accounts, but Larry requested Danny, and so of course the bank agreed. Had to, given Larry's power, though Danny has a senior mentor who reviews *every* transaction to avoid problems. Larry trusts Danny."

"Does the bank like that?"

"The last audit showed not a single problem. In fact, Danny was commended for thoroughness of his dealings with Larry's money."

"Well, where does this leave us?"

"But I think," Jimmy talked over me, "that Danny is calling some of the shots—or at least feeding Larry advice. Larry is director of an operation called AsiaAuto Investments, part of some larger corporation called AsiaConcepts Enterprises. And it was Danny who did the research on it, putting together a prospectus. With Larry's connections in the automotive world and his history and knowledge of the industry, it seemed a sure investment."

"What's it all about?"

"Well," said Jimmy, "best I can figure out is that AsiaConcepts is a kind of broker. You know, many U.S. corporations are exporting electronic trash to China because it's easier to unload it there than deal with the chemicals, toxins, you name it."

"Yeah," Hank was nodding, "I read how some Chinese cities are ringed by huge heaps of American appliances, electronics, and stuff. Corporations pay China to accept untreated trash, and the Chinese see it as a way of getting scrap metal cheaply, a source of raw material."

"But," said Jimmy, "the broken TVs, monitors, keyboards, traveling by way of Hong Kong, are ruining the health of Chinese children, respiratory problems, and so on."

"And AsiaConcepts does what?" From Liz.

"Some big corporations handle their own deals, but lately some small industries, burdened by U.S. environmental laws, want to get rid of trash, but they're small potatoes. AsiaConcepts brokers it, deals with the politicos in China, arranges delivery, and pockets a hefty percentage."

"Sounds like a good deal, if ethically questionable," I said. "But what does AsiaConcepts have to do with Larry?"

"Nothing, really," Jimmy said.

"So?"

"But AsiaConcepts has diversified. You know, China has one-fifth of the world population, with an economy growing at ten percent a year. They're coming into their own with electronics, even automobiles. Since they've become part of the World Trade Organization, they're blossoming. It's a foreign investor's dream. World Bank. Asian Development Bank. They want to be a player on the world scene but are plagued by acid rain and coal-backed pollution. They recycle little, creating trash heaps of their own—plastics, glass, metal.

"So Larry comes into this how?" I asked.

"China wants to be a leader in automobile manufacture. Already they're third, behind America and Japan. Cars are everywhere. China has decided to make car manufacturing one of its four pillars of development. They're getting ready to create a car that will be exported worldwide—even to the U.S., rivaling, eventually, Japan."

"That seems farfetched." From Hank.

"No, not really. They got the push behind them."

"And Larry?" I repeated.

Jimmy smiled. "So AsiaConcepts created a division called AsiaAuto Investments, an offshoot managed by Larry, who, with his knowledge of the industry, is perfect. Like the parent company, small-time investors, especially Larry's auto-world friends, can pool investment monies—fifty grand, even up to a half million maybe—and AsiaAuto uses the money to help develop China's car culture. Long-range hopes of a big payoff."

"So how does it work?" Liz asked.

"Investors provide the capital, Larry coordinates it, works with AsiaConcepts so that China manufacturers become partners with hundreds of small U.S. investors."

"How does Larry make money?"

"Like an agent's fee. He takes a percentage off the top, and the rest goes to AsiaConcepts with it international connections via trash dumping. Real clever. There are other subsidiaries in the mix from AsiaConcepts—pharmaceuticals, for one. But Larry was the natural to lead the car deal. He stands to make a fortune."

"He's already making money from it."

"Nothing like what he might make down the road."

"But how does Danny fit into all this?" I asked.

"On the books he's just the banker. Larry's Motorworks, licensed, does the nuts and bolts, handling the invested capital. The money is deposited in a designated Bank of America account. Danny oversees it."

"Okay," I said, "that sounds legit."

"Well," Jimmy continued, grinning, "that's where the detective part of me comes into play. You see, I did some research on AsiaAuto and AsiaConcepts, and it's a company owned by a young guy named Jack Williamson, whose cousin, by the way, is the NASCAR great that bought lunch in a crash five years back. Anyway, young Williamson, another rich pretty boy, was Danny's roommate at Harvard. I guess his daddy set him up."

"So you're saying…"

"I'm guessing that Danny brought Larry into AsiaAuto because they needed a credible automobile man, and Danny probably gets a little bit of the cut off the top."

"The one thousand smackeroos appearing in his savings account," I concluded.

"Like a finder's fee," Jimmy said,

I was nodding. "So everyone makes out. Danny and Larry helping each other out. Even if it's illegal. Maybe. I mean, Danny's not a licensed broker, right?"

"Probably not illegal, as it turns out. Business expense. Maybe a little unethical, Danny being the banker and all. But Larry can handle his profits any way he wants—feed money to Danny."

"Okay," I added, "maybe not illegal, but maybe a gray area."

Jimmy smiled broadly. "Shady dealings."

"I wonder," I said.

"But it's like a good father-and-son team," Hank said.

"You laugh." Jimmy made a harrumph sound. "Everybody in the world is getting rich but us." He narrowed his eyes. "Larry is raking it in. There is so much money here, I believe Danny has to be making more than the occasional thousand here and there."

"You think he's stashing it in a hidden account?"

"Gotta be the case," Jimmy said. "He'd know how to do that."

"Why would he do it?"

"It's *his* baby, in some way. Larry's already rich, and getting richer. Danny's got to be demanding a bigger chunk of the pie."

"But would he risk it?"

"The operation is *legit*," Jimmy insisted. "Who the hell pays attention to ethics these days?"

At that moment the check was placed on the table, and Jimmy reached for it. "Holy shit," he bellowed. "For lunch? Thank God Rick's paying."

I waved a credit card. "Someday, Jimmy, you might quality for one of these."

"Then I might have to pay for lunch."

I was intrigued by AsiaAuto Investments.

Something was bothering me, but I didn't know what. I ran through the morning talk with Jon and through the rambling conversation at lunch. Nothing. I was thinking about our tossing around the words *illegal* and *unethical* to characterize the "alleged" skimming of profits into Danny's bank account. And a secret bank account? Probably. So what? I thought. It *was* his baby. That was business as usual. Danny initiated the deal. His Harvard buddy's company.

Restless, I hopped in my car, as I always did when the ideas in my head sifted and whirled out of control. I drove through hot sticky streets. I ended up in East Hartford, pulling into the driveway of Hank's house. When you're lost, you go looking for family. Hank, I knew, had a date with a girl he'd met at, of all places, a CVS Pharmacy. They were going to get burgers and ice cream at Shady Glen in Manchester, a little mooncalf wooing over cheeseburgers. I had hoped he'd be back early, but his car wasn't parked in front.

Nobody was home but Grandma, my favorite, and Grandpa, leader of the opposition forces. Luckily Grandpa spotted me at the door, belched loudly, and disappeared with a can of Budweiser and a TV guide. Grandma, patting me on the wrist, made me sit down at the kitchen table.

"Hank's not home."

"I know. He met a new girl."

She clicked her tongue. "Last week a girl from North Vietnam, and his father loses his mind. This week a different girl. But how can American boys meet girls at a place where you fill your prescriptions and buy shampoo? We want to send him back to Vietnam to meet the daughter of old friends."

I smiled. "What does Hank say about that?"

She smiled back at me. "You know the answer to that."

I could imagine Hank's face when he heard that news. A mail-order bride who'd do nothing but serve him.

Of course, Grandma insisted on feeding me, whipping up some diced chicken with ginger slices, served over rice. *Ga kho gung.* I hadn't eaten and now, acutely aware of my hunger, I attacked the food.

"You need a wife to feed you," she told me gently.

"Maybe you should send me back to Vietnam to find a bride."

But it wasn't proper for me to say those words to her, so she didn't laugh. A *bui doi* like me, with my white American blood, would not be considered a worthy husband for any pureblood Vietnamese girl. Now, as much as Grandma loved and doted on me, she understood that, in a faraway world that she no longer approved of, I was mongrel, unfit.

"It's weeks now since Molly died," she began, sitting across from me. "And Mary died. The end of the beautiful Le sisters."

I got melancholy. "God, I haven't thought of that phrase for a while. The beautiful Le sisters."

"And they were beautiful. They died beautiful. They would have been beautiful old women."

"Like you," I said without thinking, and she shook her head.

"You flatter me when you don't have to."

I nodded, a little embarrassed.

"Hank fills me in on what's happening. The talks with family, this conversation and that. I never knew—nor wanted to know—the angers and jealousies these four children have toward each other." She sighed. "American children lose balance." She searched for words. "*Binh quan*," she said finally. "Maybe that is what I mean. Everything evens out." She looked into my face. "It would be hard for Buddha to visit America." She smiled. "Americans reject pain. They think they can pay it to go away, not understanding it is *in* us. Suffering is necessary. The First Noble Truth. You know that. It comes from being hungry for the things of this world, and, for some of us, things are all that matter. So, of course, the pain can't go away. Desire, want, grasping to hold onto things that have to change. Nirvana? It's an impossibility."

"The kids only seem to have this world."

"And so they have nothing. Families at each other's throats."

"Maybe it's because their worlds are divided so dramatically between rich and poor."

She thought for a moment. "Holding onto money lets you hold onto nothing."

"My partner Jimmy says money is the answer to these murders. To most murders."

She sighed. "Yes, money is what everyone fights for, but I think there are stronger motives for murder."

"In this case?"

"In *any* case. Money is concrete. People kill for love—because of an idea. Money may be involved but it's the passion *behind* it—behind everything—that makes someone pick up a knife or a gun."

Passion, I thought, *ai tinh*. What kind of passion?

"One family here has a lot of money."

"And the other none. They're both halves of the same coin, as you know. One and the same. And so everyone thinks everything is off balance, out of kilter. But you know as well as I do, Rick, that the extremes of poor and rich are balanced, an awful balance."

"An unhealthy balance."

"Not unhealthy. Just what it is. Everything tries to find a balance that's already there. It's that people refuse to see it, this balance. So the money is a thing that some hunger for, others try to hold onto what they have, others want more and more of it. That's all a game. Each of these people looks into a mirror and sees unhappiness."

"But it can lead to murder."

"Look beyond the money. What do you see?"

"A love of money." I was a little too flippant.

"You're right. But that doesn't explain anything here, does it? Otherwise you'd have the answers. We already *know* that these people—rich and poor—love or crave or lack money. But that knowledge hasn't helped you find the murderer."

"So what are you saying?"

"I'm saying that you're looking at the wrong kind of love. Yes, there is a love of money, and it may have killed the beautiful Le sisters. Somebody was trying to guard some money. Maybe. But *that* love doesn't tell the story."

"What does?"

"Stop looking at the money. Start asking yourself what other kinds of love are there, love that has nothing to do with money. You identify *that* love, and you will know what happened to Mary and Molly."

Chapter Thirty-one

Grandma's words got me thinking, and I was up through the night, back and forth to the computer, to my note cards, to my diagrams. My mind raced: love love love. Snatches of popular tunes swirled in my head, an unwelcome hum. *Love makes me do foolish things…love love love…love the one you're with…tell me that you love me…love to love you, baby…baby love…*Madness, all of it. I wanted to call Hank but it was four in the morning. Grandma, "Rick, stop thinking of money."

But I couldn't stop thinking about money. I couldn't. I was bothered by Danny's possible skimming a thousand here and there, most likely from AsiaAuto transactions. Was that the first crack in the golden bowl these people swam in?

Get away from the money, Grandma said. Impossible. But I did, drawing lists on a piece of paper. Two categories: Money-driven love versus other-driven love. The first list went on and on: Larry, Molly, Danny, even Jon, possibly Benny and Mary. And, at five in the morning, I only had one name in column B. Just one name. One name alone.

At nine o'clock in the morning I made phone calls. First I had to deal with the money side of the ledger. Pulling out an old day runner, I flipped the pages until I found the name I was looking for: Harry Jacobi, an erstwhile buddy of mine at Columbia, later an Assistant DA, and then a short-term commissioner of some sort in the Giuliani administration. We'd kept in touch, mainly less than more, over the years. After his messy divorce from a Broadway actress more famous for a TV commercial about some aloe vera cream than for her histrionics, he disappeared. But we always knew where the other was. I'm not sure why.

I caught him at home, where he now worked. He'd invested in dot-com properties, bailed out just in time, and was now free to do, as he said, "whatever the fuck I want to." That sounded like him. We chatted for a while, and I told him about the case, and what I needed from him.

He got excited. "I've been so bored. I sit here counting money. This'll give me lots to do. I'll get back to you. Soon." I thanked him.

Then I called Detective Ardolino, left a message, and he got right back to me. I told him a few of my suspicions, to which he made no comment other than his noncommittal but emphatic grunt—and I backed it up with what Grandma had said. I could almost *hear* his eyebrows rise on the other end. Here I was taking advice from an old Vietnamese woman, who had perhaps twenty words of serviceable English at her command, and now, based on that, I wanted his help.

"Think of it. Stop thinking about the money and think of love. Who in this cast of characters seems to be dealing purely out of love—vain, almost juvenile love maybe, but still love?"

"I don't have an answer."

I told him the name that had popped into my head as I composed my lists last night: "Kristen Torcelli."

"The dingbat girl?"

"Everything she, Danny, and the others have said points to one thing—she has a wicked crush on Danny. I think she thinks she's in love with him."

"That ain't love."

"Well, it certainly comes close."

"I dunno…"

"And she had something to do with her mother getting lost at the mall."

"How do you know?"

"I feel it."

"Asian voodoo?"

I smiled. "Probably."

He finally conceded I might have a point. But I wanted the two of us to sit down with Kristen, just her alone. Not with Hank, her relative. Not only with me, the friend of the family. But with the authority of a detective, the two of us, not bad cop-good cop to be sure, but enough of a presence to have a real conversation with her. And given her limited intelligence, such iconic authority might do the trick.

"What trick?" Detective Ardolino asked.

"Follow my lead."

"I can't have a private citizen in on my interrogations, even though you're a PI. A little unorthodox. Got to clear this with superiors."

"A conversation."

"A conversation," he echoed.

By noon Kristen was sitting in a small room at a Hartford police substation. When Ardolino asked if she wanted a lawyer, she blinked a bunch of times, then said, "Why? Am I being arrested?" No, she was told, just questioned. "I didn't do anything. Okay?" Did she want to call her father at his dealership? "Oh, God, no. He'll only yell or something. He *can't* know I'm here."

So she sat in the conference room, ill at ease but oddly happy, smiling her thanks for the diet Coke someone brought her. Dressed in shorts, sandals, and a pink lipstick that matched her nails and the necklace she wore, she looked ready to join friends at the beach. Which, in fact, she was.

"Is this gonna take long? I'm gonna be late."

"Kristen," I spoke into her smiling face, "we wanted to talk privately with you because we need to get some answers from you."

"Sure. Go ahead."

"Is it possible Danny killed your mother?" I threw the line out so fast she actually sputtered and spat out soda.

"Are you crazy?" She looked from me to Ardolino. "Is this a joke?"

"I'm just asking."

Ardolino added, "Your mother didn't like him."

She got serious, and for a second I saw panic in her eyes. "Danny wouldn't hurt a fly. Okay, Mom didn't care for him…"

"Why?" I asked.

She got quiet, looked away. "It goes back a long way. I don't know."

"Back to prep school and Tommy and the drug arrest?"

She blurted out, "Yeah, that, too."

"What else?" Ardolino asked.

"She didn't like him."

"You said that," I stressed. "Why?"

She half-rose from her chair. She looked toward the door as though she wanted to flee. "I don't know where you're going with this murder crap. Danny is loving and sweet…."

"You love him, don't you?" I rushed my words.

Tears started in the corners of her eyes. Makeup caked, got blotchy. She dabbed at her eyelids. "He loves me."

"You're a couple?"

"We sort of are." She was smiling.

"Sort of?" From Ardolino.

"Well, it's a secret, so far. No one knows. Danny said we gotta keep it under wraps. For now."

"Why?"

"Mom would have *killed* me. Even my Dad."

"Your father loves Danny."

"But he doesn't want me to date him."

"He's told you that?"

"Years ago." She sighed. "Well, you know, Danny used to be sort of a player. Liked to, you know, *brag* about girls. He used to brag about girls to Dad—to impress him. Well, Dad gave *me* a lecture about Danny and sex. That was years ago. I promised never never never to go out with him *that way*. You know. Danny, he said, was—he called him a cad. Said he'd only bring a girl misery and unhappiness. He'd use me, Dad said."

"But back in school you did sleep with him?"

She blushed. "God no! Danny was too afraid of Daddy then. Daddy was paying for school."

"But what happened?"

A smile, oddly beatific, flashed across her face. "You know, after a while it never was a thing to think about. You know. Then last year, Danny gave me a ride somewhere, and then I'm at his apartment in Hartford somewhere where he hangs out, I guess, and we made love." She closed her eyes a second. "It feels funny talking about it."

"Why?"

"It's a secret. Danny said it's *our* secret."

"So you see him a lot?"

"Now and then. He'd like to take me to the movies and dinner, like a real date, but, you know, we *can't*."

"So you just put out for him?" Ardolino threw out bluntly.

"Put out?" She looked ready to cry.

"Yours is mainly a sexual relationship?" I softened my tone.

"No, we love each other. He's the man I want to marry."

"How are you gonna marry the dude," Ardolino said, "if he can't take you out in public? You're forgetting your father."

"Once Danny is solid at the bank and has tons of money, then we'll tell Dad he wants to marry me. He'll *want* to settle *down*." She emphasized the words.

"He told you this?"

"Yes."

"He loves you."

"Yes." But the second *yes* was tentative, a little uncertain. She looked around, confused. "He wouldn't lie to me."

I looked at Ardolino. He was shaking his head. I could read his mind: lowlife Danny using this sad girl.

"Wasn't Danny afraid you'd get caught?"

She frowned. "My mother started to suspect, I think. She made remarks. Mom, you know, was afraid of him. She told me Danny has this mean streak. She said she'd seen it, but I never did. I didn't believe her. Look at him—Harvard, model looks,

killer body"—She stopped. "He loves me, that's all." She stated
it as a fact.

"Did your mother say anything to your father?"

"I think she said something but Dad never listens. It was
because she found a joint in my room."

"From Danny?"

"Yeah, we smoked. He likes to smoke when we, you know,
do it. Says it brings him—joy. He gets crazy, like. But I took
the joint from him even though he told me never never never
smoke without him. I took it from his case. I hid it. She went
snooping. I don't know *why* I took it."

"But you're not telling us something, Kristen. Because of that
one joint, your mother searched your room, no? She found an
envelope of…"

She held up her hand, her face flushed. "Oh God, you know
that? Mom yelled at me. I made her promise not to tell Dad.
I said it was a mistake. I was holding the stuff for someone. I
begged her. Dad would kill me."

"Did Jon know?"

"Know what?"

"That you had that stash?"

"I think Mom told him. She told him everything. He'd never
say a word. Mom couldn't stop crying."

"She blamed Danny?"

She nodded.

Ardolino jumped in. "So tell me, Kristen, if Danny suspected
your mom of causing trouble, maybe he killed her."

She spoke through her teeth. "I told you. You don't kill someone over *this*. A few joints—not crack or something." A weak
smile. "Danny warned me over and over not to do it, but…"
She shrugged. "Tempting."

"What happened the night your Aunt Mary got killed?" I asked.

"I can't remember." Her voice got belligerent. "I don't know."

"Your mother went out on an errand," I reminded her. "She
had a note. She went to the mall. She was supposed to pick

you up somewhere. She got confused—or lost. She went to the wrong place. What's that all about?"

Kristen fidgeted, bit her lower lip. "I didn't do anything wrong."

"You wrote that note, Kristen. Right?"

"I don't think…"

"Why would you leave that note?"

"You left that note, right?" From Ardolino.

She nodded, sucked in her breath. "I guess so."

"What did it say?" Ardolino asked.

"Well, I said a friend was dropping me off at West Farms Mall, and I didn't have a ride home—my car was in the garage—and could she pick me up in front of Ruby Tuesday's. I told her to call me. Let me know. She left a message on my cell phone and said she would."

"You didn't talk to her?"

"No, I let my machine pick up."

"Why?"

She didn't answer, just shrugged her shoulders. "I didn't want to talk to her, I guess. I don't know. I was busy, maybe."

"But she didn't meet you," I said. "When she got home, she told Jon she must have missed you."

"I got a ride home later and she went apeshit. Wasting her time and crap like that. I must have forgot that I wrote Ruby Tuesday's. I don't know. Then we learned that Mary was dead and she had other things to worry about. She left me alone."

"So you're saying it was a simple mistake?" Ardolino asked.

She nodded. "Mom got it all wrong, I guess."

I'd had enough. "Kristen," I demanded, "tell me the truth. You were never even near the mall. You were with Danny."

"I…why…"

"We can ask him, you know," Ardolino said.

"He'll say no," she said, a little smugly.

"We can find out, you know."

She got flushed. "Why else would I leave that note? I needed a ride." Her voice was tinny, scared.

"Answer me this, Kristen," I went on. "Why did Danny call your Aunt Mary at her home the night she died?"

"Did he?"

"The phone records show he called Tommy's apartment, the store, then Mary's home. Tommy wasn't there. He talked to Mary. They talked for ten minutes."

She started scratching her elbows. She looked toward the door. "I don't know."

"What don't you know?" Ardolino asked.

"Danny didn't call her. He—I think he was with me—at the mall."

"Then why did you need a ride?"

"He had to leave, I think. I…I…"

I leaned into her: "Isn't it possible Danny called, not to talk to Tommy, but to reach Mary herself. To get her to leave and go into Hartford?"

"But why?"

"You tell me."

"Danny couldn't get Aunt Mary to do that. Why would she listen to him? My mom poisoned the way she looked at Danny…"

I leaned in closer. "That's right, Kristen," I said. "Mary would never leave her home to go there. That's preposterous."

"See…I…"

"But she might if *you* were the one making the call from Danny's phone."

She sat there, rigid. Her face trembled, one hand searching for the other, then both hands touching her face. We waited. And waited.

I tapped her wrist. "Kristen, why would you tell Mary to go *there* of all places?"

"I love Danny." She closed her eyes. "He loves me. They were trying to get between us. Mom and Mary. We love each other." She started to cry. "But it has nothing to do with murder. That was an *accident*. We didn't do *that*."

"Tell us what happened. Why did you make that call?"

"Danny told me what to do. I left the note for Mom so she wouldn't be home if Aunt Mary called. I knew Mary never called Mom on her cell phone. Danny said we had to teach them both a lesson."

"What kind of lesson?"

"I'm not sure, but Mary was a troublemaker. She was talking to Mom about Danny on drugs, or something, and me on drugs, and it was all getting crazy. And sooner or later Dad would step in, and I wouldn't be able to marry Danny."

"What did you tell Mary?" Ardolino asked. "When you reached her."

"I told her Mom called me and said she had an accident in Goodwin Square. Mary didn't even know where that was, except that it was a bad neighborhood. Everybody sort of knows that. I told her Mom was going to Little Saigon and took the wrong turn because of the detour there, and now she was struck by someone. There were scary people around and she'd called the police who were slow in coming. So she called me. She couldn't drive her car, I said, but my car was in the garage. Which it was. Nobody was around. Would she pick her up? She said to call my Dad, but I said I couldn't reach him at work and besides he'd be pissed off that she was in that part of town. He'd blame the accident on *her*. I just went on and on until she asked for the address again. I had to tell her how to get there. Mom wanted company there. To help her…wait till the police and tow truck came and…and… you know…Mary said she'd pick up Mom, but she wasn't happy. She said she was tired of being Mom's servant."

"But why get Mary to that corner?" Ardolino asked.

Kristen looked confused. "I don't know. Danny said she was too nosy, asking too many questions about him and drugs. You know, Aunt Mary was a busybody. Danny said she wanted to talk to the *police* about it. Imagine, the *police*."

"What was going to happen to Mary at that corner?"

She stared at me, searching for an answer. "I dunno. Danny said he knew someone who would scare her silly. You know, tell her…"

"That makes no sense, Kristen," I said. "Think about it. She'd call your mother afterwards and find out you were lying, no? She'd learn your mother was never there."

A long silence. "I didn't think of that." But she said the line too quickly. "It was all worked out so that it all made sense."

"And how does scaring her there stop her from messing up your life with Danny?" Ardolino asked.

Another long silence, then she started to cry again. "I don't know…I think…thought…Danny told me it would work. He promised me it would work."

"But Mary got shot and killed," Ardolino said.

She spoke too fast. "Danny wasn't counting on that. He told me it was a mistake. There was a drive-by shooting that happened. She just happened to be there. Danny said drive-by shootings happen there all the time. People get killed there and… nobody pays…attention. One night we were driving and you know how they got that detour off the highway, and *we* ended up there. It was easy to make that mistake."

"Kristen, do you believe what you're telling us?"

"What?"

"That the drive-by was an accident?"

She nodded, but I could see she was faltering. There was a rehearsed quality about some of her lines now. "Danny said these things happen all the time in that neighborhood."

"You expect us to believe this?" Ardolino asked.

A whimper. "Danny said nobody could catch a cab there. No cab stops there. Otherwise Mom would have, you know, called a cab. Mary was, you know, gullible. I kept talking until she said yes."

"What else did she say?"

"She said it was the craziest thing she ever heard of. It was the last time she'd do such a thing.

"And so you went home?'

"Danny dropped me off at the bottom of my driveway, and he went to the gym for a while. I stayed in the yard, like hiding, then went inside. Mom was there. She yelled at me for the stupid note, but then we heard that Mary died and I was too afraid to say anything. I knew it was an accident."

"What did Danny say to you?"

"He called me that night and told me not to say anything because we'd look bad. He told me it was a tragic accident. 'Every week somebody is killed there,' he said. So I couldn't say anything. People would think *we* killed her. The next day he had to drive to New York so he wasn't around."

I looked at Ardolino, and he nodded. "Let's take a break." I told Kristen we'd be back in a second, and she asked for another diet Coke. Watching her through the one-way mirror, I saw a young woman drying her eyes and then reaching into her purse to repair her makeup. It seemed to take all of her attention. She applied fresh lipstick. She smiled into the compact mirror and then snapped it shut. She crossed and uncrossed her legs, looked at the ceiling, and then smiled. "She's probably thinking of Danny," I said.

"Is she this dense for real?" he asked me.

"She's not very bright."

"That's not what I asked. Even dumb people—her own little corner of humankind—know enough not to commit murder or to abet a murderer like Danny."

"Well, you combine a little-girl mentality with a little-girl puppy love infatuation, and tuck her into the Machiavellian folds of a slick operator like Danny, and, sure, she could miss the picture."

"I think she's faking all this."

"Yeah, it's possible." I glanced back at Kristen. I told him what Marcie and Vinnie had said about her days at Chesterton—how she could be manipulative. "She's a little game player. Wily."

"There were moments in there I thought she was aware of what she was saying...."

"That's my point."

I stared back into the room. Kristen was checking her face in a compact. "Danny set her up—or she really knew what was going to happen."

"How could she not, Rick?" he said. "Think about it. She's not *that* dumb." He sighed. "Ready for round two?"

"Wait. Alibis. Obviously you ran the alibis…"

"What little they were. Most were alone or unavailable. But the one solid alibi we have for that night is Danny. That night he was at the gym on New Britain Avenue.'

"For sure?"

"We checked that out. He worked one-on-one with a personal trainer. The whole time."

"How convenient."

"Nobody else has such an airtight alibi." He cleared his throat. "Real convenient."

Chapter Thirty-two

"You want anything?" I asked Kristen when we returned to the room.

She smiled. "I'm okay. Can I go home now?"

"Pretty soon. We appreciate your honesty, Kristen. There are just a few more questions. Thank you for telling us the truth."

"You gonna tell Danny?" She was wide eyed. "I did *promise* him."

"Don't worry about Danny," Ardolino said. "You take care of yourself."

"How?" It seemed a genuine question.

"By telling us the truth," I told her. "When I talked to you before, you never told me this."

She smiled. "I didn't say *anything*. I was quiet."

"Don't be quiet now." Ardolino smiled at her.

I looked at her. "We think that Danny killed your Aunt Mary."

She screamed. "No." Her voice broke.

"Tell us," Ardolino said.

"I told you, she was supposed to be *scared.*"

"That sounds a little hollow, Kristen," I said.

"What does that mean?"

I pulled my chair closer to her. I could smell her perfume, cloying and sweet. It mixed with the sweat of her body. She was nervous.

"Tell me this, Kristen, what do *you* think happened to your aunt?"

She nibbled on the corner of a nail and then stopped. "*You* know," she said to me, stressing the word. "She got herself killed in a drive-by…"

"Did Danny tell you that?"

She looked from me to Ardolino. "He says it happens all the time there."

"Then why would you send your aunt there?"

She faltered. "To scare her." But she barely whispered the words.

"We're not buying that. Maybe you bought Danny's story for Mary, but by the time your own mom was dead, you must have suspected something."

She bit her lip, said nothing. Her hand gripped the can of diet Coke. I thought she'd crunch it.

"Mary was going to the police, Kristen. Right?"

She sighed. "Well, I overheard Mom tell Dad."

"You did?"

"Yeah, I guess Aunt Mary was on Tommy's case. She was afraid Tommy was back into drugs and she wanted to—to—intervene."

"Intervene?"

"Have someone talk to him. But also to Danny. She told Mom that Tommy and Danny were doing drugs. She wanted the police to look at Danny. Selling drugs, maybe. Call the bank, in fact. She told Mom that. Talk to someone at the bank. And that pissed Danny off. I told Danny what I heard, but he already thought Mary was going over the edge. Danny didn't want the police talking to him. He kept mentioning the bank. Can you blame him?"

"But then Mary was dead."

"The drive-by."

"And then there was your mother," Ardolino said.

She nodded.

"Come on, Kristen, what did your mother say about all this?"

"She was suspicious, that's all. Why did I leave that note? Why was Danny calling? She got nervous. She said she should have been there for Mary."

"Meaning?"

"I don't know what that means."

I spoke up. "Maybe your mother realized that Mary was dead because she had talked to Mary about Tommy and Danny and drugs and you…"

"She didn't trust Danny, so she wanted to blame him for something."

"Did she tell you anything about the murder?" I asked.

Kristen clicked her tongue. "No, but I heard her tell Dad that his golden boy had to be looked at."

"What did your Dad say?"

"He said he'd talk to Danny."

"Did he?"

"I don't know. Danny was afraid of losing me, Rick. Losing *me*. And once Mary was dead, Mom got suspicious. But I couldn't tell her anything. There was nothing to tell, Rick. It was an accident. Danny didn't really *plan* it. You know that."

"What did your mother tell you to do after Mary's death?" I asked.

A pause. Then: "Stay away from Danny."

"Did you?"

"I told Danny to lay low. But you know what Danny said. 'This is a lot of nonsense.' We're talking about a couple sticks of pot. Nothing. A few dollars. I told Mom it was nothing. And do you know what she said to me?" She waited.

"What?" From Ardolino.

Her voice deepened. "She said, 'Kristen, I hope you don't think you're going to marry that man. It's just not gonna happen.'"

"And you said what?" Ardolino asked.

"I started crying and I told her nothing was going on, but I think by crying she got the answer she wanted."

"Did she ask you if Danny killed Mary?"

"Oh, no, of course not. Because Danny didn't do that. I told you."

"Don't you find it strange," Ardolino said, "that your Mom died in the same location?"

She didn't speak. She stared at her nails. Then she bit another corner of one of them.

"Your mother said you'd never marry Danny. That must have hurt."

"A little, but I didn't care. She didn't understand how much he loves me. How much I love him. I said to her—Danny is a good man. But she laughed and said, 'Your father and I are moral people. We don't do drugs or sleep around with tramps.'"

"Did that make you angry?"

"She said she was going to tell Susie that Danny couldn't come to the house any more. Even if it made Susie mad. Danny picked her up sometimes. Sometimes he stopped in to see me."

"You believe whatever Danny tells you?" Ardolino asked.

"I said Dad would never stop Danny from coming, but she said Dad would listen to her."

Kristen was out of breath, talking slowly now but swallowing her words.

"And you said?" I asked her.

Softly, almost a whisper. "I couldn't have that."

I looked at Ardolino, and he narrowed his eyes. I could read his mind. The more she talked, the more Kristen seemed aware of things. Here was a feeble intellect infused with a diabolic purpose.

"So you told Danny the conversation," I said.

"I told Danny everything."

"And so you did it again. Another phone call, this time to your mother."

"No."

"Of course you did," Ardolino said.

"But it's not what you think."

"What am I thinking?" Ardolino said.

"That I killed my own mother. God, no. I couldn't do that. I just wanted to—to scare her."

I was angry. "Kristen, you can't keep using that word *scare*. You can't. We're talking about murder here."

She pouted. "Danny said *scare*."

"So what did you do?" I asked.

"When?"

"That night your Mom died."

She was breathing heavily now and kept biting her lower lip. "I called from my cell phone." She breathed in and out, then started again. "I was at Danny's apartment. He told me what to say. I said I was driving with Danny, and she got real mad. 'Where are you?' she said. 'I told you to stay away from him.' I told her we drove to the spot where Mary died because I wanted to look around."

"What did she say to that?"

"She called me stupid. Over and over. 'Why are you there? And with Danny? Are you crazy?' She wouldn't shut up. But I said I had a fight with him—he told me to say that—and I got out of the car real mad and he drove off, mad. I told her he made me get out, and I was scared. I told her I thought he was just scaring me, but he drove off and left me there. I told her I knew he'd come back, but she started yelling about what a loser he was. I said I needed help. 'Call 911,' she said. 'Right now.' 'No,' I said, 'Dad'll kill me if he finds this out. I'm afraid. Really afraid. Come get me.' I started crying. 'No,' she said. 'Run into a store and call a taxi.' 'No,' I said, 'I don't have any money on me. Someone is watching me, coming close. Come get me. Please. I'm gonna stay in this, like, grocery store.' Wait for her, then come out. Then I hung up."

"So she went there. What did Danny do?"

"He left."

"Danny killed her," I said, flat out. "Or had someone do it."

She looked at me. "He said he wanted me to have his baby. His baby. He just wanted her to leave us alone. We're in love. We have a right to be in love."

Ardolino and I sat quietly for a while. Kristen said nothing. She stared into her lap for a minute, but I noticed a quick, almost furtive glance out the corner of her eyes. That bothered me. She was trying to think of how to handle this.

"We're in love," she mumbled.

"Did Danny return to his apartment?"

"Not—I don't know. He—he called me at his apartment. He said to drive myself home…"

"When did you fix your car?" Ardolino said.

"What?"

"You said your car was broken."

"Yes, but that was when Mary went there. My car was fixed and…"

"You knew he was going to kill your mother," Ardolino said. "That night, after you called her to come get you."

"No, I…" She reached into her purse and pulled out a handkerchief. "She was my mother. He…promised…"

"Promised what?" I asked.

"Promised that he would *talk* to her."

"About the two of you being in love?"

"Yes."

"That's stupid. Why did he have to have her go to that square?"

Silence. Then: "He said it would confuse the police. They'd, you know, think of gangs." But she listened to her own words, stopped. "I mean, the police…"

"You were sending your Mom to be killed," I said.

"No, I just wanted them to leave me and Danny alone. He promised me a baby."

"And," I raised my voice, "I'm not buying that stuff about Mary either. To scare her. To frighten her. You *knew* she'd get killed."

"I…I didn't know. I swear. It all happened so fast. Danny said nothing would happen. He said it was like…like a game we were playing."

"And you believed him when he said Mary's death was a drive-by," Ardolino said

She mumbled, "Yes."

"And you didn't doubt him afterwards?"

She looked at the wall over my shoulder. She thought about her words. "I did believe him."

"But Danny killed Mary."

"He couldn't. He was at the gym."

"Then how was he going to scare her when she arrived there?"

She looked rattled. "I didn't believe he'd hurt Aunt Mary. That was about her yapping and a few joints. And us. *Us*. Our love. You don't kill for that." She was nodding furiously. "I didn't understand it. I still don't. Danny kept saying it would be all right. Everything's all right. Just tell everyone nothing happened. He told me he just wanted to *talk*. He needed my help. Not murder. I don't know what happened."

"What happened is that you set your Aunt Mary up to be killed."

"No," she gasped, but the words were coming out gargled now, a little hysterical. "No."

"But didn't you think something else was going on—bigger than the pot and the romance?" I asked.

"What?"

"Didn't you think Danny was involved with something bigger, something he hid from you?"

"Like what?"

"He never told you?" Ardolino asked.

"He told me he loved me. And if I kept quiet he would love me forever."

"After Mary's death, didn't you worry about your mother?"

A transformation. A flash of fire in her eyes. "She was gonna get him in trouble," she yelled. "My Danny. I couldn't have that. We love each other. She was gonna call the police on him. I knew it. That was funny."

"Why funny?"

"Because he said that if Mary went to that square, the police would never look at us. That they'd look to drug people in Hartford. Danny said it was the most perfect place in the world for a…"

"Crime?"

"No, like a…"

"But then they got nosy, the police. And me," I said.

"That's when it got all mixed up. Danny said people were too nosy."

"Kristen." I looked into her face. "You knew Danny would kill your mother when you called her that night. You knew that, right?"

She said nothing.

"Come on, Kristen," Ardolino prodded. "You set your own mother up to be murdered."

She looked at him helplessly. "What else could I do? Everyone was trying to take away our happiness. That's not right, is it? When do I get a chance to be in love?"

Chapter Thirty-three

That afternoon after I left, Ardolino read Kristen her Miranda rights, had her sign off on them, and then led her through a taped confession. Then he got an arrest warrant for Danny Trinh. In her bumbling way, Kristen finally came clean.

"I sort of…you know…figured…"

She would be charged, but first Ardolino wanted to deal with Danny, who, escorted from Bank of America, said nothing, just glowered at the officers who cuffed him. In the back of a squad car he slumped down, his head folded into the folds of the Armani sports jacket.

According to an arresting officers, an older woman commented to another as Danny was led out the front door of the bank, "Good-looking young man like that!" as she shook her head.

The other, grinning, added, "Looks good even in handcuffs."

When Ardolino told me the anecdote, he laughed. "People crack me up."

I'd spoken to him before the arrest, and the two of us pondered the still-unfathomable question—what is the motive for two horrific killings? It didn't make any sense. Danny clearly had no great love for Kristen, was in fact using her for quickie sex, and obviously fed into her mushrooming delusions with talk of marriage and fidelity and kids up against a white picket fence. So her puppy love was convenient for him, I agreed, but for what end? Kristen's remarks, now being transcribed in

Hartford, identified him as the murderer, or at least provided sufficient information to begin serious questioning of Danny. But, again, why? Because Mary was too nosy? He dabbled in smoking weed—dabbled. Recreation—a great word for it, I thought cynically. Dabbled, with Tommy.

You don't murder two women because of it. You just don't. And you don't go to such bizarre strategies to mask the murders as drive-bys, attempting to throw the police way off the track. This was overkill. Worried about Bank of America? Maybe. But…overkill. Definitely. The drive-by machinations smacked of deliberate planning…and desperation.

But Mary, I said to Ardolino, was trying to contact the police. Danny *feared* that. Could it be that Danny was afraid something more sinister would emerge? That he'd be scrutinized more closely? What was going on here?

So Danny was hauled in, protested his innocence, eventually got a lawyer present during the interrogation, and said the things Ardolino and I expected him to say: Kristen was a little slow—"No," he said, "a lot slow." She "misinterpreted things." He and Kristen were playing some sort of prank, admittedly to "scare" the women. Kristen must have made those phone calls on her own. They'd joked about it, especially after taking that detour and ending up in Goodwin Square. One wrong turn and you miss Saigon, he said. Get it? Miss Saigon. So the murders were, indeed, accidental drive-bys. What evidence was there to convict him? He had nothing to do with it.

In the first hour he kept protesting his innocence, with his lawyer doing most of the talking. Then Ardolino played part of the Kristen tape and Danny winced, hearing the fragmented bits and pieces of Kristen's chatter, especially as she moved from talking in circles about what had happened, and ended with her caving in—her acknowledgement that something had to be done. Her mother was going to end their once-in-a-lifetime love affair.

After three hours Danny started to crack. An hour later, wiped out, over the protests of his lawyer, he confessed to arranging Mary's murder, and then Molly's, both done in by a hit man he'd located in New York City. Then, exhausted, he shut up. Why did you do it? Ardolino asked. But Danny had stopped talking.

I'd headed home directly after the interview with Kristen, called Hank and Liz to fill them in on Kristen's handing over of Danny, and then tried to decide what to do. There still were a number of unanswered questions. Then the phone rang, Harry Jacobi calling from New York. We talked for ten or so minutes, and I jotted down notes. When I hung up the phone, I knew where I might get some of those answers.

Larry Torcelli was busy, his secretary said, but when I told her it had to do with his dead wife, her face got long and mournful, and she buzzed him: "Go right in." Larry stood behind his desk, pointed to a chair, and thinly smiled.

I'd never been to his office before. In the North End of Hartford, off Albany Avenue, the Hartford office and showroom, the original building of his father's massive corporate empire, were dwarfed by the gaudy edifices he'd built in New Haven, Bridgeport, Greenwich, and even Agawam, Massachusetts. Yet Larry still ordered his empire out of the 1920s Hartford building, surrounded by a decaying city landscape. But his office was no cheap walnut paneling board, gray industrial carpets over old linoleum, with the obligatory awards from the Rotarians or the Elks Club lopsidedly mounted on the wall. No, this spacious office, obviously once two rooms now joined as one, was like any other elegant room in his home, with carpeting so deep I felt I'd never see my shoes again, a mahogany desk that could hold a meeting at the UN, and on the wall behind him a line of Dali prints, which I suspected were real. And though the view from the back window was of a parking lot, a corner of a shabby housing project, and a sagging stockade fence the victim of too many harsh New England winters, the window itself had draperies so effectively hung they gave the impression of cascading water. I was impressed.

"It's about Molly?" he asked impatiently as I gazed around the office. "You have some answers."

"Some. I need more."

"And?"

"And I'm hoping you can give me some."

"Well, I've talked to the police and said everything I know."

"There are new developments. Did you know that your daughter Kristen was sleeping with Danny?"

He looked confused. "Well, I had suspicions. Molly mentioned something, but Kristen has these wild fantasies, always has had, so I never knew what to believe. She can go off, you know…"

"A guy like Danny could manipulate her very easily."

"But Danny's a gentleman."

I laughed. "You know, in all my talks to people the last few weeks, and a lot of it about Danny, I've never heard anyone call him a gentleman."

"He's a success story."

"Well, that he is, which I've also heard too many times. But he's also a player, as you well know—you know his history with casual sex." Larry frowned. "He led Kristen to believe he loved her. It knocked her off-balance. Molly thought he was on drugs, and Kristen, too. Mary was already calling the police. But Kristen told Danny that Molly was going to forbid him from seeing her—from coming to the house, in fact."

"That will never happen. I wouldn't allow it. Danny is—like a son."

"So I've heard, over and over again. Another familiar linc. But things backfired on Danny. He tells her to keep their affair a secret, and she really can't. Worse, once she starts talking, she can't stop."

He looked confused. "What does this mean?"

"It means that Danny put a lot of pressure on Kristen to keep quiet about things. More so, he got hcr to *do* things she shouldn't have done—supposedly in the name of love." I paused. "Would you have allowed Kristen to marry Danny?"

"That has nothing to do with anything."

"I was just curious. She felt her mother would fight it, but you'd cave in."

"I'm not following this."

"You and Danny worked as a team."

"Not really. He's a banker in charge…"

"He introduced you to Jack Williamson."

Larry looked puzzled. "Who?"

"Danny's old roommate at Harvard. Now a resident of New York City. In fact, the creator, owner, and CEO of AsiaConcepts and its subsidiary, AsiaAuto."

"Danny isn't a *part* of that. He got me to invest. I run the AsiaAuto division out of—here. I handle it personally." He waved his hand out toward the showroom. "It's fairly lucrative."

"I'll say. In the past year moneys from that enterprise have saved your ass, got you out of near-bankruptcy, and made you a lot richer."

"I said it was a good deal."

"Did Danny get a cut?"

"No, of course not. Everything went through his bank, but no. Maybe some finder's fees at the start. A few thousand."

"He deposits periodic checks for a thousand here, a thousand there, sudden entries into his bank account."

Larry rubbed his jaw, nervous. "Okay, so I manage to keep paying him—to help him out. I give him a percentage of *my* profit. He squirrels it away somewhere. I can spend my dollar any way I want, if that's the point you're making. It's legal. But he's a kid starting out. It was *his* connection that got me into it. So who is the loser?"

"Good question."

The conversation was making him edgy. He got up, turned to look out the window. Sunlight glinted off the rows of parked cars. When he turned back, he seemed more in control. He sat back down. "I don't see how a minor business indiscretion relates to Molly's death."

"And Mary's. Don't forget her."

"They were drive-bys."

"They were, indeed."

"So?"

"But, as it turns out, not by Spanish thugs in low-slung armored Toyotas."

"Then?"

I changed the subject, determined to keep control of the conversation. "Why did Danny want you involved with Asia-Auto Enterprises?"

He looked perplexed. "Well, simple. His old roommate started AsiaConcepts, as you know. It really took off. But he wanted to tap into China's other growth—the automobile. I got connections, expertise. I flew to China last year to talk the talk with auto industry types there…" He paused. "It's a new market, a new concept, in fact, and Danny said I should jump in. I should *operate* it. It's paid off…"

"Beautifully," I finished.

"I still don't see…"

"Let me put my cards on the table. I've done some research on AsiaConcepts and AsiaAuto in New York City. Frankly, it raises a few questions. I just learned that some investigators are asking questions. The Department of Consumer Protection has something to say about it. The Feds. You see, Jack Williamson did form the company, there is an office in Soho tucked between two art galleries, and a filed prospectus explains the rationale of the company. And, quite frankly, AsiaConcepts is an idea that works. And works well."

"So?" Impatience in his voice. "That's what they do."

"The only problem is, Larry, that AsiaAuto seems to be a shadow corporation, papers filed, but largely nonfunctional. Sure, the money is there, profitable as hell, but some digging by the New York Attorney General suggests that the investing companies here in America are not real. What I'm saying is that the sources of that money are questionable. In other words, AsiaAuto is beginning to look to some investigators like a bogus corporation, tucked comfortably into the shadow of a legit operation like AsiaConcepts. Lots of money has flowed through your hands, through Danny's at the bank, and back to Jack Williamson. Millions of dollars."

For the first time I saw sweat on his upper lip. He licked it.

"I don't know where you're going with this."

"I'll tell you what I think. It strikes me as a little money laundering going on here, all seemingly legal. Fake investors pay into AsiaAuto, all documented on paper. You broker the money, deposit that money into a special account at Bank of America, Danny sends off all but twenty-five percent to New York, and you keep the rest, with a cash allotment to Danny. Nice scheme. Smoke and mirrors. Legit investment in the Chinese auto industry. Neat documentation. You pay legit taxes on it. Seamless, in fact. But fake investors, real money. Probably drug money that needs to be laundered. And Danny, at the bank, could be a watchdog for any surprises that might arise."

"You're making this up." Larry lowered his voice.

"Am I?"

"I can prove…"

"It must have been real tempting, this offer, a surefire, permanent way to ease your cash flow problems and to keep your business solvent."

"But this has nothing to do with the murder. How can it? You *don't* think I…"

I waited a moment. "Right now Danny is being questioned by the Hartford police in the murders of Molly and Mary."

He stood up. "What?"

"Sit down. Just sit."

He deliberated, but sat down.

"A couple hours ago your daughter Kristen told Detective Ardolino—and me, too—that she made the call to get Mary to that spot, calling from Danny's apartment. Then she set the trap for her own mother to go there a week later, all at Danny's bidding."

He was pale. "This has nothing to do with me."

My cell phone rang. While he watched, I answered it, turning sideway from Larry. "Yes." And then said "yes" a number of times. With a few "uh huhs" and "wells" tossed in. I said little else. Then I hung up. "That was Detective Ardolino. He told me he'd check in with me. It seems your golden boy Danny has finally confessed to orchestrating the murders. He used your own daughter to set them up…"

"No," he yelled. "No. What does this mean?"

"What do you think it means?"

"You're not saying that I had anything to do with this?"

"That's what Danny is saying right now. He says you were part of the whole horrible deal."

"That's a lie. A fucking lie."

"Is it?"

Then, sinking into his chair, his face dissolved, his shoulders slumped, and for a second his head dipped onto his hands on the desk. When he looked up, his face was awash in tears. "I had nothing to do with those murders, for God's sake. I had nothing to do with killing my Molly. She was my wife, damn it. I loved her. How can you believe that?"

I sat there, waiting. He sobbed and sobbed, started to talk, then stopped, sputtering. "Not my Molly. Not her. My beautiful wife. I loved her. Not her." Then, an edge in his voice. "That fucking Danny. He did it."

I waited.

"I still can't believe he killed my wife. Had her killed. I watched him grow into an evil…man. I couldn't stop him. This wasn't supposed to happen like this."

"What? The money laundering operation?"

"He said it was foolproof. Christ, Danny and Williamson, both Harvard business majors. Slick. Easy money. I just, well, facilitated. It seems so simple an operation. Who would know?"

"Where did the money originate from?"

He shrugged his shoulders. "I don't know. I didn't want to know. Some drug syndicate. I don't know. He set it up with the guy. He wanted to be rich."

"*You* already were."

He looked at me, eyes red and swollen. "Yeah, sure. Month to month. Out of control. This was a—guarantee. I was going to lose everything. I couldn't be poor. I couldn't."

"But what went wrong?"

He stammered. "It was that busybody, Mary. She was going to ruin everything. All over nothing. *Nothing!* Danny was stupid.

That low-level pot smoking crap. It was nothing. He had to smoke his fucking weed. But once Mary got hold of it—she was so afraid Tommy was back into it—she went nuts. Her and Molly, back and forth. I told Molly to cool it—that it wasn't a big deal. But Mary was going to call the cops, to have them talk to Tommy and even to Danny. To talk to *Danny*. To investigate. Molly even wanted to call the state police, some drug hotline. Danny said if the cops got interested, it could be trouble for us. They'd talk to the bank. They'd investigate *him*. The bank would start asking questions, they'd review accounts, maybe look at AsiaAuto because the paper work was slippery. Documents in one state don't back up documents in another state. Once the state police were brought in, the Attorney General, they'd find out things. Suddenly Danny was running scared. He got *me* scared. I couldn't shut him up. He *panicked*. I kept saying—cool it. He was *afraid*."

"But murder?"

"I learned too late that he was heartless. He got mean. Vicious. He turned on me—cold and cutthroat. I couldn't believe it was the same man. The charming boy was, well, gone. Replaced by a ruthless man who was running scared. He lost all…proportion."

"So Danny had Mary killed."

He nodded. "Christ, he never even told me. I could have stopped it. I never *thought* he was thinking murder, for Christ's sake. Murder. He said something had to be done. Okay, I'm thinking, we'll hide the accounts, put everything on hold, back off from AsiaAuto. Slick, business moves. Stuff I know how to do. But he's thinking murder. It *never* crossed my mind. You hide things and wait till everything blows over. But Danny seemed to get unhinged—like it was a make-or-break deal. I couldn't calm him down. I couldn't talk to him. I didn't know anything about it until it was over, but the minute it happened, I knew."

"Did you ask him?"

"Yeah, I talked to him, and he confessed. He laughed at me. What was I gonna do? Call the police. I should have, I know. But he said not to worry. He said it was nothing. He tells me he made sure it looked like a drive-by dumb accident, and I told him—they're gonna find out. Now they definitely will look at us. But he said no. We were safe. A drive-by. He's so fuckin' cocky. 'I got it all covered,' he said. Perfect scheme. Police would close the case."

"Why Goodwin Square?"

"He babbled about that detour off the highway that could lead a person to Goodwin Square instead of Little Saigon. Perfect situation, he said. I didn't understand what he was talking about. He told me he even told the guy to shoot someone—like that Spanish kid—in the shin. Anyone walking by. Clever, he said. The police are stupid, he said. You gotta stay one step ahead of them. *Feed* them the easy answers—a drive-by. I couldn't sleep that night, I tell you. I'm involved with a murder. I was gonna call the police in the morning, but then—it's Danny. Like my son. And he kept saying—Mary would bring us down. Now she can't talk to the cops. It's over with. God, how it backfired."

"It backfired because he killed Molly."

Fresh sobbing, anguish. "He told me everything was done, over with. Nothing to worry about. But I worried about Molly—what she knew. I worried what Danny *thought* she knew. I said to Danny—don't touch Molly. Promise me. She's my wife. This will blow over. She doesn't know anything. Okay, Mary is dead, it's over with."

"But he couldn't be stopped."

"Molly got suspicious after Mary died, suspected something with Danny and Tommy. Christ, she was thinking pot-smoking. He said there was no problem, but he lied to me. He promised me nothing would happen. Molly had gone nuts about the joint she found, but I thought the matter was over. Kristen was foolish." A deep sigh. "Every foolish thing she's ever done leads to disaster."

"This time it was murder."

He winced. "I couldn't believe it when Danny had Molly killed. He promised me he wouldn't. I *made* him promise. Promise, I said."

"You let it happen."

"I loved her. She was so beautiful. He didn't care. He didn't care what I thought. He had no conscience, no soul. But by then I couldn't open my mouth. What could I say to anyone? If they arrested Danny, they'd find out about our deal. They'd find out I knew about Mary. Then it would be all over. I didn't know what to do. Then Molly was dead, and I fell apart. He knew he had me. I was grieving for Molly's death, and I couldn't sleep knowing I was responsible." He held my eye. "I still can't make any sense of it. He said he would do what he had to do to survive. I couldn't believe it when he told me that. 'Now it's my turn to be rich,' he said to me. Nothing will stop me.'" Larry bit his lip. "I couldn't be poor. You know. I just couldn't."

"So Danny used you—and Kristen."

"Kristen," he moaned. "Oh, my God, I didn't know he did that to her. Will she be arrested?"

"That's up to Ardolino."

"When he killed Mary, I flipped. I told him I'd handle Molly, talk her out of her suspicions. One killing. Mary. Okay. No suspicion. But two—like that. Didn't he think the cops would wonder? Nobody is that stupid. The second murder made it *not* an accidental drive-by. That was clear. But he said it was covered. What bothered him, I know, was when *you* got involved. He never thought the family would do anything. The whole thing would have gone away, he said. *You* made him nervous. He tried to keep track of everything you did. But he felt you were getting too close."

"Was he gonna have me killed?"

Larry stared into my face. "He considered it. Talked of it. Another stupid act on his part. He was out of control. But I couldn't go to the police. But if I had gone to the police after Mary, Molly would be alive."

"But you would have gone down."

He looked at me. "If I had a choice between jail and Molly dying, I would have gone to jail."

"Danny thinks he's invincible."

"I made him that way." His raw, dark laugh broke at the end. "Isn't that ironic? I made him believe he could do anything." He closed his eyes. "I'm glad it's over, frankly. I'm glad. At the end I felt that Danny controlled me. I created him, and I was afraid of him. I was in over my head. What choice did I have?"

"You had a choice."

"Did I really? Have you ever been poor?" He waited.

"Yes. I've been poor."

"Then you know it sucks. I've been rich all my life. I had money and a beautiful wife and I..."

"You what?"

"For one moment I decided money was more important than love."

"But you were wrong."

He met my eyes, and dropped his chin.

Epilogue

We sit in Grandma's steamy kitchen, the three of us, Hank, Grandma, and me. The house is quiet. Hank's parents and grandfather are at Benny's tonight, sitting with him in his kitchen. Everyone has been quiet or depressed these past three days, ever since the surprising arrests of Danny, Larry, and sad, sad Kristen. Everyone has hidden from the omnipresent cameras, the intrusive microphones, the deliberate cruelties.

On TV you see pictures of Susie running from the court-house, her head covered under a jacket. You see Jon drinking coffee at Starbucks, by himself. He gives the finger to the camera, but they blur the image. The story plays itself out again and again, a delight for twenty-four-hour CNN and the Fox network. Commentators discuss it as a morality tale of greed, lust, and mendacity.

But we three sit in the kitchen, under the overhead garish light, and say little to one another. The window-box fan stirs up hot air from the clammy, awful night and sends it back into our faces. No one moves. A mosquito buzzes near my ear, its sound raw and metallic. My eyes follow its haphazard flight.

For a second I flash back to a childhood memory that comes on me unawares. I'm a young boy sitting in an orphanage in Saigon—Ho Chi Minh City now—and the night is tropical, feverish, so humid a film of water seems to cover the whole world. I've been crying, and I sit there alone, watching older kids playing some game with sticks and ball. I have a cut on my shin, not because I've played ball but because someone has tripped me, one of the older boys, a mean kid I remember now as huge and monstrous. I'm *bui doi.* Child of the dust. A black dot on the landscape. I'm crying. The swarming mosquitoes bite me. I stare into the slate-gray nighttime sky, so stark it's like a layer of rock pressing me to the earth. I can't stop crying. I shake the mosquitoes away from my head, but they stay, refuse to leave.

Suddenly I come out of my reverie. Grandma has said something. She is offering me a sesame ball, chewy and tangy. I say no, I'm not hungry. I'd spent the early evening with Jimmy, Liz, and Gracie, the three of us having a mournful dinner at Zeke's Olde Tavern. Out of the blue, crazily, I told Liz I thought we should go away for a weekend, to get away.

"Together? A weekend?"

Yes, I nodded. I don't care. I'll need her company to help me pull myself back together again.

She smiled. "I'll think it over."

Jimmy looked at her. "I wanna be best man."

We all changed the subject.

Staring at Grandma, Hank is shaking his head. "This is the worst ending."

Grandma looks at him. "Why do you say that?"

"I feel like Kristen was duped into the killings."

"She was," I say, "but there has to be a price."

Grandma shakes her head. "This madness is now over." She sits back and picks up the silk blouse I've bought her, an exquisite work of Thai embroidery in some glowing baby-blue metallic color. Earlier I gave it to her as thanks. "For telling me the answer."

She'd smiled. "You knew it all along."

You knew it all along. She means the conversation the two of us had about love and money and greed and motive. I know that. Her soft and utterly persuasive words made me dwell on Kristen's deadly infatuation.

Hank is talking. "I can't believe you got Larry to open up like that. Mr. Stoic. Mr. Hard-as-nails. I suppose when Ardolino called you and told you that Danny had confessed, well, he had no choice."

I laugh. "True. He had no choice. But Ardolino never called me."

"But didn't you say Larry cracked after you got a phone call?"

"Yeah, but I haven't told you that part of the story. It was Jimmy who called me, as planned, on schedule. I figured it might do the trick. I knew Danny was in Ardolino's care, but I needed Larry's part of it. At that point Danny was still protesting his innocence. He would be for another couple hours. I made the whole thing up. Larry fell apart, told me everything. When I left, with the Farmington cops coming to collect him, I called Ardolino. He came out of his interrogation and I told him. When he told Danny what Larry said, well, that was the beginning of Danny's caving in."

"You bluffed him?"

I nod.

Grandma is not listening. Instead she is running her old palm over the smooth silk, holding it to her wrinkled cheek. She smiles and closes her eyes.

"Grandma," Hank says, "it did turn out to be about money after all."

She puts down the silk blouse, smiles at me, and touches him on the cheek. "Tell him, Rick."

"Tell me what?"

"I think she wants me to quote the real source of these crimes. One of the maxims from my child's book of Buddha." I look at Grandma. She is grinning.

"Tell him." She is shaking her head.

I face Hank. "When there is love there must also be its opposite. The one is the other. They are parts of the whole."

"But," Grandma adds, "don't forget. It is up to you to choose love or the lack of love. Choose one to hold onto, but one that leads you to goodness. Choose."

"I still don't get it," Hank says.

She reaches out and holds both my hand and Hank's. Hank looks uncomfortable. That's because he's young, I think. I still get a kick out of him, his friendship, that boyishness. For me, I feel like I am finally home among family. A mosquito buzzes around my head, maddened, frantic, but I let it live. It is a choice I make.

To receive a free catalog of Poisoned Pen Press titles, please contact us in one of the following ways:

Phone: 1-800-421-3976
Facsimile: 1-480-949-1707
Email: info@poisonedpenpress.com
Website: www.poisonedpenpress.com

Poisoned Pen Press
6962 E. First Ave. Ste 103
Scottsdale, AZ 85251